The Borgias

CELEBRATED CRIMES
Volume I (of VIII), Part 1 (of 2)

The Borgias

Alexandre Dumas

WILDSIDE PRESS
Doylestown, Pennsylvania

The Borgias
A publication of
WILDSIDE PRESS
P.O. Box 301
Holicong, PA 18928–0301
www.wildsidepress.com

Note

Dumas's *Celebrated Crimes* was not written for children. The novelist has spared no language — has minced no words — to describe the violent scenes of a violent time.

In some instances facts appear distorted out of their true perspective, and in others the author makes unwarranted charges. It is not within our province to edit the historical side of Dumas, any more than it would be to correct the obvious errors in Dickens's *Child's History of England.* The careful, mature reader, for whom the books are intended, will recognize, and allow for, this fact.

Introduction

The contents of these volumes of *Celebrated Crimes*, as well as the motives which led to their inception, are unique. They are a series of stories based upon historical records, from the pen of Alexandre Dumas, pere, when he was not "the elder," nor yet the author of D'Artagnan or Monte Cristo, but was a rising young dramatist and a lion in the literary set and world of fashion.

Dumas, in fact, wrote his *Crimes Celebres* just prior to launching upon his wonderful series of historical novels, and they may therefore be considered as source books, whence he was to draw so much of that far-reaching and intimate knowledge of inner history which has perennially astonished his readers. The Crimes were published in Paris, in 1839–40, in eight volumes, comprising eighteen titles — all of which now appear in the present carefully translated text. The success of the original work was instantaneous. Dumas laughingly said that he thought he had exhausted the subject of famous crimes, until the work was off the press, when he immediately became deluged with letters from every province in France, supplying him with material upon other deeds of violence! The subjects which he has chosen, however, are of both historic and dramatic importance, and they have the added value of giving the modern reader a clear picture of the state of semi-lawlessness which existed in Europe, during the middle ages. "The Borgias, the Cenci, Urbain Grandier, the Marchioness of Brinvilliers, the Marchioness of Ganges, and the rest — what subjects for the pen of Dumas!" exclaims Garnett.

Space does not permit us to consider in detail the material

here collected, although each title will be found to present points of special interest. The first volume comprises the annals of the Borgias and the Cenci. The name of the noted and notorious Florentine family has become a synonym for intrigue and violence, and yet the Borgias have not been without stanch defenders in history.

Another famous Italian story is that of the Cenci. The beautiful Beatrice Cenci — celebrated in the painting of Guido, the sixteenth century romance of Guerrazi, and the poetic tragedy of Shelley, not to mention numerous succeeding works inspired by her hapless fate — will always remain a shadowy figure and one of infinite pathos.

The second volume chronicles the sanguinary deeds in the south of France, carried on in the name of religion, but drenching in blood the fair country round about Avignon, for a long period of years.

The third volume is devoted to the story of Mary Queen of Scots, another woman who suffered a violent death, and around whose name an endless controversy has waged. Dumas goes carefully into the dubious episodes of her stormy career, but does not allow these to blind his sympathy for her fate. Mary, it should be remembered, was closely allied to France by education and marriage, and the French never forgave Elizabeth the part she played in the tragedy.

The fourth volume comprises three widely dissimilar tales. One of the strangest stories is that of Urbain Grandier, the innocent victim of a cunning and relentless religious plot. His story was dramatized by Dumas, in 1850. A famous German crime is that of Karl-Ludwig Sand, whose murder of Kotzebue, Councilor of the Russian Legation, caused an international upheaval which was not to subside for many years.

An especially interesting volume is number six, containing, among other material, the famous "Man in the Iron Mask." This unsolved puzzle of history was later incorporated by Dumas in one of the D'Artagnan Romances a section of the Vicomte de Bragelonne, to which it gave its name. But in this later form, the true story of this singular man doomed to wear an iron visor over his features during his entire lifetime could only be treated episodically. While as a special subject in the Crimes, Dumas indulges his curiosity, and that of his reader, to the full. Hugo's unfinished tragedy, *Les Jumeaux*, is on the same subject; as also are others by Fournier, in French, and Zschokke, in German.

Other stories can be given only passing mention. The beautiful poisoner, Marquise de Brinvilliers, must have suggested to Dumas his later portrait of Miladi, in the Three Musketeers, the mast celebrated of his woman characters. The incredible cruelties of Ali Pacha, the Turkish despot, should not be charged entirely to Dumas, as he is said to have been largely aided in this by one of his "ghosts," Mallefille.

"Not a mere artist" — writes M. de Villemessant, founder of the Figaro, — "he has nevertheless been able to seize on those dramatic effects which have so much distinguished his theatrical career, and to give those sharp and distinct reproductions of character which alone can present to the reader the mind and spirit of an age. Not a mere historian, he has nevertheless carefully consulted the original sources of information, has weighed testimonies, elicited theories, and . . . has interpolated the poetry of history with its most thorough prose."

The Borgias

Prologue

On the 8th of April, 1492, in a bedroom of the Carneggi Palace, about three miles from Florence, were three men grouped about a bed whereon a fourth lay dying.

The first of these three men, sitting at the foot of the bed, and half hidden, that he might conceal his tears, in the gold-brocaded curtains, was Ermolao Barbaro, author of the treatise *On Celibacy,* and of *Studies in Pliny*: the year before, when he was at Rome in the capacity of ambassador of the Florentine Republic, he had been appointed Patriarch of Aquileia by Innocent VIII.

The second, who was kneeling and holding one hand of the dying man between his own, was Angelo Poliziano, the Catullus of the fifteenth century, a classic of the lighter sort, who in his Latin verses might have been mistaken for a poet of the Augustan age.

The third, who was standing up and leaning against one of the twisted columns of the bed-head, following with profound sadness the progress of the malady which he read in the face of his departing friend, was the famous Pico della Mirandola, who at the age of twenty could speak twenty-two languages, and who had offered to reply in each of these languages to any seven hundred questions that might be put to him by the twenty most learned men in the whole world, if they could be assembled at Florence.

The man on the bed was Lorenzo the Magnificent, who at the beginning of the year had been attacked by a severe and deep-seated fever, to which was added the gout, a hereditary ailment in his family. He had found at last that the draughts

containing dissolved pearls which the quack doctor, Leoni di
Spoleto, prescribed for him (as if he desired to adapt his
remedies rather to the riches of his patient than to his
necessities) were useless and unavailing, and so he had come
to understand that he must part from those gentle-tongued
women of his, those sweet-voiced poets, his palaces and their
rich hangings; therefore he had summoned to give him
absolution for his sins — in a man of less high place they
might perhaps have been called crimes — the Dominican,
Giralamo Francesco Savonarola.

It was not, however, without an inward fear, against which
the praises of his friends availed nothing, that the pleasure-
seeker and usurper awaited that severe and gloomy preacher
by whose word's all Florence was stirred, and on whose
pardon henceforth depended all his hope far another world.

Indeed, Savonarola was one of those men of stone, coming,
like the statue of the Commandante, to knock at the door of
a Don Giovanni, and in the midst of feast and orgy to
announce that it is even now the moment to begin to think
of Heaven. He had been barn at Ferrara, whither his family,
one of the most illustrious of Padua, had been called by
Niccolo, Marchese d'Este, and at the age of twenty-three,
summoned by an irresistible vocation, had fled from his
father's house, and had taken the vows in the cloister of
Dominican monks at Florence. There, where he was appointed by his superiors to give lessons in philosophy, the
young novice had from the first to battle against the defects
of a voice that was both harsh and weak, a defective pronun-
ciation, and above all, the depression of his physical powers,
exhausted as they were by too severe abstinence.

Savonarala from that time condemned himself to the most
absolute seclusion, and disappeared in the depths of his
convent, as if the slab of his tomb had already fallen over
him. There, kneeling on the flags, praying unceasingly before
a wooden crucifix, fevered by vigils and penances, he soon
passed out of contemplation into ecstasy, and began to feel
in himself that inward prophetic impulse which summoned
him to preach the reformation of the Church.

Nevertheless, the reformation of Savonarola, more rever-
ential than Luther's, which followed about five-and-twenty

years later, respected the thing while attacking the man, and had as its aim the altering of teaching that was human, not faith that was of God. He did not work, like the German monk, by reasoning, but by enthusiasm. With him logic always gave way before inspiration: he was not a theologian, but a prophet. Yet, although hitherto he had bowed his head before the authority of the Church, he had already raised it against the temporal power. To him religion and liberty appeared as two virgins equally sacred; so that, in his view, Lorenzo in subjugating the one was as culpable as Pope Innocent VIII in dishonoring the other. The result of this was that, so long as Lorenzo lived in riches, happiness, and magnificence, Savonarola had never been willing, whatever entreaties were made, to sanction by his presence a power which he considered illegitimate. But Lorenzo on his death-bed sent for him, and that was another matter. The austere preacher set forth at once, bareheaded and barefoot, hoping to save not only the soul of the dying man but also the liberty of the republic.

Lorenzo, as we have said, was awaiting the arrival of Savonarola with an impatience mixed with uneasiness; so that, when he heard the sound of his steps, his pale face took a yet more deathlike tinge, while at the same time he raised himself on his elbow and ordered his three friends to go away. They obeyed at once, and scarcely had they left by one door than the curtain of the other was raised, and the monk, pale, immovable, solemn, appeared on the threshold. When he perceived him, Lorenzo dei Medici, reading in his marble brow the inflexibility of a statue, fell back on his bed, breathing a sigh so profound that one might have supposed it was his last.

The monk glanced round the room as though to assure himself that he was really alone with the dying man; then he advanced with a slow and solemn step towards the bed. Lorenzo watched his approach with terror; then, when he was close beside him, he cried:

"O my father, I have been a very great sinner!"

"The mercy of God is infinite," replied the monk; "and I come into your presence laden with the divine mercy."

"You believe, then, that God will forgive my sins?" cried

the dying man, renewing his hope as he heard from the lips of the monk such unexpected words.

"Your sins and also your crimes, God will forgive them all," replied Savonarola. "God will forgive your vanities, your adulterous pleasures, your obscene festivals; so much for your sins. God will forgive you for promising two thousand florins reward to the man who should bring you the head of Dietisalvi, Nerone Nigi, Angelo Antinori, Niccalo Soderini, and twice the money if they were handed over alive; God will forgive you for dooming to the scaffold or the gibbet the son of Papi Orlandi, Francesco di Brisighella, Bernardo Nardi, Jacopo Frescobaldi, Amoretto Baldovinetti, Pietro Balducci, Bernardo di Banding, Francesco Frescobaldi, and more than three hundred others whose names were none the less dear to Florence because they were less renowned; so much far your crimes." And at each of these names which Savonarala pronounced slowly, his eyes fixed on the dying man, he replied with a groan which proved the monk's memory to be only too true. Then at last, when he had finished, Lorenzo asked in a doubtful tone:

"Then do you believe, my father, that God will forgive me everything, both my sins and my crimes?"

"Everything," said Savonarola, "but on three conditions."

"What are they?" asked the dying man.

"The first," said Savonarola, "is that you feel a complete faith in the power and the mercy of God."

"My father," replied Lorenzo eagerly, "I feel this faith in the very depths of my heart."

"The second," said Savonarola, "is that you give back the property of others which you have unjustly confiscated and kept."

"My father, shall I have time?" asked the dying man.

"God will give it to you," replied the monk.

Lorenzo shut his eyes, as though to reflect more at his ease; then, after a moment's silence, he replied:

"Yes, my father, I will do it."

"The third," resumed Savonarola, "is that you restore to the republic her ancient independence end her farmer liberty."

Lorenzo sat up on his bed, shaken by a convulsive movement, and questioned with his eyes the eyes of the Dominican, as though he would find out if he had deceived himself and not heard aright. Savonarola repeated the same words.

"Never! never!" exclaimed Lorenzo, falling back on his bed and shaking his head, — "never!"

The monk, without replying a single word, made a step to withdraw.

"My father, my father," said the dying man, "do not leave me thus: have pity on me!"

"Have pity on Florence," said the monk.

"But, my father," cried Lorenzo, "Florence is free, Florence is happy."

"Florence is a slave, Florence is poor," cried Savonarola, "poor in genius, poor in money, and poor in courage; poor in genius, because after you, Lorenzo, will come your son Piero; poor in money, because from the funds of the republic you have kept up the magnificence of your family and the credit of your business houses; poor in courage, because you have robbed the rightful magistrates of the authority which was constitutionally theirs, and diverted the citizens from the double path of military and civil life, wherein, before they were enervated by your luxuries, they had displayed the virtues of the ancients; and therefore, when the day shall dawn which is not far distant," continued the mark, his eyes fixed and glowing as if he were reading in the future, "whereon the barbarians shall descend from the mountains, the walls of our towns, like those of Jericho, shall fall at the blast of their trumpets."

"And do you desire that I should yield up on my deathbed the power that has made the glory of my whole life?" cried Lorenzo dei Medici.

"It is not I who desire it; it is the Lord," replied Savonarola coldly.

"Impossible, impossible!" murmured Lorenzo.

"Very well; then die as you have lived!" cried the monk, "in the midst of your courtiers and flatterers; let them ruin your soul as they have ruined your body!" And at these words, the austere Dominican, without listening to the cries of the dying man, left the room as he had entered it, with face and step unaltered; far above human things he seemed to soar, a spirit already detached from the earth.

At the cry which broke from Lorenzo dei Medici when he saw him disappear, Ermolao, Poliziano, and Pico delta Mirandola, who had heard all, returned into the room, and found their friend convulsively clutching in his arms a magnificent crucifix which he had just taken dawn from the bed-head. In vain did they try to reassure him with friendly words. Lorenzo the Magnificent only replied with sobs; and one hour after the scene which we have just related, his lips clinging to the feet of the Christ, he breathed his last in the arms of these three men, of whom the most fortunate — though all three were young — was not destined to survive him more than two years. "Since his death was to bring about many calamities," says Niccolo Macchiavelli, "it was the will of Heaven to show this by omens only too certain: the dome of the church of Santa Regarata was struck by lightning, and Roderigo Borgia was elected pope."

Chapter I

*T*owards the end of the fifteenth century — that is to say, at the epoch when our history opens the Piazza of St. Peter's at Rome was far from presenting so noble an aspect as that which is offered in our own day to anyone who approaches it by the Piazza dei Rusticucci.

In fact, the Basilica of Constantine existed no longer, while that of Michael Angelo, the masterpiece of thirty popes, which cost the labor of three centuries and the expense of two hundred and sixty millions, existed not yet. The ancient edifice, which had lasted for eleven hundred and forty-five years, had been threatening to fall in about 1440, and Nicholas V, artistic forerunner of Julius II and Leo X, had had it pulled down, together with the temple of Probus Anicius which adjoined it. In their place he had had the foundations of a new temple laid by the architects Rossellini and Battista Alberti; but some years later, after the death of Nicholas V, Paul II, the Venetian, had not been able to give more than five thousand crowns to continue the project of his predecessor, and thus the building was arrested when it had scarcely risen above the ground, and presented the appearance of a still-born edifice, even sadder than that of a ruin.

As to the piazza itself, it had not yet, as the reader will understand from the foregoing explanation, either the fine colonnade of Bernini, or the dancing fountains, or that Egyptian obelisk which, according to Pliny, was set up by the Pharaoh at Heliopolis, and transferred to Rome by Caligula, who set it up in Nero's Circus, where it remained till 1586. Now, as Nero's Circus was situate on the very ground where

St. Peter's now stands, and the base of this obelisk covered the actual site where the vestry now is, it looked like a gigantic needle shooting up from the middle of truncated columns, walls of unequal height, and half-carved stones.

On the right of this building, a ruin from its cradle, arose the Vatican, a splendid Tower of Babel, to which all the celebrated architects of the Roman school contributed their work for a thousand years: at this epoch the two magnificent chapels did not exist, nor the twelve great halls, the two-and-twenty courts, the thirty staircases, and the two thousand bedchambers; for Pope Sixtus V, the sublime swineherd, who did so many things in a five years' reign, had not yet been able to add the immense building which on the eastern side towers above the court of St. Damasius; still, it was truly the old sacred edifice, with its venerable associations, in which Charlemagne received hospitality when he was crowned emperor by Pope Leo III.

All the same, on the 9th of August, 1492, the whole of Rome, from the People's Gate to the Coliseum and from the Baths of Diocletian to the castle of Sant' Angelo, seemed to have made an appointment on this piazza: the multitude thronging it was so great as to overflow into all the neighboring streets, which started from this center like the rays of a star. The crowds of people, looking like a motley moving carpet, were climbing up into the basilica, grouping themselves upon the stones, hanging on the columns, standing up against the walls; they entered by the doors of houses and reappeared at the windows, so numerous and so densely packed that one might have said each window was walled up with heads. Now all this multitude had its eyes fixed on one single point in the Vatican; for in the Vatican was the Conclave, and as Innocent VIII had been dead for sixteen days, the Conclave was in the act of electing a pope.

Rome is the town of elections: since her foundation down to our own day — that is to say, in the course of nearly twenty-six centuries — she has constantly elected her kings, consuls, tribunes, emperors, and popes: thus Rome during the days of Conclave appears to be attacked by a strange fever which drives everyone to the Vatican or to Monte Cavallo, according as the scarlet-robed assembly is held in one or the other of these two palaces: it is, in fact, because the raising up of a new pontiff is a great event far everybody; for, according to the average established in the period between St. Peter and Gregory XVI, every pope lasts about eight years, and these eight years, according to the character of the man who is elected, are a period either of tranquility or of disorder, of justice or of venality, of peace or of war.

Never perhaps since the day when the first successor of St. Peter took his seat on the, pontifical throne until the inter-regnum which now occurred, had so great an agitation been shown as there was at this moment, when, as we have shown, all these people were thronging on the Piazza of St. Peter and in the streets which led to it. It is true that this was not without reason; for Innocent VIII — who was called the father of his people because he had added to his subjects eight sons and the same number of daughters — had, as we have said, after living a life of self-indulgence, just died, after a death-struggle during which, if the journal of Stefano Infessura may be believed, two hundred and twenty murders were committed in the streets of Rome. The authority had then devolved in the customary way upon the Cardinal Camerlengo, who during the interregnum had sovereign powers; but as he had been obliged to fulfill all the duties of his office — that is, to get money coined in his name and bearing his arms, to take the fisherman's ring from the finger of the dead pope, to dress, shave and paint him, to have the corpse embalmed, to lower the coffin after nine days' obsequies into the provi-sional niche where the last deceased pope has to remain until his successor comes to take his place and consign him to his final tomb; lastly, as he had been obliged to wall up the door of the Conclave and the window of the balcony from which the pontifical election is proclaimed, he had not had a single moment for busying himself with the police; so that the assassinations had continued in goodly fashion, and there were loud cries for an energetic hand which should make all these swords and all these daggers retire into their sheaths.

Now the eyes of this multitude were fixed, as we have said, upon the Vatican, and particularly upon one chimney, from which would come the first signal, when suddenly, at the moment of the *Ave Maria* — that is to say, at the hour when the day begins to decline — great cries went up from all the crowd mixed with bursts of laughter, a discordant murmur of threats and raillery, the cause being that they had just perceived at the top of the chimney a thin smoke, which seemed like a light cloud to go up perpendicularly into the sky. This smoke announced that Rome was still without a master, and that the world still had no pope; for this was the smoke of the voting tickets which were being burned, a proof that the cardinals had not yet come to an agreement.

Scarcely had this smoke appeared, to vanish almost immediately, when all the innumerable crowd, knowing well that there was nothing else to wait for, and that all was said and done until ten o'clock the next morning, the time when the cardinals had their first voting, went off in a tumult of noisy joking, just as they would after the last rocket of a firework display; so that at the end of one minute nobody was there where a quarter of an hour before there had been an excited crowd, except a few curious laggards, who, living in the neighborhood or on the very piazza itself, were less in a hurry than the rest to get back to their homes; again, little by little, these last groups insensibly diminished; for half-past nine had just struck, and at this hour the streets of Rome began already to be far from safe; then after these groups followed some solitary passer-by, hurrying his steps; one after another the doors were closed, one after another the windows were darkened; at last, when ten o'clock struck, with the single exception of one window in the Vatican where a lamp might be seen keeping obstinate vigil, all the houses, piazzas, and streets were plunged in the deepest obscurity.

At this moment a man wrapped in a cloak stood up like a ghost against one of the columns of the uncompleted basilica, and gliding slowly and carefully among the stones which were lying about round the foundations of the new church, advanced as far as the fountain which, formed the center of the piazza, erected in the very place where the obelisk is now set up of which we have spoken already; when he reached this spot he stopped, doubly concealed by the darkness of the night and by the shade of the monument, and after looking around him to see if he were really alone, drew his sword, and with its point rapping three times on the pavement of the piazza, each time made the sparks fly. This signal, for signal it was, was not lost: the last lamp which still kept vigil in the Vatican went out, and at the same instant an object thrown out of the window fell a few paces off from the young man in the cloak: he, guided by the silvery sound it had made in touching the flags, lost no time in laying his hands upon it in spite of the darkness, and when he had it in his possession hurried quickly away.

Thus the unknown walked without turning round half-way along the Borgo Vecchio; but there he turned to the right and took a street at the other end of which was set up a Madonna with a lamp: he approached the light, and drew from his pocket the object he had picked up, which was nothing else than a Roman crown piece; but this crown unscrewed, and in a cavity hollowed in its thickness enclosed a letter, which the man to whom it was addressed began to read at the risk of being recognized, so great was his haste to know what it contained.

We say at the risk of being recognized, for in his eagerness the recipient of this nocturnal missive had thrown back the hood of his cloak; and as his head was wholly within the luminous circle cast by the lamp, it was easy to distinguish in the light the head of a handsome young man of about five or six and twenty, dressed in a purple doublet slashed at the shoulder and elbow to let the shirt come through, and wearing on his head a cap of the same color with a long black feather falling to his shoulder. It is true that he did not stand there long; for scarcely had he finished the letter, or rather the note, which he had just received in so strange and mysterious a manner, when he replaced it in its silver receptacle, and readjusting his cloak so as to hide all the lower part of his face, resumed his walk with a rapid step, crossed Borgo San Spirito, and took the street of the Longara, which he followed as far as the church of Regina Coeli. When he arrived at this place, he gave three rapid knocks on the door of a house of good appearance, which immediately opened; then slowly mounting the stairs he entered a room where two women were awaiting him with an impatience so unconcealed that both as they saw him exclaimed together:

"Well, Francesco, what news?"

"Good news, my mother; good, my sister," replied the young man, kissing the one and giving his hand to the other. "Our father has gained three votes today, but he still needs six to have the majority."

"Then is there no means of buying them?" cried the elder of the two women, while the younger, instead of speaking, asked him with a look.

"Certainly, my mother, certainly," replied the young man; "and it is just about that that my father has been thinking. He is giving Cardinal Orsini his palace at Rome and his two castles of Monticello and Soriano; to Cardinal Colanna his abbey of Subiaca; he gives Cardinal Sant' Angelo the bishopric of Porto, with the furniture and cellar; to the Cardinal of Parma the town of Nepi; to the Cardinal of Genoa the church of Santa Maria-in-Via-Lata; and lastly, to Cardinal Savelli the church of Santa Maria Maggiore and the town of Civita Castellana; as to Cardinal Ascanio-Sforza, he knows already that the day before yesterday we sent to his house four mules laden with silver and plate, and out of this treasure he has engaged to give five thousand ducats to the Cardinal Patriarch of Venice."

"But how shall we get the others to know the intentions of Roderigo?" asked the elder of the two women.

"My father has provided for everything, and proposes an easy method; you know, my mother, with what sort of ceremonial the cardinals' dinner is carried in."

"Yes, on a litter, in a large basket with the arms of the cardinal far whom the meal is prepared."

"My father has bribed the bishop who examines it: tomorrow is a feast-day; to the Cardinals Orsini, Colonna, Savelli, Sant' Angelo, and the Cardinals of Parma and of Genoa, chickens will be sent for hot meat, and each chicken will contain a deed of gift duly drawn up, made by me in my father's name, of the houses, palaces, or churches which are destined for each."

"Capital!" said the elder of the two women; "now, I am certain, all will go well."

"And by the grace of God," added the younger, with a strangely mocking smile, "our father will be pope."

"Oh, it will be a fine day for us!" cried Francesco.

"And for Christendom," replied his sister, with a still more ironical expression.

"Lucrezia, Lucrezia," said the mother, "you do not deserve the happiness which is coming to us."

"What does that matter, if it comes all the same? Besides, you know the proverb; mother: 'Large families are blessed of the Lord'; and still more so our family, which is so patriarchal."

At the same time she cast on her brother a look so wanton that the young man blushed under it: but as at the moment he had to think of other things than his illicit loves, he ordered that four servants should be awakened; and while they were getting armed to accompany him, he drew up and signed the six deeds of gift which were to be carried the next day to the cardinals; for, not wishing to be seen at their houses, he thought he would profit by the night-time to carry them himself to certain persons in his confidence who would have them passed in, as had been arranged, at the dinner-hour. Then, when the deeds were quite ready and the servants also, Francesco went out with them, leaving the two women to dream golden dreams of their future greatness.

From the first dawn of day the people hurried anew, as ardent and interested as on the evening before, to the Piazza of the Vatican, where; at the ordinary time, that is, at ten o'clock in the morning, — the smoke rose again as usual, evoking laughter and murmuring, as it announced that none of the cardinals had secured the majority. A report, however, began to be spread about that the chances were divided between three candidates, who were Roderigo Borgia, Giuliano delta Rovera, and Ascanio Sforza; for the people as yet knew nothing of the four mules laden with plate and silver which had been led to Sforza's house, by reason of which he had given up his own votes to his rival. In the midst of the agitation excited in the crowd by this new report a solemn chanting was heard; it proceeded from a procession, led by the Cardinal Camerlengo, with the object of obtaining from Heaven the speedy election of a pope: this procession, starting from the church of Ara Coeli at the Capitol, was to make stations before the principal Madannas and the most frequented churches. As soon as the silver crucifix was perceived which went in front, the most profound silence prevailed, and everyone fell on his knees; thus a supreme calm followed the tumult and uproar which had been heard a few minutes before, and which at each appearance of the smoke had assumed a more threatening character: there was a shrewd suspicion that the procession, as well as having a religious end in view, had a political object also, and that its influence was intended to be as great on earth as in heaven. In any case, if such had been the design of the Cardinal Camerlengo, he had not deceived himself, and the effect was what he desired: when the procession had gone past, the laughing and joking continued, but the cries and threats had completely ceased.

The whole day passed thus; for in Rome nobody works. You are either a cardinal or a lackey, and you live, nobody knows how. The crowd was still extremely numerous, when, towards two o'clock in the afternoon, another procession, which had quite as much power of provoking noise as the first of imposing silence, traversed in its turn the Piazza of St. Peter's: this was the dinner procession. The people received it with the usual bursts of laughter, without suspecting, for all their irreverence, that this procession, more efficacious than the former, had just settled the election of the new pope.

The hour of the Ave Maria came as on the evening before; but, as on the evening before, the waiting of the whole day was lost; for, as half-past eight struck, the daily smoke reappeared at the top of the chimney. But when at the same moment rumors which came from the inside of the Vatican were spread abroad, announcing that, in all probability, the election would take place the next day, the good people preserved their patience. Besides, it had been very hot that day, and they were so broken with fatigue and roasted by the sun, these dwellers in shade and idleness, that they had no strength left to complain.

The morning of the next day, which was the 11th of August, 1492, arose stormy and dark; this did not hinder the multitude from thronging the piazzas, streets, doors, houses, churches. Moreover, this disposition of the weather was a real blessing from Heaven; for if there were heat, at least there would be no sun. Towards nine o'clock threatening storm-clouds were heaped up over all the Trastevere; but to this crowd what mattered rain, lightning, or thunder? They were preoccupied with a concern of a very different nature; they were waiting for their pope: a promise had been made them for today, and it could be seen by the manner of all, that if the day should pass without any election taking place, the end of it might very well be a riot; therefore, in proportion as the time advanced, the agitation grew greater. Nine o'clock, half-past nine, a quarter to ten struck, without anything happening to confirm or destroy their hopes. At last the first stroke of ten was heard; all eyes turned towards the chimney: ten o'clock struck slowly, each stroke vibrating in the heart of the multitude. At last the tenth stroke trembled, then vanished shuddering into space, and, a great cry breaking simultaneously frog a hundred thousand breasts followed the silence "Non v'e fumo! There is no smoke!" In other words, "We have a pope."

At this moment the rain began to fall; but no one paid any attention to it, so great were the transports of joy and impatience among all the people. At last a little stone was detached from the walled window which gave on the balcony and upon which all eyes were fixed: a general shout saluted its fall; little by little the aperture grew larger, and in a few minutes it was large enough to allow a man to come out on the balcony.

The Cardinal Ascanio Sforza appeared; but at the moment when he was on the point of coming out, frightened by the rain and the lightning, he hesitated an instant, and finally drew back: immediately the multitude in their turn broke out like a tempest into cries, curses, howls, threatening to tear down the Vatican and to go and seek their pope themselves. At this noise Cardinal Sforza, more terrified by the popular storm than by the storm in the heavens, advanced on the balcony, and between two thunderclaps, in a moment of silence astonishing to anyone who had just heard the clamor that went before, made the following proclamation:

"I announce to you a great joy: the most Eminent and most Reverend Signor Roderigo Lenzuolo Borgia, Archbishop of Valencia, Cardinal-Deacon of San Nicolao-in-Carcere, Vice-Chancellor of the Church, has now been elected Page, and has assumed the name of Alexander VI."

The news of this nomination was received with strange joy.

Roderigo Borgia had the reputation of a dissolute man, it is true, but libertinism had mounted the throne with Sixtus IV and Innocent VIII, so that for the Romans there was nothing new in the singular situation of a pope with a mistress and five children. The great thing for the moment was that the power fell into strong hands; and it was more important for the tranquility of Rome that the new pope inherited the sword of St. Paul than that he inherited the keys of St. Peter.

And so, in the feasts that were given on this occasion, the dominant character was much more warlike than religious, and would have appeared rather to suit with the election of some young conqueror than the exaltation of an old pontiff: there was no limit to the pleasantries and prophetic epigrams on the name of Alexander, which for the second time seemed to promise the Romans the empire of the world; and the same evening, in the midst of brilliant illuminations and bonfires, which seemed to turn the town into a lake of flame, the following epigram was read, amid the acclamation of the people:

"Rome under Caesar's rule in ancient story
  At home and o'er the world victorious trod;
  But Alexander still extends his glory:
  Caesar was man, but Alexander God."

As to the new pope, scarcely had he completed the formalities of etiquette which his exaltation imposed upon him, and paid to each man the price of his simony, when from the height of the Vatican he cast his eyes upon Europe, a vast political game of chess, which he cherished the hope of directing at the will of his own genius.

Chapter II

*T*he world had now arrived at one of those supreme moments of history when every thing is transformed between the end of one period and the beginning of another: in the East Turkey, in the South Spain, in the West France, and in the North German, all were going to assume, together with the title of great Powers, that influence which they were destined to exert in the future over the secondary States. Accordingly we too, with Alexander VI, will cast a rapid glance over them, and see what were their respective situations in regard to Italy, which they all coveted as a prize.

Constantine, Palaeologos Dragozes, besieged by three hundred thousand Turks, after having appealed in vain for aid to the whole of Christendom, had not been willing to survive the loss of his empire, and had been found in the midst of the dead, close to the Tophana Gate; and on the 30th of May, 1453, Mahomet II had made his entry into Constantinople, where, after a reign which had earned for him the surname of 'Fatile', or the Conqueror, he had died leaving two sons, the elder of whom had ascended the throne under the name of Bajazet II.

The accession of the new sultan, however, had not taken place with the tranquility which his right as elder brother and his father's choice of him should have promised. His younger brother, D'jem, better known under the name of Zizimeh, had argued that whereas he was born in the purple — that is, born during the reign of Mahomet — Bajazet was born prior to his epoch, and was therefore the son of a private individual. This was rather a poor trick; but where force is all and right

is naught, it was good enough to stir up a war. The two
brothers, each at the head of an army, met accordingly in Asia
in 1482. D'jem was defeated after a seven hours' fight, and
pursued by his brother, who gave him no time to rally his
army: he was obliged to embark from Cilicia, and took refuge
in Rhodes, where he implored the protection of the Knights
of St. John. They, not daring to give him an asylum in their
island so near to Asia, sent him to France, where they had
him carefully guarded in one of their commanderies, in spite
of the urgency of Cait Bey, Sultan of Egypt, who, having
revolted against Bajazet, desired to have the young prince in
his army to give his rebellion the appearance of legitimate
warfare. The same demand, moreover, with the same political
object, had been made successively by Mathias Corvinus,
King of Hungary, by Ferdinand, King of Aragon and Sicily,
and by Ferdinand, King of Naples.

On his side Bajazet, who knew all the importance of such
a rival, if he once allied himself with any one of the princes
with whom he was at war, had sent ambassadors to Charles
VIII, offering, if he would consent to keep D'jem with him,
to give him a considerable pension, and to give to France the
sovereignty of the Holy Land, so soon as Jerusalem should
be conquered by the Sultan of Egypt. The King of France had
accepted these terms.

But then Innocent VIII had intervened, and in his turn
had claimed D'jem, ostensibly to give support by the claims
of the refugee to a crusade which he was preaching against
the Turks, but in reality to appropriate the pension of 40,000
ducats to be given by Bajazet to any one of the Christian
princes who would undertake to be his brother's jailer. Charles VIII had not dared to refuse to the spiritual head of
Christendom a request supported by such holy reasons; and
therefore D'jem had quitted France, accompanied by the
Grand Master d'Aubusson, under whose direct charge he was;
but his guardian had consented, for the sake of a cardinal's
hat, to yield up his prisoner. Thus, on the 13th of March,
1489, the unhappy young man, cynosure of so many interested eyes, made his solemn entry into Rome, mounted on a
superb horse, clothed in a magnificent oriental costume,
between the Prior of Auvergne, nephew of the Grand Master

d'Aubusson, and Francesco Cibo, the son of the pope.

After this he had remained there, and Bajazet, faithful to promises which it was so much his interest to fulfill, had punctually paid to the sovereign pontiff a pension of 40,000 ducats.

So much for Turkey.

Ferdinand and Isabella were reigning in Spain, and were laying the foundations of that vast power which was destined, five-and-twenty years later, to make Charles V declare that the sun never set on his dominions. In fact, these two sovereigns, on whom history has bestowed the name of Catholic, had reconquered in succession nearly all Spain, and driven the Moors out of Granada, their last entrenchment; while two men of genius, Bartolome Diaz and Christopher Columbus, had succeeded, much to the profit of Spain, the one in recovering a lost world, the other in conquering a world yet unknown. They had accordingly, thanks to their victories in the ancient world and their discoveries in the new, acquired an influence at the court of Rome which had never been enjoyed by any of their predecessors.

So much for Spain.

In France, Charles VIII had succeeded his father, Louis XI, on the 30th of August, 1483. Louis by dint of executions, had tranquillized his kingdom and smoothed the way for a child who ascended the throne under the regency of a woman. And the regency had been a glorious one, and had put down the pretensions of princes of the blood, put an end to civil wars, and united to the crown all that yet remained of the great independent fiefs. The result was that at the epoch where we now are, here was Charles VIII, about twenty-two years of age, a prince (if we are to believe La Tremouille) little of body but great of heart; a child (if we are to believe Commines) only now making his first flight from the nest, destitute of both sense and money, feeble in person, full of self-will, and consorting rather with fools than with the wise; lastly, if we are to believe Guicciardini, who was an Italian, might well have brought a somewhat partial judgment to bear upon the subject, a young man of little wit concerning the actions of men, but carried away by an ardent desire for rule and the acquisition of glory, a desire based far more on his shallow character and impetuosity than on any consciousness of genius: he was an enemy to all fatigue and all business, and when he tried to give his attention to it he showed himself always totally wanting in prudence and judgment. If anything in him appeared at first sight to be worthy of praise, on a closer inspection it was found to be something nearer akin to vice than to virtue. He was liberal, it is true, but without thought, with no measure and no discrimination. He was sometimes inflexible in will; but this was through obstinacy rather than a constant mind; and what his flatterers called goodness deserved far more the name of insensibility to injuries or poverty of spirit.

As to his physical appearance, if we are to believe the same author, it was still less admirable, and answered marvelously to his weakness of mind and character. He was small, with a large head, a short thick neck, broad chest, and high shoulders; his thighs and legs were long and thin; and as his face also was ugly — and was only redeemed by the dignity and force of his glance — and all his limbs were disproportionate with one another, he had rather the appearance of a monster than a man. Such was he whom Fortune was destined to make a conqueror, for whom Heaven was reserving more glory than he had power to carry.

So much for France.

The Imperial throne was occupied by Frederic III, who had been rightly named the Peaceful, not for the reason that he had always maintained peace, but because, having constantly been beaten, he had always been forced to make it. The first proof he had given of this very philosophical forbearance was during his journey to Rome, whither he betook himself to be consecrated. In crossing the Apennines he was attacked by brigands. They robbed him, but he made no pursuit. And so, encouraged by example and by the impunity of lesser thieves, the greater ones soon took part in the robberies. Amurath seized part of Hungary. Mathias Corvinus took Lower Austria, and Frederic consoled himself for these usurpations by repeating the maxim, Forgetfulness is the best cure for the losses we suffer. At the time we have now reached, he had just, after a reign of fifty-three years, affianced his son Maximilian to Marie of Burgundy and had put under the ban of the

Empire his son-in-law, Albert of Bavaria, who laid claim to the ownership of the Tyrol. He was therefore too full of his family affairs to be troubled about Italy. Besides, he was busy looking for a motto for the house of Austria, an occupation of the highest importance for a man of the character of Frederic III. This motto, which Charles V was destined almost to render true, was at last discovered, to the great joy of the old emperor, who, judging that he had nothing more to do on earth after he had given this last proof of sagacity, died on the 19th of August, 1493; leaving the empire to his son Maximilian.

This motto was simply founded on the five vowels, a, e, i, o, u, the initial letters of these five words

"AUSTRIAE EST IMPERARE ORBI UNIVERSO"

This means

"It is the destiny of Austria to rule over the whole world."

So much for Germany.

Now that we have cast a glance over the four nations which were on the way, as we said before, to become European Powers, let us turn our attention to those secondary States which formed a circle more contiguous to Rome, and whose business it was to serve as armor, so to speak, to the spiritual queen of the world, should it please any of these political giants whom we have described to make encroachments with a view to an attack, on the seas or the mountains, the Adriatic Gulf or the Alps, the Mediterranean or the Apennines.

These were the kingdom of Naples, the duchy of Milan, the magnificent republic of Florence, and the most serene republic of Venice.

The kingdom of Naples was in the hands of the old Ferdinand, whose birth was not only illegitimate, but probably also well within the prohibited degrees. His father, Alfonso of Aragon, received his crown from Giovanna of Naples, who had adopted him as her successor. But since, in the fear of having no heir, the queen on her deathbed had named two instead of one, Alfonso had to sustain his rights against Rene. The two aspirants for some time disputed the crown. At last the house of Aragon carried the day over the house of Anjou, and in the course of the year 1442, Alfonso definitely secured his seat on the throne. Of this sort were the claims of the defeated rival which we shall see Charles VIII maintaining later on. Ferdinand had neither the courage nor the genius of his father, and yet he triumphed over his enemies, one after another he had two rivals, both far superior in merit to him self. The one was his nephew, the Count of Viana, who, basing his claim on his uncle's shameful birth, commanded the whole Aragonese party; the other was Duke John of Calabria, who commanded the whole Angevin party. Still he managed to hold the two apart, and to keep himself on the throne by dint of his prudence, which often verged upon duplicity. He had a cultivated mind, and had studied the sciences — above all, law. He was of middle height, with a large handsome head, his brow open and admirably framed in beautiful white hair, which fell nearly down to his shoulders. Moreover, though he had rarely exercised his physical strength in arms, this strength was so great that one day, when he happened to be on the square of the Mercato Nuovo at Naples, he seized by the horns a bull that had escaped and stopped him short, in spite of all the efforts the animal made to escape from his hands. Now the election of Alexander had caused him great uneasiness, and in spite of his usual prudence he had not been able to restrain himself from saying before the bearer of the news that not only did he fail to rejoice in this election, but also that he did not think that any Christian could rejoice in it, seeing that Borgia, having always been a bad man, would certainly make a bad pope. To this he added that, even were the choice an excellent one and such as would please everybody else, it would be none the less fatal to the house of Aragon, although Roderigo was born her subject and owed to her the origin and progress of his fortunes; for wherever reasons of state come in, the ties of blood and parentage are soon forgotten, and, 'a fortiori', relations arising from the obligations of nationality.

Thus, one may see that Ferdinand judged Alexander VI with his usual perspicacity; this, however, did not hinder him, as we shall soon perceive, from being the first to contract an alliance with him.

The duchy of Milan belonged nominally to John Galeazzo, grandson of Francesco Sforza, who had seized it by violence on the 26th of February, 1450, and bequeathed it to his son, Galeazzo Maria, father of the young prince now reigning; we say nominally, because the real master of the Milanese was at this period not the legitimate heir who was supposed to possess it, but his uncle Ludovico, surnamed 'il Moro', because of the mulberry tree which he bore in his arms. After being exiled with his two brothers, Philip who died of poison in 1479, and Ascanio who became the cardinal, he returned to Milan some days after the assassination of Galeazzo Maria, which took place on the 26th of December 1476, in St. Stephen's Church, and assumed the regency for the young duke, who at that time was only eight years old. From now onward, even after his nephew had reached the age of two-and-twenty, Ludovico continued to rule, and according to all probabilities was destined to rule a long time yet; for, some days after the poor young man had shown a desire to take the reins himself, he had fallen sick, and it was said, and not in a whisper, that he had taken one of those slow but mortal poisons of which princes made so frequent a use at this period, that, even when a malady was natural, a cause was always sought connected with some great man's interests. However it may have been, Ludovico had relegated his nephew, now too weak to busy himself henceforward with the affairs of his duchy, to the castle of Pavia, where he lay and languished under the eyes of his wife Isabella, daughter of King Ferdinand of Naples.

As to Ludovico, he was an ambitious man, full of courage and astuteness, familiar with the sword and with poison, which he used alternately, according to the occasion, without feeling any repugnance or any predilection for either of them; but quite decided to be his nephew's heir whether he died or lived.

Florence, although she had preserved the name of a republic, had little by little lost all her liberties, and belonged in fact, if not by right, to Piero dei Medici, to whom she had been bequeathed as a paternal legacy by Lorenzo, as we have seen, at the risk of his soul's salvation.

The son, unfortunately, was far from having the genius of his father: he was handsome, it is true, whereas Lorenzo, on the contrary, was remarkably ugly; he had an agreeable, musical voice, whereas Lorenzo had always spoken through his nose; he was instructed in Latin and Greek, his conversation was pleasant and easy, and he improvised verses almost as well as the so-called Magnificent; but he was both ignorant of political affairs and haughtily insolent in his behavior to those who had made them their study. Added to this, he was an ardent lover of pleasure, passionately addicted to women, incessantly occupied with bodily exercises that should make him shine in their eyes, above all with tennis, a game at which he very highly excelled: he promised himself that, when the period of mourning was fast, he would occupy the attention not only of Florence but of the whole of Italy, by the splendor of his courts and the renown of his fetes. Piero dei Medici had at any rate formed this plan; but Heaven decreed otherwise.

As to the most serene republic of Venice, whose doge was Agostino Barbarigo, she had attained, at the time we have reached, to her highest degree of power and splendor. From Cadiz to the Palus Maeotis, there was no port that was not open to her thousand ships; she possessed in Italy, beyond the coastline of the canals and the ancient duchy of Venice, the provinces of Bergamo, Brescia, Crema, Verona, Vicenza, and Padua; she owned the marches of Treviso, which comprehend the districts of Feltre, Belluno, Cadore, Polesella of Rovigo, and the principality of Ravenna; she also owned the Friuli, except Aquileia; Istria, except Trieste; she owned, on the east side of the Gulf, Zara, Spalatra, and the shore of Albania; in the Ionian Sea, the islands of Zante and Corfu; in Greece, Lepanto and Patras; in the Morea, Morone, Corone, Neapolis, and Argos; lastly, in the Archipelago, besides several little towns and stations on the coast, she owned Candia and the kingdom of Cyprus.

Thus from the mouth of the Po to the eastern extremity of the Mediterranean, the most serene republic was mistress of the whole coastline, and Italy and Greece seemed to be mere suburbs of Venice.

In the intervals of space left free between Naples, Milan,

Florence, and Venice, petty tyrants had arisen who exercised an absolute sovereignty over their territories: thus the Colonnas were at Ostia and at Nettuna, the Montefeltri at Urbino, the Manfredi at Faenza, the Bentivogli at Bologna, the Malatesta family at Rimini, the Vitelli at Citta di Castello, the Baglioni at Perugia, the Orsini at Vicovaro, and the princes of Este at Ferrara.

Finally, in the center of this immense circle, composed of great Powers, of secondary States, and of little tyrannies, Rome was set on high, the most exalted, yet the weakest of all, without influence, without lands, without an army, without gold. It was the concern of the new pope to secure all this: let us see, therefore, what manner of man was this Alexander VI, for undertaking and accomplishing such a project.

Chapter III

RODERIGO LENZUOLO was barn at Valencia, in Spain, in 1430 or 1431, and on his mother's side was descended, as some writers declare, of a family of royal blood, which had cast its eyes on the tiara only after cherishing hopes of the crowns of Aragon and Valencia. Roderigo from his infancy had shown signs of a marvelous quickness of mind, and as he grew older he exhibited an intelligence extremely apt far the study of sciences, especially law and jurisprudence: the result was that his first distinctions were gained in the law, a profession wherein he soon made a great reputation by his ability in the discussion of the most thorny cases. All the same, he was not slow to leave this career, and abandoned it quite suddenly far the military profession, which his father had followed; but after various actions which served to display his presence of mind and courage, he was as much disgusted with this profession as with the other; and since it happened that at the very time he began to feel this disgust his father died, leaving a considerable fortune, he resolved to do no more work, but to live according to his own fancies and caprices. About this time he became the lover of a widow who had two daughters. The widow dying, Roderigo took the girls under his protection, put one into a convent, and as the other was one of the loveliest women imaginable, made her his mistress. This was the notorious Rosa Vanozza, by whom he had five children — Francesco, Caesar, Lucrezia, and Goffredo; the name of the fifth is unknown.

Roderigo, retired from public affairs, was given up entirely to the affections of a lover and a father, when he heard that his uncle, who loved him like a son, had been elected pope under the name of Calixtus III. But the young man was at this time so much a lover that love imposed silence on ambition; and indeed he was almost terrified at the exaltation of his uncle, which was no doubt destined to force him once more into public life. Consequently, instead of hurrying to Rome, as anyone else in his place would have done, he was content to indite to His Holiness a letter in which he begged for the continuation of his favors, and wished him a long and happy reign.

This reserve on the part of one of his relatives, contrasted with the ambitious schemes which beset the new pope at every step, struck Calixtus III in a singular way: he knew the stuff that was in young Roderigo, and at a time when he was besieged on all sides by mediocrities, this powerful nature holding modestly aside gained new grandeur in his eyes so he replied instantly to Roderigo that on the receipt of his letter he must quit Spain for Italy, Valencia for Rome.

This letter uprooted Roderigo from the center of happiness he had created for himself, and where he might perhaps have slumbered on like an ordinary man, if fortune had not thus interposed to drag him forcibly away. Roderigo was happy, Roderigo was rich; the evil passions which were natural to him had been, if not extinguished, — at least lulled; he was frightened himself at the idea of changing the quiet life he was leading for the ambitious, agitated career that was promised him; and instead of obeying his uncle, he delayed the preparations for departure, hoping that Calixtus would forget him. It was not so: two months after he received the letter from the pope, there arrived at Valencia a prelate from Rome, the bearer of Roderigo's nomination to a benefice worth 20,000 ducats a year, and also a positive order to the holder of the post to come and take possession of his charge as soon as possible.

Holding back was no longer feasible: so Roderigo obeyed; but as he did not wish to be separated from the source whence had sprung eight years of happiness, Rosa Vanozza also left Spain, and while he was going to Rome, she betook herself to Venice, accompanied by two confidential servants, and under the protection of a Spanish gentleman named Manuel

Melchior.

Fortune kept the promises she had made to Roderigo: the pope received him as a son, and made him successively Archbishop of Valencia, Cardinal-Deacon, and Vice-Chancellor. To all these favors Calixtus added a revenue of 20,000 ducats, so that at the age of scarcely thirty-five Roderigo found himself the equal of a prince in riches and power.

Roderigo had had some reluctance about accepting the cardinalship, which kept him fast at Rome, and would have preferred to be General of the Church, a position which would have allowed him more liberty for seeing his mistress and his family; but his uncle Calixtus made him reckon with the possibility of being his successor some day, and from that moment the idea of being the supreme head of kings and nations took such hold of Roderigo, that he no longer had any end in view but that which his uncle had made him entertain.

From that day forward, there began to grow up in the young cardinal that talent for hypocrisy which made of him the most perfect incarnation of the devil that has perhaps ever existed; and Roderigo was no longer the same man: with words of repentance and humility on his lips, his head bowed as though he were bearing the weight of his past sins, disparaging the riches which he had acquired and which, according to him, were the wealth of the poor and ought to return to the poor, he passed his life in churches, monasteries, and hospitals, acquiring, his historian tells us, even in the eyes of his enemies, the reputation of a Solomon for wisdom, of a Job for patience, and of a very Moses for his promulgation of the word of God: Rosa Vanozza was the only person in the world who could appreciate the value of this pious cardinal's conversion.

It proved a lucky thing for Roderiga that he had assumed this pious attitude, for his protector died after a reign of three years three months and nineteen days, and he was now sustained by his own merit alone against the numerous enemies he had made by his rapid rise to fortune: so during the whole of the reign of Pius II he lived always apart from public affairs, and only reappeared in the days of Sixtus IV, who made him the gift of the abbacy of Subiaco, and sent him in the capacity of ambassador to the kings of Aragon and Portugal. On his return, which took place during the pontificate of Innocent VIII, he decided to fetch his family at last to Rome: thither they came, escorted by Don Manuel Melchior, who from that moment passed as the husband of Rosa Vanozza, and took the name of Count Ferdinand of Castile. The Cardinal Roderigo received the noble Spaniard as a countryman and a friend; and he, who expected to lead a most retired life, engaged a house in the street of the Lungara, near the church of Regina Coeli, on the banks of the Tiber. There it was that, after passing the day in prayers and pious works, Cardinal Roderigo used to repair each evening and lay aside his mask. And it was said, though nobody could prove it, that in this house infamous scenes passed: Report said the dissipations were of so dissolute a character that their equals had never been seen in Rome. With a view to checking the rumors that began to spread abroad, Roderigo sent Caesar to study at Pisa, and married Lucrezia to a young gentleman of Aragon; thus there only remained at home Rosa Vanozza and her two sons: such was the state of things when Innocent VIII died and Roderigo Borgia was proclaimed pope.

We have seen by what means the nomination was effected; and so the five cardinals who had taken no part in this simony — namely, the Cardinals of Naples, Sierra, Portugal, Santa Maria-in-Porticu, and St. Peter-in-Vinculis — protested loudly against this election, which they treated as a piece of jobbery; but Roderigo had none the less, however it was done, secured his majority; Roderigo was none the less the two hundred and sixtieth successor of St. Peter.

Alexander VI, however, though he had arrived at his object, did not dare throw off at first the mask which the Cardinal Bargia had worn so long, although when he was apprised of his election he could not dissimulate his joy; indeed, on hearing the favorable result of the scrutiny, he lifted his hands to heaven and cried, in the accents of satisfied ambition, "Am I then pope? Am I then Christ's vicar? Am I then the keystone of the Christian world?"

"Yes, holy father," replied Cardinal Ascanio Sforza, the same who had sold to Roderigo the nine votes that were at his disposal at the Conclave for four mules laden with silver;

"and we hope by your election to give glory to God, repose to the Church, and joy to Christendom, seeing that you have been chosen by the Almighty Himself as the most worthy among all your brethren."

But in the short interval occupied by this reply, the new pope had already assumed the papal authority, and in a humble voice and with hands crossed upon his breast, he spoke:

"We hope that God will grant us His powerful aid, in spite of our weakness, and that He will do for us that which He did for the apostle when aforetime He put into his hands the keys of heaven and entrusted to him the government of the Church, a government which without the aid of God would prove too heavy a burden for mortal man; but God promised that His Spirit should direct him; God will do the same, I trust, for us; and for your part we fear not lest any of you fail in that holy obedience which is due unto the head of the Church, even as the flock of Christ was bidden to follow the prince of the apostles."

Having spoken these words, Alexander donned the pontifical robes, and through the windows of the Vatican had strips of paper thrown out on which his name was written in Latin. These, blown by the wind, seemed to convey to the whole world the news of the great event which was about to change the face of Italy. The same day couriers started far all the courts of Europe.

Caesar Borgia learned the news of his father's election at the University of Pisa, where he was a student. His ambition had sometimes dreamed of such good fortune, yet his joy was little short of madness. He was then a young man, about twenty-two or twenty-four years of age, skilful in all bodily exercises, and especially in fencing; he could ride barebacked the most fiery steeds, could cut off the head of a bull at a single sword-stroke; moreover, he was arrogant, jealous, and insincere. According to Tammasi, he was great among the godless, as his brother Francesco was good among the great. As to his face, even contemporary authors have left utterly different descriptions; for same have painted him as a monster of ugliness, while others, on the contrary, extol his beauty. This contradiction is due to the fact that at certain times of the year, and especially in the spring, his face was covered with an eruption which, so long as it lasted, made him an object of horror and disgust, while all the rest of the year he was the somber, black-haired cavalier with pale skin and tawny beard whom Raphael shows us in the fine portrait he made of him. And historians, both chroniclers and painters, agree as to his fixed and powerful gaze, behind which burned a ceaseless flame, giving to his face something infernal and superhuman. Such was the man whose fortune was to fulfill all his desires. He had taken for his motto, 'Aut Caesar, aut nihil': Caesar or nothing.

Caesar posted to Rome with certain of his friends, and scarcely was he recognized at the gates of the city when the deference shown to him gave instant proof of the change in his fortunes: at the Vatican the respect was twice as great; mighty men bowed down before him as before one mightier than themselves. And so, in his impatience, he stayed not to visit his mother or any other member of his family, but went straight to the pope to kiss his feet; and as the pope had been forewarned of his coming, he awaited him in the midst of a brilliant and numerous assemblage of cardinals, with the three other brothers standing behind him. His Holiness received Caesar with a gracious countenance; still, he did not allow himself any demonstration of his paternal love, but, bending towards him, kissed him an the forehead, and inquired how he was and how he had fared on his journey. Caesar replied that he was wonderfully well, and altogether at the service of His Holiness: that, as to the journey, the trifling inconveniences and short fatigue had been compensated, and far mare than compensated, by the joy which he felt in being able to adore upon the papal throne a pope who was so worthy. At these words, leaving Caesar still on his knees, and reseating himself — for he had risen from his seat to embrace him — the pope assumed a grave and composed expression of face, and spoke as follows, loud enough to be heard by all, and slowly enough far everyone present to be able to ponder and retain in his memory even the least of his words:

"We are convinced, Caesar, that you are peculiarly rejoiced in beholding us on this sublime height, so far above our deserts, whereto it has pleased the Divine goodness to exalt us. This joy of yours is first of all our due because of the love we have always borne you and which we bear you still, and in the second place is prompted by your own personal interest, since henceforth you may feel sure of receiving from our pontifical hand those benefits which your own good works shall deserve. But if your joy — and this we say to you as we have even now said to your brothers — if your joy is founded on ought else than this, you are very greatly mistaken, Caesar, and you will find yourself sadly deceived. Perhaps we have been ambitious — we confess this humbly before the face of all men — passionately and immoderately ambitious to attain to the dignity of sovereign pontiff, and to reach this end we have followed every path that is open to human industry; but we have acted thus, vowing an inward vow that when once we had reached our goal, we would follow no other path but that which conduces best to the service of God and to the advancement of the Holy See, so that the glorious memory of the deeds that we shall do may efface the shameful recollection of the deeds we have already done. Thus shall we, let us hope, leave to those who follow us a track where upon if they find not the footsteps of a saint, they may at least tread in the path of a true pontiff. God, who has furthered the means, claims at our hands the fruits, and we desire to discharge to the full this mighty debt that we have incurred to Him; and accordingly we refuse to arouse by any deceit the stern rigor of His judgments. One sole hindrance could have power to shake our good intentions, and that might happen should we feel too keen an interest in your fortunes. Therefore are we armed beforehand against our love, and therefore have we prayed to God beforehand that we stumble not because of you; for in the path of favoritism a pope cannot slip without a fall, and cannot fall without injury and dishonor to the Holy See. Even to the end of our life we shall deplore the faults which have brought this experience home to us; and may it please Gad that our uncle Calixtus of blessed memory bear not this day in purgatory the burden of our sins, more heavy, alas, than his own! Ah, he was rich in every virtue, he was full of good intentions; but he loved too much his own people, and among them he loved me chief. And so he suffered this love to lead him blindly astray, all this love that he bore to his kindred, who to him were too truly flesh of his flesh, so that he heaped upon the heads of a few persons only, and those perhaps the least worthy, benefits which would more fittingly have rewarded the deserts of many. In truth, he bestowed upon our house treasures that should never have been amassed at the expense of the poor, or else should have been turned to a better purpose. He severed from the ecclesiastical State, already weak and poor, the duchy of Spoleto and other wealthy properties, that he might make them fiefs to us; he confided to our weak hands the vice-chancellorship, the vice-prefecture of Rome, the generalship of the Church, and all the other most important offices, which, instead of being monopolized by us, should have been conferred on those who were most meritorious. Moreover, there were persons who were raised on our recommendation to posts of great dignity, although they had no claims but such as our undue partiality accorded them; others were left out with no reason for their failure except the jealousy excited in us by their virtues. To rob Ferdinand of Aragon of the kingdom of Naples, Calixtus kindled a terrible war, which by a happy issue only served to increase our fortune, and by an unfortunate issue must have brought shame and disaster upon the Holy See. Lastly, by allowing himself to be governed by men who sacrificed public good to their private interests, he inflicted an injury, not only upon the pontifical throne and his own reputation, but what is far worse, far more deadly, upon his own conscience. And yet, O wise judgments of God! hard and incessantly though he toiled to establish our fortunes, scarcely had he left empty that supreme seat which we occupy today, when we were cast down from the pinnacle whereon we had climbed, abandoned to the fury of the rabble and the vindictive hatred of the Roman barons, who chose to feel offended by our goodness to their enemies. Thus, not only, we tell you, Caesar, not only did we plunge headlong from the summit of our grandeur, losing the worldly goods and dignities which our uncle had heaped at our feet, but for very peril of our life we were condemned to a voluntary exile, we and our friends, and in this way only did we contrive to escape the storm which our too good

fortune had stirred up against us. Now this is a plain proof
that God mocks at men's designs when they are bad ones.
How great an error is it for any pope to devote more care to
the welfare of a house, which cannot last more than a few
years, than to the glory of the Church, which will last forever!
What utter folly for any public man whose position is not
inherited and cannot be bequeathed to his posterity, to support the edifice of his grandeur on any other basis than the
noblest virtue practiced for the general good, and to suppose
that he can ensure the continuance of his own fortune otherwise than by taking all precautions against sudden whirl-
winds which are want to arise in the midst of a calm, and to
blow up the storm-clouds I mean the host of enemies. Now
any one of these enemies who does his worst can cause
injuries far more powerful than any help that is at all likely
to come from a hundred friends and their lying promises. If
you and your brothers walk in the path of virtue which we
shall now open for you, every wish of your heart shall be
instantly accomplished; but if you take the other path, if you
have ever hoped that our affection will wink at disorderly life,
then you will very soon find out that we are truly pope, Father
of the Church, not father of the family; that, vicar of Christ
as we are, we shall act as we deem best for Christendom, and
not as you deem best for your own private good. And now
that we have come to a thorough understanding, Caesar,
receive our pontifical blessing." And with these words, Alexander VI rose up, laid his hands upon his son's head, for
Caesar was still kneeling, and then retired into his apartments, without inviting him to follow.

The young man remained awhile stupefied at this discourse, so utterly unexpected, so utterly destructive at one fell
blow to his most cherished hopes. He rose giddy and stagger-
ing like a drunken man, and at once leaving the Vatican,
hurried to his mother, whom he had forgotten before, but
sought now in his despair. Rosa Vanozza possessed all the
vices and all the virtues of a Spanish courtesan; her devotion
to the Virgin amounted to superstition, her fondness for her
children to weakness, and her love for Roderigo to sensuality.
In the depth of her heart she relied on the influence she had
been able to exercise over him for nearly thirty years; and like

a snake, she knew haw to envelop him in her coils when the
fascination of her glance had lost its power. Rosa knew of old
the profound hypocrisy of her lover, and thus she was in no
difficulty about reassuring Caesar.

Lucrezia was with her mother when Caesar arrived; the two
young people exchanged a lover-like kiss beneath her very
eyes: and before he left Caesar had made an appointment for
the same evening with Lucrezia, who was now living apart
from her husband, to whom Roderigo paid a pension in her
palace of the Via del Pelegrino, opposite the Campo dei Fiori,
and there enjoying perfect liberty.

In the evening, at the hour fixed, Caesar appeared at
Lucrezia's; but he found there his brother Francesco. The two
young men had never been friends. Still, as their tastes were
very different, hatred with Francesco was only the fear of the
deer for the hunter; but with Caesar it was the desire for
vengeance and that lust for blood which lurks perpetually in
the heart of a tiger. The two brothers none the less embraced,
one from general kindly feeling, the other from hypocrisy;
but at first sight of one another the sentiment of a double
rivalry, first in their father's and then in their sister's good
graces, had sent the blood mantling to the cheek of Francesco,
and called a deadly pallor into Caesar's. So the two young
men sat on, each resolved not to be the first to leave, when
all at once there was a knock at the door, and a rival was
announced before whom both of them were bound to give
way: it was their father.

Rosa Vanazza was quite right in comforting Caesar. Indeed,
although Alexander VI had repudiated the abuses of nepo-
tism, he understood very well the part that was to be played
for his benefit by his sons and his daughter; for he knew he
could always count on Lucrezia and Caesar, if not on
Francesco and Goffredo. In these matters the sister was quite
worthy of her brother. Lucrezia was wanton in imagination,
godless by nature, ambitious and designing: she had a craving
for pleasure, admiration, honors, money, jewels, gorgeous
stuffs, and magnificent mansions. A true Spaniard beneath
her golden tresses, a courtesan beneath her frank looks, she
carried the head of a Raphael Madonna, and concealed the
heart of a Messalina. She was dear to Roderigo both as

daughter and as mistress, and he saw himself reflected in her as in a magic mirror, every passion and every vice. Lucrezia and Caesar were accordingly the best beloved of his heart, and the three composed that diabolical trio which for eleven years occupied the pontifical throne, like a mocking parody of the heavenly Trinity.

Nothing occurred at first to give the lie to Alexander's professions of principle in the discourse he addressed to Caesar, and the first year of his pontificate exceeded all the hopes of Rome at the time of his election. He arranged for the provision of stores in the public granaries with such liberality, that within the memory of man there had never been such astonishing abundance; and with a view to extending the general prosperity to the lowest class, he organized numerous doles to be paid out of his private fortune, which made it possible for the very poor to participate in the general banquet from which they had been excluded for long enough. The safety of the city was secured, from the very first days of his accession, by the establishment of a strong and vigilant police force, and a tribunal consisting of four magistrates of irreproachable character, empowered to prosecute all nocturnal crimes, which during the last pontificate had been so common that their very numbers made impunity certain: these judges from the first showed a severity which neither the rank nor the purse of the culprit could modify. This presented such a great contrast to the corruption of the last reign, — in the course of which the vice-chamberlain one day remarked in public, when certain people were complaining of the venality of justice, "God wills not that a sinner die, but that he live and pay," — that the capital of the Christian world felt for one brief moment restored to the happy days of the papacy. So, at the end of a year, Alexander VI had reconquered that spiritual credit, so to speak, which his predecessors lost. His political credit was still to be established, if he was to carry out the first part of his gigantic scheme. To arrive at this, he must employ two agencies — alliances and conquests. His plan was to begin with alliances. The gentleman of Aragon who had married Lucrezia when she was only the daughter of Cardinal Roderigo Borgia was not a man powerful enough, either by birth and fortune or by intellect, to

enter with any sort of effect into the plots and plans of
Alexander VI; the separation was therefore changed into a
divorce, and Lucrezia Borgia was now free to remarry. Alexander opened up two negotiations at the same time: he
needed an ally to keep a watch on the policy of the neighboring States. John Sforza, grandson of Alexander Sforza,
brother of the great Francis I, Duke of Milan, was lord of
Pesaro; the geographical situation of this place, an the coast,
on the way between Florence and Venice, was wonderfully
convenient for his purpose; so Alexander first cast an eye
upon him, and as the interest of both parties was evidently
the same, it came about that John Sforza was very soon
Lucrezia's second husband.

At the same time overtures had been made to Alfonso of
Aragon, heir presumptive to the crown of Naples, to arrange
a marriage between Dana Sancia, his illegitimate daughter,
and Goffreda, the pope's third son; but as the old Ferdinand
wanted to make the best bargain he could out of it; he dragged
on the negotiations as long as possible, urging that the two
children were not of marriageable age, and so, highly honored
as he felt in such a prospective alliance, there was no hurry
about the engagement. Matters stopped at this point, to the
great annoyance of Alexander VI, who saw through this
excuse, and understood that the postponement was nothing
more or less than a refusal. Accordingly Alexander and Ferdinand remained in statu quo, equals in the political game,
both on the watch till events should declare for one or other.
The turn of fortune was for Alexander.

Italy, though tranquil, was instinctively conscious that her
calm was nothing but the lull which goes before a storm. She
was too rich and too happy to escape the envy of other
nations. As yet the plains of Pisa had not been reduced to
marsh-lands by the combined negligence and jealousy of the
Florentine Republic, neither had the rich country that lay
around Rome been converted into a barren desert by the wars
of the Colonna and Orsini families; not yet had the Marquis
of Marignan razed to the ground a hundred and twenty
villages in the republic of Siena alone; and though the
Maremma was unhealthy, it was not yet a poisonous marsh:
it is a fact that Flavio Blando, writing in 1450, describes Ostia

as being merely less flourishing than in the days of the Romans, when she had numbered 50,000 inhabitants, whereas now in our own day there are barely 30 in all.

The Italian peasants were perhaps the most blest on the face of the earth: instead of living scattered about the country in solitary fashion, they lived in villages that were enclosed by walls as a protection for their harvests, animals, and farm implements; their houses — at any rate those that yet stand — prove that they lived in much more comfortable and beautiful surroundings than the ordinary townsman of our day. Further, there was a community of interests, and many people collected together in the fortified villages, with the result that little by little they attained to an importance never acquired by the boorish French peasants or the German serfs; they bore arms, they had a common treasury, they elected their own magistrates, and whenever they went out to fight, it was to save their common country.

Also commerce was no less flourishing than agriculture; Italy at this period was rich in industries — silk, wool, hemp, fur, alum, sulfur, bitumen; those products which the Italian soil could not bring forth were imported, from the Black Sea, from Egypt, from Spain, from France, and often returned whence they came, their worth doubled by labor and fine workmanship. The rich man brought his merchandise, the poor his industry: the one was sure of finding workmen, the other was sure of finding work.

Art also was by no means behindhand: Dante, Giotto, Brunelleschi, and Donatello were dead, but Ariosto, Raphael, Bramante, and Michael Angelo were now living. Rome, Florence, and Naples had inherited the masterpieces of antiquity; and the manuscripts of Aeschylus, Sophocles, and Euripides had come (thanks to the conquest of Mahomet II) to rejoin the statue of Xanthippus and the works of Phidias and Praxiteles. The principal sovereigns of Italy had come to understand, when they let their eyes dwell upon the fat harvests, the wealthy villages, the flourishing manufactories, and the marvelous churches, and then compared with them the poor and rude nations of fighting men who surrounded them on all sides, that some day or other they were destined to become for other countries what America was for Spain, a vast gold-mine for them to work. In consequence of this, a league offensive and defensive had been signed, about 1480, by Naples, Milan, Florence, and Ferrara, prepared to take a stand against enemies within or without, in Italy or outside. Ludovico Sforza, who was more than anyone else interested in maintaining this league, because he was nearest to France, whence the storm seemed to threaten, saw in the new pope's election means not only of strengthening the league, but of making its power and unity conspicuous in the sight of Europe.

Chapter IV

On the occasion of each new election to the papacy, it is the custom for all the Christian States to send a solemn embassy to Rome, to renew their oath of allegiance to the Holy Father. Ludovico Sforza conceived the idea that the ambassadors of the four Powers should unite and make their entry into Rome on the same day, appointing one of their envoy, viz. the representative of the King of Naples, to be spokesman for all four. Unluckily, this plan did not agree with the magnificent projects of Piero dei Medici. That proud youth, who had been appointed ambassador of the Florentine Republic, had seen in the mission entrusted to him by his fellow-citizens the means of making a brilliant display of his own wealth. From the day of his nomination onwards, his palace was constantly filled with tailors, jewelers, and merchants of priceless stuffs; magnificent clothes had been made for him, embroidered with precious stones which he had selected from the family treasures. All his jewels, perhaps the richest in Italy, were distributed about the liveries of his pages, and one of them, his favorite, was to wear a collar of pearls valued by itself at 100,000 ducats, or almost, a million of our francs. In his party the Bishop of Arezzo, Gentile, who had once been Lorenzo dei Medici's tutor, was elected as second ambassador, and it was his duty to speak. Now Gentile, who had prepared his speech, counted on his eloquence to charm the ear quite as much as Piero counted on his riches to dazzle the eye. But the eloquence of Gentile would be lost completely if nobody was to speak but the ambassador of the King of Naples; and the magnificence of Piero dei Medici would never be noticed at all if he went to Rome mixed up with all the other ambassadors. These two important interests, compromised by the Duke of Milan's proposition, changed the whole face of Italy.

Ludovico Sforza had already made sure of Ferdinand's promise to conform to the plan he had invented, when the old king, at the solicitation of Piero, suddenly drew back. Sforza found out how this change had come about, and learned that it was Piero's influence that had overmastered his own. He could not disentangle the real motives that had promised the change, and imagined there was some secret league against himself: he attributed the changed political program to the death of Lorenzo dei Medici. But whatever its cause might be, it was evidently prejudicial to his own interests: Florence, Milan's old ally, was abandoning her for Naples. He resolved to throw a counter weight into the scales; so, betraying to Alexander the policy of Piero and Ferdinand, he proposed to form a defensive and offensive alliance with him and admit the republic of Venice; Duke Hercules III of Ferrara was also to be summoned to pronounce for one or other of the two leagues. Alexander VI, wounded by Ferdinand's treatment of himself, accepted Ludovico Sforza's proposition, and an Act of Confederation was signed on the 22nd of April, 1493, by which the new allies pledged themselves to set on foot for the maintenance of the public peace an army of 20,000 horse and 6,000 infantry.

Ferdinand was frightened when he beheld the formation of this league; but he thought he could neutralize its effects by depriving Ludovico Sforza of his regency, which he had already kept beyond the proper time, though as yet he was not strictly an usurper. Although the young Galeazzo, his nephew, had reached the age of two-and-twenty, Ludovico Sforza none the less continued regent. Now Ferdinand definitely proposed to the Duke of Milan that he should resign the sovereign power into the hands of his nephew, on pain of being declared an usurper.

This was a bold stroke; but there was a risk of inciting Ludovico Sforza to start one of those political plots that he was so familiar with, never recoiling from any situation, however dangerous it might be. This was exactly what happened: Sforza, uneasy about his duchy, resolved to threaten Ferdinand's kingdom.

Nothing could be easier: he knew the warlike nations of Charles VIII, and the pretensions of the house of France to the kingdom of Naples. He sent two ambassadors to invite the young king to claim the rights of Anjou usurped by Aragon; and with a view to reconciling Charles to so distant and hazardous an expedition, offered him a free and friendly passage through his own States.

Such a proposition was welcome to Charles VIII, as we might suppose from our knowledge of his character; a magnificent prospect was opened to him as by an enchanter: what Ludovica Sforza was offering him was virtually the command of the Mediterranean, the protectorship of the whole of Italy; it was an open road, through Naples and Venice, that well might lead to the conquest of Turkey or the Holy Land, if he ever had the fancy to avenge the disasters of Nicapolis and Mansourah. So the proposition was accepted, and a secret alliance was signed, with Count Charles di Belgiojasa and the Count of Cajazza acting for Ludovica Sforza, and the Bishop of St. Malo and Seneschal de Beaucaire far Charles VIII. By this treaty it was agreed: —

That the King of France should attempt the conquest of the kingdom of Naples;

That the Duke of Milan should grant a passage to the King of France through his territories, and accompany him with five hundred lances;

That the Duke of Milan should permit the King of France to send out as many ships of war as he pleased from Genoa;

Lastly, that the Duke of Milan should lend the King of France 200,000 ducats, payable when he started.

On his side, Charles VIII agreed: —

To defend the personal authority of Ludowico Sforza over the duchy of Milan against anyone who might attempt to turn him out;

To keep two hundred French lances always in readiness to help the house of Sforza, at Asti, a town belonging to the Duke of Orleans by the inheritance of his mother, Valentina Visconti;

Lastly, to hand over to his ally the principality of Tarentum immediately after the conquest of Naples was effected.

This treaty was scarcely concluded when Charles VIII, who exaggerated its advantages, began to dream of freeing himself from every let or hindrance to the expedition. Precautions were necessary; for his relations with the great Powers were far from being what he could have wished.

Indeed, Henry VII had disembarked at Calais with a formidable army, and was threatening France with another invasion.

Ferdinand and Isabella of Spain, if they had not assisted at the fall of the house of Anjou, had at any rate helped the Aragon party with men and money.

Lastly, the war with the emperor acquired a fresh impetus when Charles VIII sent back Margaret of Burgundy to her father Maximilian, and contracted a marriage with Anne of Brittany.

By the treaty of Etaples, on the 3rd of November, 1492, Henry VII cancelled the alliance with the King of the Romans, and pledged himself not to follow his conquests.

This cost Charles VIII 745,000 gold crowns and the expenses of the war with England.

By the treaty of Barcelona, dated the 19th of January, 1493, Ferdinand the Catholic and Isabella agreed never to grant aid to their cousin, Ferdinand of Naples, and never to put obstacles in the way of the French king in Italy.

This cost Charles VIII Perpignan, Roussillon, and the Cerdagne, which had all been given to Louis XI as a hostage for the sum of 300,000 ducats by John of Aragon; but at the time agreed upon, Louis XI would not give them up for the money, for the old fox knew very well how important were these doors to the Pyrenees, and proposed in case of war to keep them shut.

Lastly, by the treaty of Senlis, dated the 23rd of May, 1493, Maximilian granted a gracious pardon to France for the insult her king had offered him.

It cost Charles VIII the counties of Burgundy, Artois, Charalais, and the seigniory of Noyers, which had come to him as Margaret's dowry, and also the towns of Aire, Hesdin, and Bethune, which he promised to deliver up to Philip of Austria on the day he came of age.

By dint of all these sacrifices the young king made peace with his neighbors, and could set on foot the enterprise that Ludavico Sforza had proposed. We have already explained that the project came into Sforza's mind when his plan about the deputation was refused, and that the refusal was due to Piero dei Medici's desire to make an exhibition of his magnificent jewels, and Gentile's desire to make his speech.

Thus the vanity of a tutor and the pride of his scholar together combined to agitate the civilized world from the Gulf of Tarentum to the Pyrenees.

Alexander VI was in the very center of the impending earthquake, and before Italy had any idea that the earliest shocks were at hand he had profited by the perturbed preoccupation of other people to give the lie to that famous speech we have reported. He created cardinal John Borgia, a nephew, who during the last pontificate had been elected Archbishop of Montreal and Governor of Rome. This promotion caused no discontent, because of John's antecedents; and Alexander, encouraged by the success of this, promised to Caesar Borgia the archbishopric of Valencia, a benefice he had himself enjoyed before his elevation to the papacy. But here the difficulty arose an the side of the recipient. The young man, full-blooded, with all the vices and natural instincts of a captain of condottieri, had very great trouble in assuming even the appearance of a Churchman's virtue; but as he knew from his own father's mouth that the highest secular dignities were reserved far his elder brother, he decided to take what he could get, for fear of getting nothing; but his hatred for Francesco grew stronger, for from henceforth he was doubly his rival, both in love and ambition.

Suddenly Alexander beheld the old King Ferdinand returning to his side, and at the very moment when he least expected it. The pope was too clever a politician to accept a reconciliation without finding out the cause of it; he soon learned what plots were hatching at the French court against the kingdom of Naples, and the whole situation was explained.

Now it was his turn to impose conditions.

He demanded the completion of a marriage between Goffreda, his third son, and Dada Sancia, Alfonso's illegitimate daughter.

He demanded that she should bring her husband as dowry the principality of Squillace and the county of Cariati, with an income of 10,000 ducats and the office of protonotary, one of the seven great crown offices which are independent of royal control.

He demanded for his eldest son, whom Ferdinand the Catholic had just made Duke of Gandia, the principality of Tricarico, the counties of Chiaramonte, Lauria, and Carinola, an income of 12,000 ducats, and the first of the seven great offices which should fall vacant.

He demanded that Virginio Orsini, his ambassador at the Neapolitan court, should be given a third great office, viz. that of Constable, the most important of them all.

Lastly, he demanded that Giuliano delta Rovere, one of the five cardinals who had opposed his election and was now taking refuge at Ostia, where the oak whence he took his name and bearings is still to be seen carved on all the walls, should be driven out of that town, and the town itself given over to him.

In exchange, he merely pledged himself never to withdraw from the house of Aragon the investiture of the kingdom of Naples accorded by his predecessors. Ferdinand was paying somewhat dearly for a simple promise; but on the keeping of this promise the legitimacy of his power wholly depended. For the kingdom of Naples was a fief of the Holy See; and to the pope alone belonged the right of pronouncing on the justice of each competitor's pretensions; the continuance of this investiture was therefore of the highest conceivable importance to Aragon just at the time when Anjou was rising up with an army at her back to dispossess her.

For a year after he mounted the papal throne, Alexander VI had made great strides, as we see, in the extension of his temporal power. In his own hands he held, to be sure, only the least in size of the Italian territories; but by the marriage of his daughter Lucrezia with the lord of Pesaro he was stretching out one hand as far as Venice, while by the marriage of the Prince of Squillace with Dona Sancia, and the territories conceded to the Duke of Sandia, he was touching with the other hand the boundary of Calabria.

When this treaty, so advantageous for himself, was duly

signed, he made Caesar Cardinal of Santa Maria Novella, for Caesar was always complaining of being left out in the distribution of his father's favors.

Only, as there was as yet no precedent in Church history for a bastard's donning the scarlet, the pope hunted up four false witnesses who declared that Caesar was the son of Count Ferdinand of Castile; who was, as we know, that valuable person Don Manuel Melchior, and who played the father's part with just as much solemnity as he had played the husband's.

The wedding of the two bastards was most splendid, rich with the double pomp of Church and King. As the pope had settled that the young bridal pair should live near him, Caesar Borgia, the new cardinal, undertook to manage the ceremony of their entry into Rome and the reception, and Lucrezia, who enjoyed at her father's side an amount of favor hitherto unheard of at the papal court, desired on her part to contribute all the splendor she had it in her power to add. He therefore went to receive the young people with a stately and magnificent escort of lords and cardinals, while she awaited them attended by the loveliest and noblest ladies of Rome, in one of the halls of the Vatican. A throne was there prepared for the pope, and at his feet were cushions far Lucrezia and Dona Sancia. "Thus," writes Tommaso Tommasi, "by the look of the assembly and the sort of conversation that went on for hours, you would suppose you were present at some magnificent and voluptuous royal audience of ancient Assyria, rather than at the severe consistory of a Roman pontiff, whose solemn duty it is to exhibit in every act the sanctity of the name he bears. But," continues the same historian, "if the Eve of Pentecost was spent in such worthy functions, the celebrations of the coming of the Holy Ghost on the following day were no less decorous and becoming to the spirit of the Church; for thus writes the master of the ceremonies in his journal:

"'The pope made his entry into the Church of the Holy Apostles, and beside him on the marble steps of the pulpit where the canons of St. Peter are wont to chant the Epistle and Gospel, sat Lucrezia his daughter and Sancia his son's wife: round about them, a disgrace to the Church and a public scandal, were grouped a number of other Roman ladies far more fit to dwell in Messalina's city than in St. Peter's.'"

So at Rome and Naples did men slumber while ruin was at hand; so did they waste their time and squander their money in a vain display of pride; and this was going on while the French, thoroughly alive, were busy laying hands upon the torches with which they would presently set Italy on fire.

Indeed, the designs of Charles VIII for conquest were no longer for anybody a matter of doubt. The young king had sent an embassy to the various Italian States, composed of Perrone dei Baschi, Brigonnet, d'Aubigny, and the president of the Provencal Parliament. The mission of this embassy was to demand from the Italian princes their co-operation in recovering the rights of the crown of Naples for the house of Anjou.

The embassy first approached the Venetians, demanding aid and counsel for the king their master. But the Venetians, faithful to their political tradition, which had gained for them the sobriquet of "the Jews of Christendom," replied that they were not in a position to give any aid to the young king, so long as they had to keep ceaselessly on guard against the Turks; that, as to advice, it would be too great a presumption in them to give advice to a prince who was surrounded by such experienced generals and such able ministers.

Perrone dei Baschi, when he found he could get no other answer, next made for Florence. Piero dei Medici received him at a grand council, for he summoned on this occasion not only the seventy, but also the gonfalonieri who had sat for the last thirty-four years in the Signoria. The French ambassador put forward his proposal, that the republic should permit their army to pass through her States, and pledge herself in that case to supply for ready money all the necessary victual and fodder. The magnificent republic replied that if Charles VIII had been marching against the Turks instead of against Ferdinand, she would be only too ready to grant everything he wished; but being bound to the house of Aragon by a treaty, she could not betray her ally by yielding to the demands of the King of France.

The ambassadors next turned their steps to Siena. The poor little republic, terrified by the honor of being considered at all, replied that it was her desire to preserve a strict neutrality, that she was too weak to declare beforehand either for or against such mighty rivals, for she would naturally be obliged to join the stronger party. Furnished with this reply, which had at least the merit of frankness, the French envoys proceeded to Rome, and were conducted into the pope's presence, where they demanded the investiture of the kingdom of Naples for their king.

Alexander VI replied that, as his predecessors had granted this investiture to the house of Aragon, he could not take it away, unless it were first established that the house of Anjou had a better claim than the house that was to be dispossessed. Then he represented to Perrone dei Baschi that, as Naples was a fief of the Holy See, to the pope alone the choice of her sovereign properly belonged, and that in consequence to attack the reigning sovereign was to attack the Church itself.

The result of the embassy, we see, was not very promising for Charles VIII; so he resolved to rely on his ally Ludovico Sforza alone, and to relegate all other questions to the fortunes of war.

A piece of news that reached him about this time strengthened him in this resolution: this was the death of Ferdinand. The old king had caught a severe cold and cough on his return from the hunting field, and in two days he was at his last gasp. On the 25th of January, 1494, he passed away, at the age of seventy, after a thirty-six years' reign, leaving the throne to his elder son, Alfonso, who was immediately chosen as his successor.

Ferdinand never belied his title of "the happy ruler." His death occurred at the very moment when the fortune of his family was changing.

The new king, Alfonso, was not a novice in arms: he had already fought successfully against Florence and Venice, and had driven the Turks out of Otranto; besides, he had the name of being as cunning as his father in the tortuous game of politics so much in vogue at the Italian courts. He did not despair of counting among his allies the very enemy he was at war with when Charles VIII first put forward his pretensions, we mean Bajazet II. So he dispatched to Bajazet one of his confidential ministers, Camillo Pandone, to give the

Turkish emperor to understand that the expedition to Italy
was to the King of France nothing but a blind for approaching the scene of Mohammedan conquests, and that if Charles
VIII were once at the Adriatic it would only take him a day
or two to get across and attack Macedonia; from there he
could easily go by land to Constantinople. Consequently he
suggested that Bajazet for the maintenance of their common
interests should supply six thousand horse and six thousand
infantry; he himself would furnish their pay so long as they
were in Italy. It was settled that Pandone should be joined at
Tarentum by Giorgia Bucciarda, Alexander VI's envoy, who
was commissioned by the pope to engage the Turks to help
him against the Christians. But while he was waiting for
Bajazet's reply, which might involve a delay of several
months, Alfonso requested that a meeting might take place
between Piero dei Medici, the pope, and himself, to take
counsel together about important affairs. This meeting was
arranged at Vicovaro, near Tivoli, and the three interested
parties duly met on the appointed day.

The intention of Alfonso, who before leaving Naples had
settled the disposition of his naval forces, and given his
brother Frederic the command of a fleet that consisted of
thirty-six galleys, eighteen large and twelve small vessels, with
injunctions to wait at Livorno and keep a watch on the fleet
Charles VIII was getting ready at the port of Genoa, was above
all things to check with the aid of his allies the progress of
operations on land. Without counting the contingent he
expected his allies to furnish, he had at his immediate disposal a hundred squadrons of heavy cavalry, twenty men in
each, and three thousand bowmen and light horse. He proposed, therefore, to advance at once into Lombardy, to get
up a revolution in favor of his nephew Galeazzo, and to drive
Ludovico Sforza out of Milan before he could get help from
France; so that Charles VIII, at the very time of crossing the
Alps, would find an enemy to fight instead of a friend who
had promised him a safe passage, men, and money.

This was the scheme of a great politician and a bold
commander; but as everybody had came in pursuit of his own
interests, regardless of the common this plan was very coldly
received by Piero dei Medici, who was afraid lest in the war

he should play only the same poor part he had been threatened with in the affair of the embassy; by Alexander VI it was rejected, because he reckoned on employing the troops of Alfonso an his own account. He reminded the King of Naples of one of the conditions of the investiture he had promised him, viz. that he should drive out the Cardinal Giuliano delta Rovere from the town of Ostia, and give up the town to him, according to the stipulation already agreed upon. Besides, the advantages that had accrued to Virginio Orsini, Alexander's favorite, from his embassy to Naples had brought upon him the ill-will of Prospero and Fabrizio Colonna, who owned nearly all the villages round about Rome. Now the pope could not endure to live in the midst of such powerful enemies, and the most important matter was to deliver him from all of them, seeing that it was really of moment that he should be at peace who was the head and soul of the league whereof the others were only the body and limbs.

Although Alfonso had clearly seen through the motives of Piero's coldness, and Alexander had not even given him the trouble of seeking his, he was none the less obliged to bow to the will of his allies, leaving the one to defend the Apennines against the French, and helping the other to shake himself free of his neighbors in the Romagna. Consequently he, pressed on the siege of Ostia, and added to Virginio's forces, which already amounted to two hundred men of the papal army, a body of his own light horse; this little army was to be stationed round about Rome, and was to enforce obedience from the Colonnas. The rest of his troops Alfonso divided into two parties: one he left in the hands of his son Ferdinand, with orders to scour the Romagna and worry, the petty princes into levying and supporting the contingent they had promised, while with the other he himself defended the defiles of the Abruzzi.

On the 23rd of April, at three o'clock in the morning, Alexander VI was freed from the first and fiercest of his foes; Giuliano delta Rovere, seeing the impossibility of holding out any longer against Alfonso's troops, embarked on a brigantine which was to carry him to Savona.

From that day forward Virginio Orsini began that famous partisan warfare which reduced the country about Rome to the most pathetic desolation the world has ever seen. During all this time Charles VIII was at Lyons, not only uncertain as to the route he ought to take for getting into Italy, but even beginning to reflect a little on the chances and risks of such an expedition. He had found no sympathy anywhere except with Ludovico Sforza; so it appeared not unlikely that he would have to fight not the kingdom of Naples alone, but the whole of Italy to boot. In his preparations for war he had spent almost all the money at his disposal; the Lady of Beaujeu and the Duke of Bourbon both condemned his enterprise; Briconnet, who had advised it, did not venture to support it now; at last Charles, more irresolute than ever, had recalled several regiments that had actually started, when Cardinal Giuliano delta Rovere, driven out of Italy by the pope, arrived at Lyons, and presented himself before the king.

The cardinal, full of hatred, full of hope, hastened to Charles, and found him on the point of abandoning that enterprise on which, as Alexander's enemy, delta Rovere rested his whole expectation of vengeance. He informed Charles of the quarrelling among his enemies; he showed him that each of them was seeking his own ends — Piero dei Medici the gratification of his pride, the pope the aggrandizement of his house. He pointed out that armed fleets were in the ports of Villefranche, Marseilles, and Genoa, and that these armaments would be lost; he reminded him that he had sent Pierre d'Urfe, his grand equerry, on in advance, to have splendid accommodation prepared in the Spinola and Doria palaces. Lastly, he urged that ridicule and disgrace would fall on him from every side if he renounced an enterprise so loudly vaunted beforehand, for whose successful execution, moreover, he had been obliged to sign three treaties of peace that were all vexatious enough, viz. with Henry VII, with Maximilian, and with Ferdinand the Catholic. Giuliano della Rovere had exercised true insight in probing the vanity of the young king, and Charles did not hesitate for a single moment. He ordered his cousin, the Duke of Orleans (who later on became Louis XII) to take command of the French fleet and bring it to Genoa; he dispatched a courier to Antoine de Bessay, Baron de Tricastel, bidding him take to Asti the 2000 Swiss foot-soldiers he had levied in the cantons; lastly, he started himself from Vienne, in Dauphine, on the 23rd of August, 1494, crossed the Alps by Mont Genevre, without encountering a single body of troops to dispute his passage, descended into Piedmont and Monferrato, both just then governed by women regents, the sovereigns of both principalities being children, Charles John Aime and William John, aged respectively six and eight.

The two regents appeared before Charles VIII, one at Turin, one at Casale, each at the head of a numerous and brilliant court, and both glittering with jewels and precious stones. Charles, although he quite well knew that for all these friendly demonstrations they were both bound by treaty to his enemy, Alfonso of Naples, treated them all the same with the greatest politeness, and when they made protestations of friendship, asked them to let him have a proof of it, suggesting that they should lend him the diamonds they were covered with. The two regents could do no less than obey the invitation which was really a command. They took off necklaces, rings, and earrings. Charles VIII gave them a receipt accurately drawn up, and pledged the jewels for 20,000 ducats. Then, enriched by this money, he resumed his journey and made his way towards Asti. The Duke of Orleans held the sovereignty of Asti, as we said before, and hither came to meet Charles both Ludovico Sforza and his father-in-law, Hercules d'Este, Duke of Ferrara. They brought with them not only the promised troops and money, but also a court composed of the loveliest women in Italy.

The balls, fetes, and tourneys began with a magnificence surpassing anything that Italy had ever seen before. But suddenly they were interrupted by the king's illness. This was the first example in Italy of the disease brought by Christopher Columbus from the New World, and was called by Italians the French, by Frenchmen the Italian disease. The probability is that some of Columbus's crew who were at Genoa or thereabouts had already brought over this strange and cruel complaint that counter balanced the gains of the American gold-mines.

The king's indisposition, however, did not prove so grave as was at first supposed. He was cured by the end of a few weeks, and proceeded on his way towards Pavia, where the young Duke John Galeazzo lay dying. He and the King of France were first cousins, sons of two sisters of the house of Savoy. So Charles VIII was obliged to see him, and went to visit him in the castle where he lived more like prisoner than lord. He found him half reclining on a couch, pale and emaciated, some said in consequence of luxurious living, others from the effects of a slow but deadly poison. But whether or not the poor young man was desirous of pouring out a complaint to Charles, he did not dare say a word; for his uncle, Ludovico Sforza, never left the King of France for an instant. But at the very moment when Charles VIII was getting up to go, the door opened, and a young woman appeared and threw herself at the king's feet; she was the wife of the unlucky John Galeazzo, and came to entreat his cousin to do nothing against her father Alfonso, nor against her brother Ferdinand. At sight of her; Sforza scowled with an anxious and threatening aspect, far he knew not what impression might be produced on his ally by this scene. But he was soon reassured; far Charles replied that he had advanced too far to draw back now, and that the glory of his name was at stake as well as the interests of his kingdom, and that these two motives were far too important to be sacrificed to any sentiment of pity he might feel, however real and deep it might be and was. The poor young woman, who had based her last hope an this appeal, then rose from her knees and threw herself sobbing into her husband's arms. Charles VIII and Ludavico Sforza, took their leave: John Galeazzo was doomed.

Two days after, Charles VIII left for Florence, accompanied by his ally; but scarcely had they reached Parma when a messenger caught them up, and announced to Ludovico that his nephew was just dead: Ludovico at once begged Charles to excuse his leaving him to finish the journey alone; the interests which called him back to Milan were so important, he said, that he could not under the circumstances stay away a single day longer. As a fact he had to make sure of succeeding the man he had assassinated.

But Charles VIII continued his road not without some uneasiness. The sight of the young prince on his deathbed had moved him deeply, for at the bottom of his heart he was convinced that Ludovico Sforza was his murderer; and a murderer might very well be a traitor. He was going forward into an unfamiliar country, with a declared enemy in front of him and a doubtful friend behind: he was now at the entrance to the mountains, and as his army had no store of provisions and only lived from hand to mouth, a forced delay, however short, would mean famine. In front of him was Fivizzano, nothing, it is true, but a village surrounded by walls, but beyond Fivizzano lay Sarzano and Pietra Santa, both of them considered impregnable fortresses; worse than this, they were coming into a part of the country that was especially unhealthy in October, had no natural product except oil, and even procured its own corn from neighboring provinces; it was plain that a whole army might perish there in a few days either from scarcity of food or from the unwholesome air, both of which were more disastrous than the impediments offered at every step by the nature of the ground. The situation was grave; but the pride of Piero dei Medici came once more to the rescue of the fortunes of Charles VIII.

Chapter V

*P*IERO DEI MEDICI had, as we may remember, undertaken to hold the entrance to Tuscany against the French; when, however, he saw his enemy coming dawn from the Alps, he felt less confident about his own strength, and demanded help from the pope; but scarcely had the rumor of foreign invasion began to spread in the Romagna, than the Colonna family declared themselves the French king's men, and collecting all their forces seized Ostia, and there awaited the coming of the French fleet to offer a passage through Rome. The pope, therefore, instead of sending troops to Florence, was obliged to recall all his soldiers to be near the capital; the only promise he made to Piero was that if Bajazet should send him the troops that he had been asking for, he would dispatch that army for him to make use of. Piero dei Medici had not yet taken any resolution or formed any plan, when he suddenly heard two startling pieces of news. A jealous neighbor of his, the Marquis of Torderiovo, had betrayed to the French the weak side of Fivizzano, so that they had taken it by storm, and had put its soldiers and inhabitants to the edge of the sword; on another side, Gilbert of Montpensier, who had been lighting up the sea-coast so as to keep open the communications between the French army and their fleet, had met with a detachment sent by Paolo Orsini to Sarzano, to reinforce the garrison there, and after an hour's fighting had cut it to pieces. No quarter had been granted to any of the prisoners; every man the French could get hold of they had massacred.

This was the first occasion on which the Italians, accustomed as they were to the chivalrous contests of the fifteenth century, found themselves in contact with savage foreigners who, less advanced in civilization, had not yet come to consider war as a clever game, but looked upon it as simply a mortal conflict. So the news of these two butcheries produced a tremendous sensation at Florence, the richest city in Italy, and the most prosperous in commerce and in art. Every Florentine imagined the French to be like an army of those ancient barbarians who were wont to extinguish fire with blood. The prophecies of Savonarola, who had predicted the foreign invasion and the destruction that should follow it, were recalled to the minds of all; and so much perturbation was evinced that Piero dei Medici, bent on getting peace at any price, forced a decree upon the republic whereby she was to send an embassy to the conqueror; and obtained leave, resolved as he was to deliver himself in person into the hands of the French monarch, to act as one of the ambassadors. He accordingly quitted Florence, accompanied by four other messengers, and an his arrival at Pietra Santa, sent to ask from Charles VIII a safe-conduct for himself alone. The day after he made this request, Brigonnet and de Piennes came to fetch him, and led him into the presence of Charles VIII.

Piero dei Medici, in spite of his name and influence, was in the eyes of the French nobility, who considered it a dishonorable thing to concern oneself with art or industry, nothing more than a rich merchant, with whom it would be absurd to stand upon any very strict ceremony. So Charles VIII received him on horseback, and addressing him with a haughty air, as a master might address a servant, demanded whence came this pride of his that made him dispute his entrance into Tuscany. Piero dei Medici replied, that, with the actual consent of Louis XI, his father Lorenzo had concluded a treaty of alliance with Ferdinand of Naples; that accordingly he had acted in obedience to prior obligations, but as he did, not wish to push too far his devotion to the house of Aragon or his opposition to France, he was ready to do whatever Charles VIII might demand of him. The king, who had never looked for such humility in his enemy, demanded that Sarzano should be given up to him: to this Piero dei Medici at once consented. Then the conqueror, wishing to see how far the ambassador of the magnificent republic would extend his politeness, replied that this concession was far from satisfying him, and that he still must have the keys of Pietra Santa, Pisa, Librafatta, and Livorno. Piero saw no more difficulty about these than about Sarzano, and consented on Charles's mere promise by word of mouth to restore the town when he had achieved the conquest of Naples. At last Charles VIII, seeing that this man who had been sent out to negotiate with him was very easy to manage, exacted as a final condition, a 'sine qua non', however, of his royal protection, that the magnificent republic should lend him the sum of 200,000 florins. Piero found it no harder to dispose of money than of fortresses, and replied that his fellow-citizens would be happy to render this service to their new ally. Then Charles VIII set him on horseback, and ordered him to go on in front, so as to begin to carry out his promises by yielding up the four fortresses he had insisted on having. Piero obeyed, and the French army, led by the grandson of Cosimo the Great and the son of Lorenzo the Magnificent, continued its triumphal march through Tuscany.

On his arrival at Lucca, Piero dei Medici learnt that his concessions to the King of France were making a terrible commotion at Florence. The magnificent republic had supposed that what Charles VIII wanted was simply a passage through her territory, so when the news came there was a general feeling of discontent, which was augmented by the return of the other ambassadors, whom Piero had not even consulted when he took action as he did. Piero considered it necessary that he should return, so he asked Charles's permission to precede him to the capital. As he had fulfilled all his promises, except the matter of the loan, which could not be settled anywhere but at Florence, the king saw no objection, and the very evening after he quitted the French army Piero returned incognito to his palace in the Via Largo.

The next day he proposed to present himself before the Signoria, but when he arrived at the Piazza del Palazzo Vecchio, he perceived the gonfaloniere Jacopo de Nerli coming towards him, signaling to him that it was useless to attempt to go farther, and pointing out to him the figure of

Luca Corsini standing at the gate, sword in hand: behind him stood guards, ordered, if need-were, to dispute his passage. Piero dei Medici, amazed by an opposition that he was experiencing for the first time in his life, did not attempt resistance. He went home, and wrote to his brother-in-law, Paolo Orsini, to come and help him with his gendarmes. Unluckily for him, his letter was intercepted. The Signoria considered that it was an attempt at rebellion. They summoned the citizens to their aid; they armed hastily, sallied forth in crowds, and thronged about the piazza of the palace. Meanwhile Cardinal Gian dei Medici had mounted on horseback, and under the impression that the Orsini were coming to the rescue, was riding about the streets of Florence, accompanied by his servants and uttering his battle cry, "Palle, Palle." But times had changed: there was no echo to the cry, and when the cardinal reached the Via dei Calizaioli, a threatening murmur was the only response, and he understood that instead of trying to arouse Florence he had much better get away before the excitement ran too high. He promptly retired to his own palace, expecting to find there his two brothers, Piero and Giuliano. But they, under the protection of Orsini and his gendarmes, had made their escape by the Porto San Gallo. The peril was imminent, and Gian dei Medici wished to follow their example; but wherever he went he was met by a clamor that grew more and more threatening. At last, as he saw that the danger was constantly increasing, he dismounted from his horse and ran into a house that he found standing open. This house by a lucky chance communicated with a convent of Franciscans; one of the friars lent the fugitive his dress, and the cardinal, under the protection of this humble incognito, contrived at last to get outside Florence, and joined his two brothers in the Apennines.

The same day the Medici were declared traitors and rebels, and ambassadors were sent to the King of France. They found him at Pisa, where he was granting independence to the town which eighty-seven years ago had fallen under the rule of the Florentines. Charles VIII made no reply to the envoys, but merely announced that he was going to march on Florence.

Such a reply, one may easily understand, terrified the republic. Florence, had no time to prepare a defense, and no strength in her present state to make one. But all the powerful houses assembled and armed their own servants and retainers, and awaited the issue, intending not to begin hostilities, but to defend themselves should the French make an attack. It was agreed that if any necessity should arise for taking up arms, the bells of the various churches in the town should ring a peal and so serve as a general signal. Such a resolution was perhaps of more significant moment in Florence than it could have been in any other town. For the palaces that still remain from that period are virtually fortresses and the eternal fights between Guelphs and Ghibellines had familiarized the Tuscan people with street warfare.

The king appeared, an the 17th of November, in the evening, at the gate of San Friano. He found there the nobles of Florence clad in their most magnificent apparel, accompanied by priests chanting hymns, and by a mob who were full of joy at any prospect of change, and hoped for a return of liberty after the fall of the Medici. Charles VIII stopped for a moment under a sort of gilded canopy that had been prepared for him, and replied in a few evasive words to the welcoming speeches which were addressed to him by the Signoria; then he asked for his lance, he set it in rest, and gave the order to enter the town, the whole of which he paraded with his army following him with arms erect, and then went down to the palace of the Medici, which had been prepared for him.

The next day negotiations commenced; but everyone was out of his reckoning. The Florentines had received Charles VIII as a guest, but he had entered the city as a conqueror. So when the deputies of the Signoria spoke of ratifying the treaty of Piero dei Medici, the king replied that such a treaty no longer existed, as they had banished the man who made it; that he had conquered Florence, as he proved the night before, when he entered lance in hand; that he should retain the sovereignty, and would make any further decision whenever it pleased him to do so; further, he would let them know later on whether he would reinstate the Medici or whether he would delegate his authority to the Signoria: all they had to do was to come back the next day, and he would give them his ultimatum in writing.

This reply threw Florence into a great state of consternation; but the Florentines were confirmed in their resolution of making a stand. Charles, for his part, had been astonished by the great number of the inhabitants; not only was every street he had passed through thickly lined with people, but every house from garret to basement seemed overflowing with human beings. Florence indeed, thanks to her rapid increase in population, could muster nearly 150,000 souls.

The next day, at the appointed hour, the deputies made their appearance to meet the king. They were again introduced into his presence, and the discussion was reopened. At last, as they were coming to no sort of understanding, the royal secretary, standing at the foot of the throne upon which Charles viii sat with covered head, unfolded a paper and began to read, article by article, the conditions imposed by the King of France. But scarcely had he read a third of the document when the discussion began more hotly than ever before. Then Charles VIII said that thus it should be, or he would order his trumpets to be sounded. Hereupon Piero Capponi, secretary to the republic, commonly called the Scipio of Florence, snatched from the royal secretary's hand the shameful proposal of capitulation, and tearing it to pieces, exclaimed: —

"Very good, sire; blow your trumpets, and we will ring our bells."

He threw the pieces in the face of the amazed reader, and dashed out of the room to give the terrible order that would convert the street of Florence into a battlefield.

Still, against all probabilities, this bold answer saved the town. The French supposed, from such audacious words, addressed as they were to men who so far had encountered no single obstacle, that the Florentines were possessed of sure resources, to them unknown: the few prudent men who retained any influence over the king advised him accordingly to abate his pretensions; the result was that Charles VIII offered new and more reasonable conditions, which were accepted, signed by both parties, and proclaimed on the 26th of November during mass in the cathedral of Santa Maria Del Fiore.

These were the conditions:

The Signoria were to pay to Charles VIII, as subsidy, the sum of 120,000 florins, in three installments;

The Signoria were to remove the sequestration imposed upon the property of the Medici, and to recall the decree that set a price on their heads;

The Signoria were to engage to pardon the Pisans, on condition of their again submitting to the rule of Florence;

Lastly, the Signoria were to recognize the claims of the Duke of Milan over Sarzano and Pietra Santa, and these claims thus recognized, were to be settled by arbitration.

In exchange for this, the King of France pledged himself to restore the fortresses that had been given up to him, either after he had made himself master of the town of Naples, or when this war should be ended by a peace or a two years' truce, or else when, for any reason whatsoever, he should have quitted Italy.

Two days after this proclamation, Charles VIII, much to the joy of the Signoria, left Florence, and advanced towards Rome by the route of Poggibondi and Siena.

The pope began to be affected by the general terror: he had heard of the massacres of Fivizzano, of Lunigiane, and of Imola; he knew that Piero dei Medici had handed over the Tuscan fortresses, that Florence had succumbed, and that Catherine Sforza had made terms with the conqueror; he saw the broken remnants of the Neapolitan troops pass disheartened through Rome, to rally their strength in the Abruzzi, and thus he found himself exposed to an enemy who was advancing upon him with the whole of the Romagna under his control from one sea to the other, in a line of march extending from Piombina to Ancona.

It was at this juncture that Alexander VI received his answer from Bajazet II: the reason of so long a delay was that the pope's envoy and the Neapolitan ambassador had been stopped by Gian della Rovere, the Cardinal Giuliano's brother, just as they were disembarking at Sinigaglia. They were charged with a verbal answer, which was that the sultan at this moment was busied with a triple war, first with the Sultan of Egypt, secondly with the King of Hungary, and thirdly with the Greeks of Macedonia and Epirus; and therefore he could not, with all the will in the world, help His

Holiness with armed men. But the envoys were accompanied by a favorite of the sultan's bearing a private letter to Alexander VI, in which Bajazet offered on certain conditions to help him with money. Although, as we see, the messengers had been stopped on the way, the Turkish envoy had all the same found a means of getting his dispatch sent to the pope: we give it here in all its naïveté.

"Bajazet the Sultan, son of the Sultan Mahomet II, by the grace of God Emperor of Asia and Europe, to the Father and Lord of all the Christians, Alexander VI, Roman pontiff and pope by the will of heavenly Providence, first, greetings that we owe him and bestow with all our heart. We make known to your Highness, by the envoy of your Mightiness, Giorgio Bucciarda, that we have been apprised of your convalescence, and received the news thereof with great joy and comfort. Among other matters, the said Bucciarda has brought us word that the King of France, now marching against your Highness, has shown a desire to take under his protection our brother D'jem, who is now under yours — a thing which is not only against our will, but which would also be the cause of great injury to your Highness and to all Christendom. In turning the matter over with your envoy Giorgio we have devised a scheme most conducive to peace and most advantageous and honorable for your Highness; at the same time satisfactory to ourselves personally; it would be well if our aforesaid brother D'jem, who being a man is liable to death, and who is now in the hands of your Highness, should quit this world as soon as possible, seeing that his departure, a real good to him in his position, would be of great use to your Highness, and very conducive to your peace, while at the same time it would be very agreeable to us, your friend. If this proposition is favorably received, as we hope, by your Highness, in your desire to be friendly towards us, it would be advisable both in the interests of your Highness and for our own satisfaction that it should occur rather sooner than later, and by the surest means you might be pleased to employ; so that our said brother D'jem might pass from the pains of this world into a better and more peaceful life, where at last he may find repose. If your Highness should adapt this plan and send us the body of our brother, We, the above-named Sultan

Bajazet, pledge ourselves to send to your Highness, wheresoever and by whatsoever hands you please, the sum of 300,000
ducats, With which sum you could purchase some fair domain for your children. In order to facilitate this purchase,
we would be willing, while awaiting the issue, to place the
300,000 ducats in the hands of a third party, so that your
Highness might be quite certain of receiving the money on
an appointed day, in return for the dispatch of our brother's
body. Moreover, we promise your Highness herewith, for
your greater satisfaction, that never, so long as you shall
remain on the pontifical throne, shall there be any hurt done
to the Christians, neither by us, nor by our servants, nor by
any of our compatriots, of whatsoever kind or condition they
may be, neither on sea nor on land. And for the still further
satisfaction of your Highness, and in order that no doubt
whatever may remain concerning the fulfillment of our
promises, we have sworn and affirmed in the presence of
Bucciarda, your envoy, by the true God whom we adore and
by our holy Gospels, that they shall be faithfully kept from
the first point unto the last. And now for the final and
complete assurance of your Highness, in order that no doubt
may still remain in your heart, and that you may be once
again and profoundly convinced of our good faith, we the
aforesaid Sultan Bajazet do swear by the true God, who has
created the heavens and the earth and all that therein is, that
we will religiously observe all that has been above said and
declared, and in the future will do nothing and undertake
nothing that may be contrary to the interests of your Highness.

"Given at Constantinople, in our palace, on the 12th of
September A.D. 1494."

*T*his letter was the cause of great joy to the Holy Father:
the aid of four or five thousand Turks would be insufficient
under the present circumstances, and would only serve to
compromise the head of Christendom, while the sum of
300,000 ducats — that is, nearly a million francs — was good
to get in any sort of circumstances. It is true that, so long as

D'jem lived, Alexander was drawing an income of 180,000 livres, which as a life annuity represented a capital of nearly two millions; but when one needs ready mangy, one ought to be able to make a sacrifice in the wav of discount. All the same, Alexander formed no definite plan, resolved on acting as circumstances should indicate.

But it was a more pressing business to decide how he should behave to the King of France: he had never anticipated the success of the French in Italy, and we have seen that he laid all the foundations of his family's future grandeur upon his alliance with the house of Aragon. But here was this house tattering, and a volcano more terrible than her own Vesuvius was threatening to swallow up Naples. He must therefore change his policy, and attach himself to the victor, — no easy matter, for Charles VIII was bitterly annoyed with the pope for having refused him the investiture and given it to Aragon.

In consequence, he sent Cardinal Francesco Piccolomini as an envoy to the king. This choice looked like a mistake at first, seeing that the ambassador was a nephew of Pius II, who had vigorously opposed the house of Anjou; but Alexander in acting thus had a second design, which could not be discerned by those around him. In fact, he had divined that Charles would not be quick to receive his envoy, and that, in the parleyings to which his unwillingness must give rise, Piccolomini would necessarily be brought into contact with the young king's advisers. Now, besides his ostensible mission to the king, Piccalamini had also secret instructions for the more influential among his counselors. These were Briconnet and Philippe de Luxembourg; and Piccolomini was authorized to promise a cardinal's hat to each of them. The result was just what Alexander had foreseen: his envoy could not gain admission to Charles, and was obliged to confer with the people about him. This was what the pope wished. Piccolomini returned to Rome with the king's refusal, but with a promise from Briconnet and Philippe de Luxembourg that they would use all their influence with Charles in favor of the Holy Father, and prepare him to receive a fresh embassy.

But the French all this time were advancing, and never stopped more than forty-eight hours in any town, so that it became more and more urgent to get something settled with

Charles. The king had entered Siena and Viterbo without striking a blow; Yves d' Alegre and Louis de Ligny had taken over Ostia from the hands of the Colonnas; Civita Vecchia and Corneto had opened their gates; the Orsini had submitted; even Gian Sforza, the pope's son-in-law, had retired from the alliance with Aragon. Alexander accordingly judged that the moment had came to abandon his ally, and sent to Charles the Bishops of Concordia and Terni, and his confessor, Mansignore Graziano. They were charged to renew to Briconnet and Philippe de Luxembourg the promise of the cardinalship, and had full powers of negotiation in the name of their master, both in case Charles should wish to include Alfonso II in the treaty, and in case he should refuse to sign an agreement with any other but the pope alone. They found the mind of Charles influenced now by the insinuation of Giuliano della Ravere, who, himself a witness of the pope's simony, pressed the king to summon a council and depose the head of the Church, and now by the secret support given him by the Bishops of Mans and St. Malo. The end of it was that the king decided to form his own opinion about the matter and settle nothing beforehand, and continued this route, sending the ambassadors back to the pope, with the addition of the Marechal de Gie, the Seneschal de Beaucaire, and Jean de Gannay, first president of the Paris Parliament. They were ordered to say to the pope —

(1) That the king wished above all things to be admitted into Rome without resistance; that, an condition of a voluntary, frank, and loyal admission, he would respect the authority of the Holy Father and the privileges of the Church;

(2) That the king desired that D'jem should be given up to him, in order that he might make use of him against the sultan when he should carry the war into Macedonia or Turkey or the Holy Land;

(3) That the remaining conditions were so unimportant that they could be brought forward at the first conference.

The ambassadors added that the French army was now only two days distant from Rome, and that in the evening of the day after next Charles would probably arrive in person to demand an answer from His Holiness.

It was useless to think of parleying with a prince who acted in such expeditious fashion as this. Alexander accordingly warned Ferdinand to quit Rome as soon as possible, in the interests of his own personal safety. But Ferdinand refused to listen to a word, and declared that he would not go out at one gate while Charles VIII came in at another. His sojourn was not long. Two days later, about eleven o'clock in the morning, a sentinel placed on a watch-tower at the top of the Castle S. Angelo, whither the pope had retired, cried out that the vanguard of the enemy was visible on the horizon. At once Alexander and the Duke of Calabria went up an the terrace which tops the fortress, and assured themselves with their own eyes that what the soldier said was true. Then, and not till then, did the duke of Calabria mount an horseback, and, to use his own words, went out at the gate of San Sebastiana, at the same moment that the French vanguard halted five hundred feet from the Gate of the People. This was on the 31st of December 1494.

At three in the afternoon the whole army had arrived, and the vanguard began their march, drums beating, ensigns unfurled. It was composed, says Paolo Giove, an eye-witness (book ii, p. 41 of his History), of Swiss and German soldiers, with short tight coats of various colors: they were armed with short swords, with steel edges like those of the ancient Romans, and carried ashen lances ten feet long, with straight and sharp iron spikes: only one-fourth of their number bore halberds instead of lances, the spikes cut into the form of an axe and surmounted by a four-cornered spike, to be used both for cutting like an axe and piercing like a bayonet: the first row of each battalion wore helmets and cuirasses which protected the head and chest, and when the men were drawn up for battle they presented to the enemy a triple array of iron spikes, which they could raise or lower like the spines of a porcupine. To each thousand of the soldiery were attached a hundred fusiliers: their officers, to distinguish them from the men, wore lofty plumes on their helmets.

After the Swiss infantry came the archers of Gascony: there were five thousand of them, wearing a very simple dress, that contrasted with the rich costume of the Swiss soldiers, the shortest of whom would have been a head higher than the tallest of the Gascons. But they were excellent soldiers, full of courage, very light, and with a special reputation for quickness in stringing and drawing their iron bows.

Behind them rode the cavalry, the flower of the French nobility, with their gilded helmets and neck bands, their velvet and silk surcoats, their swords each of which had its own name, their shields each telling of territorial estates, and their colors each telling of a lady-love. Besides defensive arms, each man bore a lance in his hand, like an Italian gendarme, with a solid grooved end, and on his saddle bow a quantity of weapons, some for cutting and same for thrusting. Their horses were large and strong, but they had their tails and ears cropped according to the French custom. These horses, unlike those of the Italian gendarmes, wore no caparisons of dressed leather, which made them more exposed to attack. Every knight was followed by three horses — the first ridden by a page in armor like his own, the two others by equerries who were called lateral auxiliaries, because in a fray they fought to right and left of their chief. This troop was not only the most magnificent, but the most considerable in the whole army; for as there were 2500 knights, they formed each with their three followers a total of 10,000 men. Five thousand light horse rode next, who carried huge wooden bows, and shot long arrows from a distance like English archers. They were a great help in battle, for moving rapidly wherever aid was required, they could fly in a moment from one wing to another, from the rear to the van, then when their quivers were empty could go off at so swift a gallop that neither infantry or heavy cavalry could pursue them. Their defensive armor consisted of a helmet and half-cuirass; some of them carried a short lance as well, with which to pin their stricken foe to the ground; they all wore long cloaks adorned with shoulder-knots, and plates of silver whereon the arms of their chief were emblazoned.

At last came the young king's escort; there were four hundred archers, among whom a hundred Scots formed a line on each side, while two hundred of the most illustrious knights marched on foot beside the prince, carrying heavy arms on their shoulders. In the midst of this magnificent escort advanced Charles VIII, both he and his horse covered with splendid armor; an his right and left marched Cardinal

Ascanio Sforza, the Duke of Milan's brother, and Cardinal
Giuliano della Rovere, of whom we have spoken so often,
who was afterwards Pope Julius II. The Cardinals Colonna
and Savelli followed immediately after, and behind them
came Prospero and Fabrizia Colonna, and all the Italian
princes and generals who had thrown in their lot with the
conqueror, and were marching intermingled with the great
French lords.

For a long time the crowd that had collected to see all these
foreign soldiers go by, a sight so new and strange, listened
uneasily to a dull sound which got nearer and nearer. The
earth visibly trembled, the glass shook in the windows, and
behind the king's escort thirty-six bronze cannons were seen
to advance, bumping along as they lay on their gun-carriages.
These cannons were eight feet in length; and as their mouths
were large enough to hold a man's head, it was supposed that
each of these terrible machines, scarcely known as yet to the
Italians, weighed nearly six thousand pounds. After the cannons came culverins sixteen feet long, and then falconets, the
smallest of which shot balls the size of a grenade. This
formidable artillery brought up the rear of the procession,
and formed the hindmost guard of the French army.

It was six hours since the front guard entered the town;
and as it was now night and for every six artillery-men there
was a torch-bearer, this illumination gave to the objects
around a more gloomy character than they would have shown
in the sunlight. The young king was to take up his quarters
in the Palazzo di Venezia, and all the artillery was directed
towards the plaza and the neighboring streets. The remainder
of the army was dispersed about the town. The same evening,
they brought to the king, less to do honor to him than to
assure him of his safety, the keys of Rome and the keys of
the Belvedere Garden just the same thing had been done for
the Duke of Calabria.

The pope, as we said, had retired to the Castle S. Angelo
with only six cardinals, so from the day after his arrival the
young king had around him a court of very different bril-
liance from that of the head of the Church. Then arose anew
the question of a convocation to prove Alexander's simony
and proceed to depose him; but the king's chief counselors,

gained over, as we know, pointed out that this was a bad moment to excite a new schism in the Church, just when preparations were being made for war against the infidels. As this was also the king's private opinion, there was not much trouble in persuading him, and he made up his mind to treat with His Holiness.

But the negotiations had scarcely begun when they had to be broken off; for the first thing Charles VIII demanded was the surrender of the Castle S. Angelo, and as the pope saw in this castle his only refuge, it was the last thing he chose to give up. Twice, in his youthful impatience, Charles wanted to take by force what he could not get by goodwill, and had his cannons directed towards the Holy Father's dwelling-place; but the pope was unmoved by these demonstrations; and obstinate as he was, this time it was the French king who gave way.

This article, therefore, was set aside, and the following conditions were agreed upon:

That there should be from this day forward between His Majesty the King of France and the Holy Father a sincere friendship and a firm alliance;

Before the completion of the conquest of the kingdom of Naples, the King of France should occupy, for the advantage and accommodation of his army, the fortresses of Civita Vecchia, Terracina, and Spoleto;

Lastly, the Cardinal Valentino (this was now the name of Caesar Borgia, after his archbishopric of Valencia) should accompany the king in the capacity of apostolic ambassador, really as a hostage.

These conditions fixed, the ceremonial of an interview was arranged. The king left the Palazzo di Venezia and went to live in the Vatican. At the appointed time he entered by the door of a garden that adjoined the palace, while the pope, who had not had to quit the Castle S. Angelo, thanks to a corridor communicating between the two palaces, came down into the same garden by another gate. The result of this arrangement was that the king the next moment perceived the pope, and knelt down, but the pope pretended not to see him, and the king advancing a few paces, knelt a second time; as His Holiness was at that moment screened by some masonry, this supplied him with another excuse, and the king went on with the performance, got up again, once mare advanced several steps, and was on the point of kneeling down the third time face to face, when the Holy Father at last perceived him, and, walking towards him as though he would prevent him from kneeling, took off his own hat, and pressing him to his heart, raised him up and tenderly kissed his forehead, refusing to cover until the king had put his cap upon his head, with the aid of the pope's own hands. Then, after they had stood for a moment, exchanging polite and friendly speeches, the king lost no time in praying His Holiness to be so good as to receive into the Sacred College William Bricannet, the Bishop of St. Malo. As this matter had been agreed upon beforehand by that prelate and His Holiness, though the king was not aware of it, Alexander was pleased to get credit by promptly granting the request; and he instantly ordered one of his attendants to go to the house of his son, Cardinal Valentino, and fetch a cape and hat. Then taking the king by the hand, he conducted him into the hall of Papagalli, where the ceremony was to take place of the admission of the new cardinal. The solemn oath of obedience which was to be taken by Charles to His Holiness as supreme head of the Christian Church was postponed till the following day.

When that solemn day arrived, every person important in Rome, noble, cleric, or soldier, assembled around His Holiness. Charles, on his side, made his approach to the Vatican with a splendid following of princes, prelates, and captains. At the threshold of the palace he found four cardinals who had arrived before him: two of them placed. themselves one on each side of him, the two others behind him, and all his retinue following, they traversed a long line of apartments full of guards and servants, and at last arrived in the reception-room, where the pope was seated on his throne, with his son, Caesar Borgia; behind him. On his arrival at the door, the King of France began the usual ceremonial, and when he had gone on from genuflections to kissing the feet, the hand, and the forehead, he stood up, while the first president of the Parliament of Paris, in his turn stepping forward, said in a loud voice:

"Very Holy Father, behold my king ready to offer to your Holiness that oath of obedience that he owes to you; but in France it is customary that he who offers himself as vassal to his lord shall receive in exchange therefore such boons as he may demand. His Majesty, therefore, while he pledges himself for his own part to behave unto your Holiness with a munificence even greater than that wherewith your Holiness shall behave unto him, is here to beg urgently that you accord him three favors. These favors are: first, the confirmation of privileges already granted to the king, to the queen his wife, and to the dauphin his son; secondly, the investiture, for himself and his successors, of the kingdom of Naples; lastly, the surrender to him of the person of the sultan D'jem, brother of the Turkish emperor."

At this address the pope was for a moment stupefied, for he did not expect these three demands, which were moreover made so publicly by Charles that no manner of refusal was possible. But quickly recovering his presence of mind, he replied to the king that he would willingly confirm the privileges that had been accorded to the house of France by his predecessors; that he might therefore consider his first demand granted; that the investiture of the kingdom was an affair that required deliberation in a council of cardinals, but he would do all he possibly could to induce them to accede to the king's desire; lastly, he must defer the affair of the sultan's brother till a time more opportune for discussing it with the Sacred College, but would venture to say that, as this surrender could not fail to be for the good of Christendom, as it was demanded for the purpose of assuring further the success of a crusade, it would not be his fault if on this point also the king should not be satisfied.

At this reply, Charles bowed his head in sign of satisfaction, and the first president stood up, uncovered, and resumed his discourse as follows.

"Very Holy Father, it is an ancient custom among Christian kings, especially the Most Christian kings of France, to signify, through their ambassadors, the respect they feel for the Holy See and the sovereign pontiffs whom Divine Providence places thereon; but the Most Christian king, having felt a desire to visit the tombs of the holy apostles, has been pleased to pay this religious debt, which he regards as a sacred duty, not by ambassadors or by delegates, but in his own person. This is why, Very Holy Father, His Majesty the King of France is here to acknowledge you as the true vicar of Christ, the legitimate successor of the apostles St. Peter and St. Paul, and with promise and vow renders you that filial and respectful devotion which the kings his predecessors have been accustomed to promise and vow, devoting himself and all his strength to the service of your Holiness and the interests of the Holy See."

The pope arose with a joyful heart; for this oath, so publicly made, removed all his fears about a council; so inclined from this moment to yield to the King of France anything he might choose to ask, he took him by his left hand and made him a short and friendly reply, dubbing him the Church's eldest son. The ceremony over, they left the hall, the pope always holding the king's hand in his, and in this way they walked as far as the room where the sacred vestments are put off; the pope feigned a wish to conduct the king to his own apartments, but the king would not suffer this, and, embracing once more, they separated, each to retire to his own domicile.

The king remained eight days longer at the Vatican, then returned to the Palazzo San Marco. During these eight days all his demands were debated and settled to his satisfaction. The Bishop of Mans was made cardinal; the investiture of the kingdom of Naples was promised to the conqueror; lastly, it was agreed that on his departure the King of France should receive from the pope's hand the brother of the Emperor of Constantinople, for a sum of 120,000 livres. But — the pope, desiring to extend to the utmost the hospitality he had been bestowing, invited D'jem to dinner on the very day that he was to leave Rome with his new protector.

When the moment of departure arrived, Charles mounted his horse in full armor, and with a numerous and brilliant following made his way to the Vatican; arrived at the door, he dismounted, and leaving his escort at the Piazza of St. Peter, went up with a few gentlemen only. He found His Holiness waiting for him, with Cardinal Valentino on his right, and on his left D'jem, who, as we said before, was dining with him, and round the table thirteen cardinals. The king at once, bending on his knee, demanded the pope's benediction, and stooped to kiss his feet. But this Alexander would not suffer; he took him in his arms, and with the lips of a father and heart of an enemy, kissed him tenderly on his forehead. Then the pope introduced the son of Mahomet II, who was a fine young man, with something noble and regal in his air, presenting in his magnificent oriental costume a great contrast in its fashion and amplitude to the narrow, severe cut of the Christian apparel. D'jem advanced to Charles without humility and without pride, and, like an emperor's son treating with a king, kissed his hand and then his shoulder; then, turning towards the Holy Father, he said in Italian, which he spoke very well, that he entreated he would recommend him to the young king, who was prepared to take him under his protection, assuring the pontiff that he should never have to repent giving him his liberty, and telling Charles that he hoped he might some day be proud of him, if after taking Naples he carried out his intention of going on to Greece. These words were spoken with so much dignity and at the same time with such gentleness, that the King of France loyally and frankly grasped the young sultan's hand, as though he were his companion-in-arms. Then Charles took a final farewell of the pope, and went down to the piazza. There he was awaited by Cardinal Valentino, who was about to accompany him, as we know, as a hostage, and who had remained behind to exchange a few words with his father. In a moment Caesar Borgia appeared, riding on a splendidly harnessed mule, and behind him were led six magnificent horses, a present from the Holy Father to the King of France. Charles at once mounted one of these, to do honor to the gift. The pope had just conferred on him, and leaving Rome with the rest of his troops, pursued his way towards Marino, where he arrived the same evening.

He learned there that Alfonso, belying his reputation as a clever politician and great general, had just embarked with all his treasures in a flotilla of four galleys, leaving the care of the war and the management of his kingdom to his son Ferdinand. Thus everything went well for the triumphant march of Charles: the gates of towns opened of themselves at his approach, his enemies fled without waiting for his coming, and before he had fought a single battle he had won for himself the surname of Conqueror.

The day after at dawn the army started once more, and after marching the whole day, stopped in the evening at Velletri. There the king, who had been on horseback since the morning, with Cardinal Valentine and D'jem, left the former at his lodging, and taking D'jem with him, went on to his own. Then Caesar Borgia, who among the army baggage had twenty very heavy wagons of his own, had one of these opened, took out a splendid cabinet with the silver necessary for his table, and gave orders for his supper to be prepared, as he had done the night before. Meanwhile, night had come on, and he shut himself up in a private chamber, where, stripping off his cardinal's costume, he put on a groom's dress. Thanks to this disguise, he issued from the house that had been assigned for his accommodation without being recognized, traversed the streets, passed through the gates, and gained the open country. Nearly half a league outside the town, a servant awaited him with two swift horses. Caesar, who was an excellent rider, sprang to the saddle, and he and his companion at full gallop retraced the road to Rome, where they arrived at break of day. Caesar got down at the house of one Flores, auditor of the rota, where he procured a fresh horse and suitable clothes; then he flew at once to his mother, who gave a cry of joy when she saw him; for so silent and mysterious was the cardinal for all the world beside, and even for her, that he had not said a word of his early return to Rome. The cry of joy uttered by Rosa Vanozza when she beheld her son was far mare a cry of vengeance than of love. One evening, while everybody was at the rejoicings in the Vatican, when Charles VIII and Alexander VI were swearing a friendship which neither of them felt, and exchanging oaths that were broken beforehand, a messenger from Rosa Vanozza had arrived with a letter to Caesar, in which she begged him to come at once to her house in the Via delta Longara. Caesar questioned the messenger, but he only replied that he could tell him nothing, that he would learn all he cared to know from his mother's own lips. So, as soon as he was at liberty, Caesar, in layman's dress and wrapped in a large cloak, quitted the Vatican and made his way towards the church of Regina Coeli, in the neighborhood of which, it will be remembered, was the house where the pope's mistress lived.

As he approached his mother's house, Caesar began to observe the signs of strange devastation. The street was scattered with the wreck of furniture and strips of precious stuffs. As he arrived at the foot of the little flight of steps that led to the entrance gate, he saw that the windows were broken and the remains of torn curtains were fluttering in front of them. Not understanding what this disorder could mean, he rushed into the house and through several deserted and wrecked apartments. At last, seeing light in one of the rooms, he went in, and there found his mother sitting on the remains of a chest made of ebony all inlaid with ivory and silver. When she saw Caesar, she rose, pale and disheveled, and pointing to the desolation around her, exclaimed:

"Look, Caesar; behold the work of your new friends."

"But what does it mean, mother?" asked the cardinal. "Whence comes all this disorder?"

"From the serpent," replied Rosa Vanozza, gnashing her teeth, — "from the serpent you have warmed in your bosom. He has bitten me, fearing no doubt that his teeth would be broken on you."

"Who has done this?" cried Caesar. "Tell me, and, by Heaven, mother, he shall pay, and pay indeed!"

"Who?" replied Rosa. "King Charles VIII has done it, by the hands of his faithful allies, the Swiss. It was well known that Melchior was away, and that I was living alone with a few wretched servants; so they came and broke in the doors, as though they were taking Rome by storm, and while Cardinal Valentino was making holiday with their master, they pillaged his mother's house, loading her with insults and outrages which no Turks or Saracens could possibly have improved upon."

"Very good, very good, mother," said Caesar; "be calm; blood shall wash out disgrace. Consider a moment; what we have lost is nothing compared with what we might lose; and my father and I, you may be quite sure, will give you back more than they have stolen from you."

"I ask for no promises," cried Rosa; "I ask for revenge."

"My mother," said the cardinal, "you shall be avenged, or

I will lose the name of son."

Having by these words reassured his mother, he took her
to Lucrezia's palace, which in consequence of her marriage
with Pesaro was unoccupied, and himself returned to the
Vatican, giving orders that his mother's house should be
refurnished more magnificently than before the disaster.
These orders were punctually executed, and it was among her
new luxurious surroundings, but with the same hatred in her
heart, that Caesar on this occasion found his mother. This
feeling prompted her cry of joy when she saw him once more.

The mother and son exchanged a very few words; then
Caesar, mounting on horseback, went to the Vatican, whence
as a hostage he had departed two days before. Alexander, who
knew of the flight beforehand, and not only approved, but
as sovereign pontiff had previously absolved his son of the
perjury he was about to commit, received him joyfully, but
all the same advised him to lie concealed, as Charles in all
probability would not be slow to reclaim his hostage:

Indeed, the next day, when the king got up, the absence of
Cardinal Valentino was observed, and as Charles was uneasy
at not seeing him, he sent to inquire what had prevented his
appearance. When the messenger arrived at the house that
Caesar had left the evening before, he learned that he had
gone out at nine o'clock in the evening and not returned
since. He went back with this news to the king, who at once
suspected that he had fled, and in the first flush of his anger
let the whole army know of his perjury. The soldiers then
remembered the twenty wagons, so heavily laden, from one
of which the cardinal, in the sight of all, had produced such
magnificent gold and silver plate; and never doubting that
the cargo of the others was equally precious, they fetched
them down and broke them to pieces; but inside they found
nothing but stones and sand, which proved to the king that
the flight had been planned a long time back, and incensed
him doubly against the pope. So without loss of time he
dispatched to Rome Philippe de Bresse, afterwards Duke of
Savoy, with orders to intimate to the Holy Father his displeasure at this conduct. But the pope replied that he knew
nothing whatever about his son's flight, and expressed the
sincerest regret to His Majesty, declaring that he knew noth-

ing of his whereabouts, but was certain that he was not in Rome. As a fact, the pope was speaking the truth this time, for Caesar had gone with Cardinal Orsino to one of his estates, and was temporarily in hiding there. This reply was conveyed to Charles by two messengers from the pope, the Bishops of Nepi and of Sutri, and the people also sent an ambassador in their own behalf. He was Monsignore Porcari, dean of the rota, who was charged to communicate to the king the displeasure of the Romans when they learned of the cardinal's breach of faith. Little as Charles was disposed to content himself with empty words, he had to turn his attention to mare serious affairs; so he continued his march to Naples without stopping, arriving there on Sunday, the 22nd of February, 1495.

Four days later, the unlucky D'jem, who had fallen sick at Capua died at Castel Nuovo. When he was leaving, at the farewell banquet, Alexander had tried on his guest the poison he intended to use so often later on upon his cardinals, and whose effects he was destined to feel himself, — such is poetical justice. In this way the pope had secured a double haul; for, in his twofold speculation in this wretched young man, he had sold him alive to Charles for 120,000 livres and sold him dead to Bajazet for 300,00 ducats. . . .

But there was a certain delay about the second payment; for the Turkish emperor, as we remember, was not bound to pay the price of fratricide till he received the corpse, and by Charles's order the corpse had been buried at Gaeta.

When Caesar Borgia learned the news, he rightly supposed that the king would be so busy settling himself in his new capital that he would have too much to think of to be worrying about him; so he went to Rome again, and, anxious to keep his promise to his mother, he signalized his return by a terrible vengeance.

Cardinal Valentino had in his service a certain Spaniard whom he had made the chief of his bravoes; he was a man of five-and-thirty or forty, whose whole life had been one long rebellion against society's laws; he recoiled from no action, provided only he could get his price. This Don Michele Correglia, who earned his celebrity for bloody deeds under the name of Michelotto, was just the man Caesar wanted; and whereas Michelotto felt an unbounded admiration for Caesar, Caesar had unlimited confidence in Michelotto. It was to him the cardinal entrusted the execution of one part of his vengeance; the other he kept for himself.

Don Michele received orders to scour the Campagna and cut every French throat he could find. He began his work at once; and very few days elapsed before he had obtained most satisfactory results: more than a hundred persons were robbed or assassinated, and among the last the son of Cardinal de St. Malo, who was en his way back to France, and on whom Michelotto found a sum of 3000 crowns.

For himself, Caesar reserved the Swiss; for it was the Swiss in particular who had despoiled his mother's house. The pope had in his service about a hundred and fifty soldiers belonging to their nation, who had settled their families in Rome, and had grown rich partly by their pay and partly in the exercise of various industries. The cardinal had every one of them dismissed, with orders to quit Rome within twenty-four hours and the Roman territories within three days. The poor wretches had all collected together to obey the order, with their wives and children and baggage, on the Piazza of St. Peter, when suddenly, by Cardinal Valentino's orders, they were hemmed in on all sides by two thousand Spaniards, who began to fire on them with their guns and charge them with their sabers, while Caesar and his mother looked down upon the carnage from a window. In this way they killed fifty or perhaps sixty; but the rest coming up, made a charge at the assassins, and then, without suffering any loss, managed to beat a retreat to a house, where they stood a siege, and made so valiant a defense that they gave the pope time — he knew nothing of the author of this butchery — to send the captain of his guard to the rescue, who, with a strong detachment, succeeded in getting nearly forty of them safely out of the town: the rest had been massacred on the piazza or killed in the house.

But this was no real and adequate revenge; for it did not touch Charles himself, the sole author of all the troubles that the pope and his family had experienced during the last year. So Caesar soon abandoned vulgar schemes of this kind and busied himself with loftier concerns, bending all the force of his genius to restore the league of Italian princes that had been broken by the defection of Sforza, the exile of Piero dei Medici, and the defeat of Alfonso. The enterprise was more easily accomplished than the pope could have anticipated. The Venetians were very uneasy when Charles passed so near, and they trembled lest, when he was once master of Naples, he might conceive the idea of conquering the rest of Italy. Ludovico Sforza, on his side, was beginning to tremble, seeing the rapidity with which the King of France had dethroned the house of Aragon, lest he might not make much difference between his allies and his enemies. Maximilian, for his part, was only seeking an occasion to break the temporary peace which he had granted for the sake of the concession made to him. Lastly, Ferdinand and Isabella were allies of the dethroned house. And so it came about that all of them, for different reasons, felt a common fear, and were soon in agreement as to the necessity of driving out Charles VIII, not only from Naples, but from Italy, and pledged themselves to work together to this end, by every means in their power, by negotiations, by trickery, or by actual force. The Florentines alone refused to take part in this general levy of arms, and remained faithful to their promises.

According to the articles of the treaty agreed upon by the confederates, the alliance was to last for five-and-twenty years, and had for ostensible object the upholding of the majority of the pope, and the interests of Christendom; and these preparations might well have been taken for such as would precede a crusade against the Turks, if Bajazet's ambassador had not always been present at the deliberations, although the Christian princes could not have dared for very shame to admit the, sultan by name into their league. Now the confederates had to set on foot an army of 30,000 horse and 20,000 infantry, and each of them was taxed for a contingent; thus the pope was to furnish 4000 horse, Maximilian 6000, the King of Spain, the Duke of Milan, and the republic of Venice, 8000 each. Every confederate was, in addition to this, to levy and equip 4000 infantry in the six weeks following the signature of the treaty. The fleets were to be equipped by the Maritime States; but any expenses they should incur later on were to be defrayed by all in equal shares.

The formation of this league was made public on the 12th of April, 1495, Palm Sunday, and in all the Italian States, especially at Rome, was made the occasion of fetes and immense rejoicings. Almost as soon as the publicly known articles were announced the secret ones were put into execution. These obliged Ferdinand and Isabella to send a fleet of sixty galleys to Ischia, where Alfonso's son had retired, with six hundred horsemen on board and five thousand infantry, to help him to ascend the throne once more. Those troops were to be put under the command of Gonzalvo of Cordova, who had gained the reputation of the greatest general in Europe after the taking of Granada. The Venetians with a fleet of forty galleys under the command of Antonio Grimani, were to attack all the French stations on the coast of Calabria and Naples. The Duke of Milan promised for his part to check all reinforcements as they should arrive from France, and to drive the Duke of Orleans out of Asti.

Lastly, there was Maximilian, who had promised to make invasions on the frontiers, and Bajazet, who was to help with money, ships, and soldiers either the Venetians or the Spaniards, according as he might be appealed to by Barberigo or by Ferdinand the Catholic.

This league was all the more disconcerting for Charles, because of the speedy abatement of the enthusiasm that had hailed his first appearance. What had happened to him was what generally happens to a conqueror who has more good luck than talent; instead of making himself a party among the great Neapolitan and Calabrian vassals, whose roots would be embedded in the very soil, by confirming their privileges and augmenting their power, he had wounded their feelings by bestowing all the titles, offices, and fiefs on those alone who had followed him from France, so that all the important positions in the kingdom were filled by strangers.

The result was that just when the league was made known, Tropea and Amantea, which had been presented by Charles to the Seigneur de Precy, rose in revolt and hoisted the banner of Aragon; and the Spanish fleet had only to present itself at Reggio, in Calabria, for the town to throw open its gates, being more discontented with the new rule than the old; and Don Federiga, Alfonso's brother and Ferdinand's uncle, who had hitherto never quitted Brindisi, had only to appear at Tarentum to be received there as a liberator.

Chapter VI

Charles learned all this news at Naples, and, tired of his late conquests, which necessitated a labor in organization for which he was quite unfitted, turned his eyes towards France, where victorious fetes and rejoicings were awaiting the victor's return. So he yielded at the first breath of his advisers, and retraced his road to his kingdom, threatened, as was said, by the Germans on the north and the Spaniards on the south. Consequently, he appointed Gilbert de Montpensier, of the house of Bourbon, viceroy; d'Aubigny, of the Scotch Stuart family, lieutenant in Calabria; Etienne de Vese, commander at Gaeta; and Don Juliano, Gabriel de Montfaucon, Guillaume de Villeneuve, George de Lilly, the bailiff of Vitry, and Graziano Guerra respectively governors of Sant' Angelo, Manfredonia, Trani, Catanzaro, Aquila, and Sulmone; then leaving behind in evidence of his claims the half of his Swiss, a party of his Gascons, eight hundred French lances, and about five hundred Italian men-at-arms, the last under the command of the prefect of Rome, Prospero and Fabrizio Colonna, and Antonio Savelli, he left Naples on the 20th of May at two o'clock in the afternoon, to traverse the whole of the Italian peninsula with the rest of his army, consisting of eight hundred French lances, two hundred gentlemen of his guard, one hundred Italian men-at-arms, three thousand Swiss infantry, one thousand French and one thousand Gascon. He also expected to be joined by Camillo Vitelli and his brothers in Tuscany, who were to contribute two hundred and fifty men-at-arms.

A week before he left Naples, Charles had sent to Rome

Monseigneur de Saint-Paul, brother of Cardinal de Luxembourg; and just as he was starting he dispatched thither the
new Archbishop of Lyons. They both were commissioned to
assure Alexander that the King of France had the most sincere
desire and the very best intention of remaining his friend. In
truth, Charles wished for nothing so much as to separate the
pope from the league, so as to secure him as a spiritual and
temporal support; but a young king, full of fire, ambition,
and courage, was not the neighbor to suit Alexander; so the
latter would listen to nothing, and as the troops he had
demanded from the doge and Ludavico Sforza had not been
sent in sufficient number for the defense of Rome, he was
content with provisioning the castle of S. Angelo, putting in
a formidable garrison, and leaving Cardinal Sant' Anastasio
to receive Charles while he himself withdrew with Caesar to
Orvieto. Charles only stayed in Rome three days, utterly
depressed because the pope had refused to receive him in spite
of his entreaties. And in these three days, instead of listening
to Giuliano delta Rovere, who was advising him once more
to call a council and depose the pope, he rather hoped to
bring the pope round to his side by the virtuous act of
restoring the citadels of Terracina and Civita Vecchia to the
authorities of the Romagna, only keeping for himself Ostia,
which he had promised Giuliano to give back to him. At last,
when the three days had elapsed, he left Rome, and resumed
his march in three columns towards Tuscany, crossed the
States of the Church, and on the 13th reached Siena, where
he was joined by Philippe de Commines, who had gone as
ambassador extraordinary to the Venetian Republic, and now
announced that the enemy had forty thousand men under
arms and were preparing for battle. This news produced no
other effect an the king and the gentlemen of his army than
to excite their amusement beyond measure; for they had
conceived such a contempt for their enemy by their easy
conquest, that they could not believe that any army, however
numerous, would venture to oppose their passage.

Charles, however, was forced to give way in the face of facts,
when he heard at San Teranza that his vanguard, commanded
by Marechal de Gie, and composed of six hundred lances and
fifteen hundred Swiss, when it arrived at Fornova had come

face to face with the confederates, who had encamped at Guiarole. The marechal had ordered an instant halt, and he too had pitched his tents, utilizing for his defense the natural advantages of the hilly ground. When these first measures had been taken, he sent out, first, a herald to the enemy's camp to ask from Francesco di Gonzaga, Marquis of Mantua, generalissimo of the confederate troops, a passage for his king's army and provisions at a reasonable price; and secondly, he dispatched a courier to Charles VIII, pressing him to hurry on his march with the artillery and rearguard. The confederates had given an evasive answer, for they were pondering whether they ought to jeopardize the whole Italian force in a single combat, and, putting all to the hazard, attempt to annihilate the King of France and his army together, so overwhelming the conqueror in the ruins of his ambition. The messenger found Charles busy superintending the passage of the last of his cannon over the mountain of Pontremoli. This was no easy matter, seeing that there was no sort of track, and the guns had to be lifted up and lowered by main farce, and each piece needed the arms of as many as two hundred men. At last, when all the artillery had arrived without accident on the other side of the Apennines, Charles started in hot haste for Fornovd, where he arrived with all his following on the morning of the next day.

From the top of the mountain where the Marechai de Gie had pitched his tents, the king beheld both his own camp and the enemy's. Both were on the right bank of the Taro, and were at either end of a semicircular chain of hills resembling an amphitheater; and the space between the two camps, a vast basin filled during the winter floods by the torrent which now only marked its boundary, was nothing but a plain covered with gravel, where all maneuvers must be equally difficult for horse and infantry. Besides, on the western slope of the hills there was a little wood which extended from the enemy's army to the French, and was in the possession of the Stradiotes, who, by help of its cover, had already engaged in several skirmishes with the French troops during the two days of halt while they were waiting for the king.

The situation was not reassuring. From the top of the mountain which overlooked Fornovo, one could get a view,

as we said before, of the two camps, and could easily calculate
the numerical difference between them. The French army,
weakened by the establishment of garrisons in the various
towns and fortresses they had won in Italy, were scarcely eight
thousand strong, while the combined forces of Milan and
Venice exceeded a total of thirty-five thousand. So Charles
decided to try once more the methods of conciliation, and
sent Commines, who, as we know, had joined him in Tuscany, to the Venetian 'proveditori', whose acquaintance he
had made when on his embassy; he having made a great
impression on these men, thanks to a general high opinion
of his merits. He was commissioned to tell the enemy's
generals, in the name of the King of France, that his master
only desired to continue his road without doing or receiving
any harm; that therefore he asked to be allowed a free passage
across the fair plains of Lombardy, which he could see from
the heights where he now stood, stretching as far as the eye
could reach, away to the foot of the Alps. Commines found
the confederate army deep in discussion: the wish of the
Milanese and Venetian party being to let the king go by, and
not attack him; they said they were only too happy that he
should leave Italy in this way, without causing any further
harm; but the ambassadors of Spain and Germany took quite
another view. As their masters had no troops in the army,
and as all the money they had promised was already paid,
they must be the gainer in either case from a battle, whichever
way it went: if they won the day they would gather the fruits
of victory, and if they lost they would experience nothing of
the evils of defeat. This want of unanimity was the reason
why the answer to Commines was deferred until the following
day, and why it was settled that on the next day he should
hold another conference with a plenipotentiary to be appointed in the course of that night. The place of this conference was to be between the two armies.

The king passed the night in great uneasiness. All day the
weather had threatened to turn to rain, and we have already
said how rapidly the Taro could swell; the river, fordable
today, might from tomorrow onwards prove an insurmount-
able obstacle; and possibly the delay had only been asked for
with a view to putting the French army in a worse position.

As a fact the night had scarcely come when a terrible storm arose, and so long as darkness lasted, great rumblings were heard in the Apennines, and the sky was brilliant with lightning. At break of day, however, it seemed to be getting a little calmer, though the Taro, only a streamlet the day before, had become a torrent by this time, and was rapidly rising. So at six in the morning, the king, ready armed and on horseback, summoned Commines and bade him make his way to the rendezvous that the Venetian 'proveditori' had assigned. But scarcely had he contrived to give the order when loud cries were heard coming from the extreme right of the French army. The Stradiotes, under cover of the wood stretching between the two camps, had surprised an outpost, and first cutting the soldiers' throats, were carrying off their heads in their usual way at the saddle-bow. A detachment of cavalry was sent in pursuit; but, like wild animals, they had retreated to their lair in the woods, and there disappeared.

This unexpected engagement, in all probability arranged beforehand by the Spanish and German envoys, produced on the whole army the effect of a spark applied to a train of gunpowder. Commines and the Venetian 'proveditori' each tried in vain to arrest the combat an either side. Light troops, eager for a skirmish, and, in the usual fashion of those days, prompted only by that personal courage which led them on to danger, had already come to blows, rushing down into the plain as though it were an amphitheater where they might make a fine display of arms. Far a moment the young king, drawn on by example, was an the point of forgetting the responsibility of a general in his zeal as a soldier; but this first impulse was checked by Marechal de Gie, Messire Claude de la Chatre de Guise, and M. de la Trimauille, who persuaded Charles to adopt the wiser plan, and to cross the Taro without seeking a battle, — at the same time without trying to avoid it, should the enemy cross the river from their camp and attempt to block his passage. The king accordingly, following the advice of his wisest and bravest captains, thus arranged his divisions.

The first comprised the van and a body of troops whose duty it was to support them. The van consisted of three hundred and fifty men-at-arms, the best and bravest of the

army, under the command of Marechal de Gie and Jacques
Trivulce; the corps following them consisted of three thousand Swiss, under the command of Engelbert der Cleves and
de Larnay, the queen's grand equerry; next came three hundred archers of the guard, whom the king had sent to help
the cavalry by fighting in the spaces between them.

The second division, commanded by the king in person
and forming the middle of the army, was composed of the
artillery, under Jean de Lagrange, a hundred gentlemen of the
guard with Gilles Carrone far standard-bearer, pensioners of
the king's household under Aymar de Prie, some Scots, and
two hundred cross-bowmen an horseback, with French archers besides, led by M. de Crussol.

Lastly, the third division, i.e. the rear, preceded by six
thousand beasts of burden bearing the baggage, was composed of only three hundred men-at-arms, commanded by de
Guise and by de la Trimouille: this was the weakest part of
the army.

When this arrangement was settled, Charles ordered the
van to cross the river, just at the little town of Fornovo. This
was done at once, the riders getting wet up to their knees, and
the footmen holding to the horses' tails. As soon as he saw
the last soldiers of his first division on the opposite bank, he
started himself to follow the same road and cross at the same
ford, giving orders to de Guise and de la Trimouille to regulate
the march of the rear guard by that of the center, just as he
had regulated their march by that of the van. His orders were
punctually carried out; and about ten o'clock in the morning
the whole French army was on the left bank of the Taro: at
the same time, when it seemed certain from the enemy's
arrangements that battle was imminent, the baggage, led by
the captain, Odet de Reberac, was separated from the rear
guard, and retired to the extreme left.

Now, Francisco de Gonzaga, general-in-chief of the confederate troops, had modeled his plans on those of the King of
France; by his orders, Count de Cajazzo, with four hundred
men-at-arms and two thousand infantry, had crossed the Taro
where the Venetian camp lay, and was to attack the French
van; while Gonzaga himself, following the right bank as far
as Fornovo, would go over the river by the same ford that

Charles had used, with a view to attacking his rear. Lastly, he had placed the Stradiotes between these two fords, with orders to cross the river in their turn, so soon as they saw the French army attacked both in van and in the rear, and to fall upon its flank. Not content with offensive measures, Gonzaga had also made provision for retreat by leaving three reserve corps on the right bank, one to guard the camp under the instruction of the Venetian 'provveditori', and the other two arranged in echelon to support each other, the first commanded by Antonio di Montefeltro, the second by Annibale Bentivoglio.

Charles had observed all these arrangements, and had recognized the cunning Italian strategy which made his opponents the finest generals in the world; but as there was no means of avoiding the danger, he had decided to take a sideway course, and had given orders to continue the match; but in a minute the French army was caught between Count di Cajazzo, barring the way with his four hundred men-at-arms and his two thousand infantry, and Gonzaga in pursuit of the rear, as we said before; leading six hundred men-at-arms, the flower of his army, a squadron of Stradiotes, and more than five thousand infantry: this division alone was stronger than the whole of the French army.

When, however, M. de Guise and M. de la Trimouille found themselves pressed in this way, they ordered their two hundred men-at-arms to turn right about face, while at the opposite end — that is, at the head of the army-Marechal de Gie and Trivulce ordered a halt and lances in rest. Meanwhile, according to custom, the king, who, as we said, was in the center, was conferring knighthood on those gentlemen who had earned the favor either by virtue of their personal powers or the king's special friendship.

Suddenly there was heard a terrible clash behind it was the French rearguard coming to blows with the Marquis of Mantua. In this encounter, where each man had singled out his own foe as though it were a tournament, very many lances were broken, especially those of the Italian knights; for their lances were hollowed so as to be less heavy, and in consequence had less solidity. Those who were thus disarmed at once seized their swords. As they were far more numerous than the French, the king saw them suddenly outflanking his right wing and apparently prepared to surround it; at the same moment loud cries were heard from a direction facing the center: this meant that the Stradiotes were crossing the river to make their attack.

The king at once ordered his division into two detachments, and giving one to Bourbon the bastard, to make head against the Stradiotes, he hurried with the second to the rescue of the van, flinging himself into the very midst of the melee, striking out like a king, and doing as steady work as the lowest in rank of his captains. Aided by the reinforcement, the rearguard made a good stand, though the enemy were five against one, and the combat in this part continued to rage with wonderful fury.

Obeying his orders, Bourbon had thrown himself upon the Stradiotes; but unfortunately, carried off by his horse, he had penetrated so far into the enemy's ranks that he was lost to sight: the disappearance of their chief, the strange dress of their new antagonists, and the peculiar method of their fighting produced a considerable effect on those who were to attack them; and for the moment disorder was the consequence in the center, and the horse men scattered instead of serrying their ranks and fighting in a body. This false move would have done them serious harm, had not most of the Stradiotes, seeing the baggage alone and undefended, rushed after that in hope of booty, instead of following up their advantage. A great part of the troop nevertheless stayed behind to fight, pressing on the French cavalry and smashing their lances with their fearful scimitars. Happily the king, who had just repulsed the Marquis of Mantua's attack, perceived what was going on behind him, and riding back at all possible speed to the succor of the center, together with the gentlemen of his household fell upon the Stradiotes, no longer armed with a lance, for that he had just broken, but brandishing his long sword, which blazed about him like lightning, and — either because he was whirled away like Bourbon by his own horse, or because he had allowed his courage to take him too far — he suddenly found himself in the thickest ranks of the Stradiotes, accompanied only by eight of the knights he had just now created, one equerry called Antoine des Ambus, and his standard-bearer. "France, France!" he cried aloud, to rally round him all the others who had scattered; they, seeing at last that the danger was less than they had supposed, began to take their revenge and to pay back with interest the blows they had received from the Stradiotes. Things were going still better, for the van, which the Marquis de Cajazzo was to attack; for although he had at first appeared to be animated with a terrible purpose, he stopped short about ten or twelve feet from the French line and turned right about face without breaking a single lance. The French wanted to pursue, but the Marechal de Gie, fearing that this flight might be only a trick to draw off the vanguard from the center, ordered every man to stay in his place. But the Swiss, who were German, and did not understand the order, or thought it was not meant for them, followed upon their heels, and although on foot caught them up and killed a hundred of them. This was quite enough to throw them into disorder, so that some were scattered about the plain, and others made a rush for the water, so as to cross the river and rejoin their camp.

*W*hen the Marechal de Gie saw this, he detached a hundred of his own men to go to the aid of the king, who was continuing to fight with unheard-of courage and running the greatest risks, constantly separated as he was from his gentlemen, who could not follow him; for wherever there was danger, thither he rushed, with his cry of "France," little troubling himself as to whether he was followed or not. And it was no longer with his sword that he fought; that he had long ago broken, like his lance, but with a heavy battle-axe, whose every blow was mortal whether cut or pierced. Thus the Stradiotes, already hard pressed by the king's household and his pensioners, soon changed attack for defense and defense for flight. It was at this moment that the king was really in the greatest danger; for he had let himself be carried away in pursuit of the fugitives, and presently found himself all alone, surrounded by these men, who, had they not been struck with a mighty terror, would have had nothing to do

but unite and crush him and his horse together; but, as
Commines remarks, "He whom God guards is well guarded,
and God was guarding the King of France."

All the same, at this moment the French were sorely pressed
in the rear; and although de Guise and de la Trimouille held
out as firmly as it was possible to hold, they would probably
have been compelled to yield to superior numbers had not a
double aid arrived in time: first the indefatigable Charles,
who, having nothing more to do among the fugitives, once
again dashed into the midst of the fight, next the servants of
the army, who, now that they were set free from the Stradiotes
and saw their enemies put to flight, ran up armed with the
axes they habitually used to cut down wood for building their
huts: they burst into the middle of the fray, slashing at the
horses' legs and dealing heavy blows that smashed in the
visors of the dismounted horsemen.

The Italians could not hold out against this double attack;
the 'furia francese' rendered all their strategy and all their
calculations useless, especially as for more than a century they
had abandoned their fights of blood and fury for a kind of
tournament they chose to regard as warfare; so, in spite of all
Gonzaga's efforts, they turned their backs upon the French
rear and took to flight; in the greatest haste and with much
difficulty they recrossed the torrent, which was swollen even
more now by the rain that had been falling during the whole
time of the battle.

Some thought fit to pursue the vanquished, for there was
now such disorder in their ranks that they were fleeing in all
directions from the battlefield where the French had gained
so glorious a victory, blocking up the roads to Parma and
Bercetto. But Marechal de Gie and de Guise and de la Trimouille, who had done quite enough to save them from the
suspicion of quailing before imaginary dangers, put a stop to
this enthusiasm, by pointing out that it would only be risking
the loss of their present advantage if they tried to push it
farther with men and horses so worn out. This view was
adopted in spite of the opinion of Trivulce, Camillo Vitelli,
and Francesco Secco, who were all eager to follow up the
victory.

The king retired to a little village an the left bank of the

Taro, and took shelter in a poor house. There he disarmed, being perhaps among all the captains and all the soldiers the man who had fought best.

During the night the torrent swelled so high that the Italian army could not have pursued, even if they had laid aside their fears. The king did not propose to give the appearance of flight after a victory, and therefore kept his army drawn up all day, and at night went on to sleep at Medesano, a little village only a mile lower down than the hamlet where he rested after the fight. But in the course of the night he reflected that he had done enough for the honor of his arms in fighting an army four times as great as his own and killing three thousand men, and then waiting a day and a half to give them time to take their revenge; so two hours before daybreak he had the fires lighted, that the enemy might suppose he was remaining in camp; and every man mounting noiselessly, the whole French army, almost out of danger by this time, proceeded on their march to Borgo San Donnino.

While this was going on, the pope returned to Rome, where news highly favorable to his schemes was not slow to reach his ears. He learned that Ferdinand had crossed from Sicily into Calabria with six thousand volunteers and a considerable number of Spanish horse and foot, led, at the command of Ferdinand and Isabella, by the famous Gonzalva de Cordova, who arrived in Italy with a great reputation, destined to suffer somewhat from the defeat at Seminara. At almost the same time the French fleet had been beaten by the Aragonese; moreover, the battle of the Taro, though a complete defeat for the confederates, was another victory for the pope, because its result was to open a return to France for that man whom he regarded as his deadliest foe. So, feeling that he had nothing more to fear from Charles, he sent him a brief at Turin, where he had stopped for a short time to give aid to Novara, therein commanding him, by virtue of his pontifical authority, to depart out of Italy with his army, and to recall within ten days those of his troops that still remained in the kingdom of Naples, on pain of excommunication, and a summons to appear before him in person.

Charles VIII replied:

(1) That he did not understand how the pope, the chief of

the league, ordered him to leave Italy, whereas the confederates had not only refused him a passage, but had even attempted, though unsuccessfully, as perhaps His Holiness
knew, to cut off his return into France;

(2) That, as to recalling his troops from Naples, he was not
so irreligious as to do that, since they had not entered the
kingdom without the consent and blessing of His Holiness;

(3) That he was exceedingly surprised that the pope should
require his presence in person at the capital of the Christian
world just at the present time, when six weeks previously, at
the time of his return from Naples, although he ardently
desired an interview with His Holiness, that he might offer
proofs of his respect and obedience, His Holiness, instead of
according this favor, had quitted Rome so hastily on his
approach that he had not been able to come up with him by
any efforts whatsoever. On this point, however, he promised
to give His Holiness the satisfaction he desired, if he would
engage this time to wait for him: he would therefore return
to Rome so soon as the affairs that brought him back to his
own kingdom had been satisfactorily, settled.

Although in this reply there was a touch of mockery and
defiance, Charles was none the less compelled by the circumstances of the case to obey the pope's strange brief. His
presence was so much needed in France that, in spite of the
arrival of a Swiss reinforcement, he was compelled to con-
clude a peace with Ludovico Sforza, whereby he yielded
Novara to him; while Gilbert de Montpensier and d'Aubigny,
after defending, inch by inch, Calabria, the Basilicate, and
Naples, were obliged to sign the capitulation of Atella, after
a siege of thirty-two days, on the 20th of July, 1496. This
involved giving back to Ferdinand II, King of Naples, all the
palaces and fortresses of his kingdom; which indeed he did
but enjoy for three months, dying of exhaustion on the 7th
of September following, at the Castello della Somma, at the
foot of Vesuvius; all the attentions lavished upon him by his
young wife could not repair the evil that her beauty had
wrought.

His uncle Frederic succeeded; and so, in the three years of
his papacy, Alexander VI had seen five kings upon the throne
of Naples, while he was establishing himself more firmly

upon his own pontifical seat — Ferdinand I, Alfonso I, Charles VIII, Ferdinand II, and Frederic. All this agitation about his throne, this rapid succession of sovereigns, was the best thing possible for Alexander; for each new monarch became actually king only on condition of his receiving the pontifical investiture. The consequence was that Alexander was the only gainer in power and credit by these changes; for the Duke of Milan and the republics of Florence and Venice had successively recognized him as supreme head of the Church, in spite of his simony; moreover, the five kings of Naples had in turn paid him homage. So he thought the time had now come for founding a mighty family; and for this he relied upon the Duke of Gandia, who was to hold all the highest temporal dignities; and upon Caesar Borgia, who was to be appointed to all the great ecclesiastical offices. The pope made sure of the success of these new projects by electing four Spanish cardinals, who brought up the number of his compatriots in the Sacred College to twenty-two, thus assuring him a constant and certain majority.

The first requirement of the pope's policy was to clear away from the neighborhood of Rome all those petty lords whom most people call vicars of the Church, but whom Alexander called the shackles of the papacy. We saw that he had already begun this work by rousing the Orsini against the Colonna family, when Charles VIII's enterprise compelled him to concentrate all his mental resources, and also the forces of his States, so as to secure his own personal safety.

It had come about through their own imprudent action that the Orsini, the pope's old friends, were now in the pay of the French, and had entered the kingdom of Naples with them, where one of them, Virginio, a very important member of their powerful house, had been taken prisoner during the war, and was Ferdinand II's captive. Alexander could not let this opportunity escape him; so, first ordering the King of Naples not to release a man who, ever since the 1st of June, 1496, had been a declared rebel, he pronounced a sentence of confiscation against Virginio Orsini and his whole family in a secret consistory, which sat on the 26th of October following — that is to say, in the early days of the reign of Frederic, whom he knew to be entirely at his command, owing to the

King's great desire of getting the investiture from him; then, as it was not enough to declare the goods confiscated, without also dispossessing the owners, he made overtures to the Colonna family, saying he would commission them, in proof of their new bond of friendship, to execute the order given against their old enemies under the direction of his son Francesco, Duke of Gandia. In this fashion he contrived to weaken his neighbors each by means of the other, till such time as he could safely attack and put an end to conquered and conqueror alike.

The Colonna family accepted this proposition, and the Duke of Gandia was named General of the Church: his father in his pontifical robes bestowed on him the insignia of this office in the church of St. Peter's at Rome.

Chapter VII

Matters went forward as Alexander had wished, and before the end of the year the pontifical army had, seized a great number of castles and fortresses that belonged to the Orsini, who thought themselves already lost when Charles VIII came to the rescue. They had addressed themselves to him without much hope that he could be of real use to there, with his want of armed troops and his preoccupation with his own affairs. He, however, sent Carlo Orsini, son of Virginio, the prisoner, and Vitellozzo Vitelli, brother of Camillo Vitelli, one of the three valiant Italian condottieri who had joined him and fought for him at the crossing of the Taro: These two captains, whose courage and skill were well known, brought with them a considerable sum of money from the liberal coffers of Charles VIII. Now, scarcely had they arrived at Citta di Castello, the center of their little sovereignty, and expressed their intention of raising a band of soldiers, when men presented themselves from all sides to fight under their banner; so they very soon assembled a small army, and as they had been able during their stay among the French to study those matters of military organization in which France excelled, they now applied the result of their learning to their own troops: the improvements were mainly certain changes in the artillery which made their maneuvers easier, and the substitution for their ordinary weapons of pikes similar in form to the Swiss pikes, but two feet longer. These changes effected, Vitellozzo Vitelli spent three or four months in exercising his men in the management of their new weapons; then, when he thought them fit to make good use of these, and when he had collected more or less help from the towns of Perugia, Todi, and Narni, where the inhabitants trembled lest their turn should come after the Orsini's, as the Orsini's had followed on the Colonnas', he marched towards Braccianno, which was being besieged by the Duke of Urbino, who had been lent to the pope by the Venetians, in virtue of the treaty quoted above.

The Venetian general, when he heard of Vitelli's approach, thought he might as well spare him half his journey, and marched out to confront him: the two armies met in the Soriano road, and the battle straightway began. The pontifical army had a body of eight hundred Germans, on which the Dukes of Urbino and Gandia chiefly relied, as well they might, for they were the best troops in the world; but Vitelli attacked these picked men with his infantry, who, armed with their formidable pikes, ran them through, while they with arms four feet shorter had no chance even of returning the blows they received; at the same time Vitelli's light troops wheeled upon the flank, following their most rapid movements, and silencing the enemy's artillery by the swiftness and accuracy of their attack. The pontifical troops were put to flight, though after a longer resistance than might have been expected when they had to sustain the attack of an army so much better equipped than their own; with them they bore to Ronciglione the Duke of Gandia, wounded in the face by a pike-thrust, Fabrizia Calonna, and the envoy; the Duke of Urbino, who was fighting in the rear to aid the retreat, was taken prisoner with all his artillery and the baggage of the conquered army. But this success, great as it was, did not so swell the pride of Vitellozza Vitelli as to make him oblivious of his position. He knew that he and the Orsini together were too weak to sustain a war of such magnitude; that the little store of money to which he owed the existence of his army would very soon be expended and his army would disappear with it. So he hastened to get pardoned far the victory by making propositions which he would very likely have refused had he been the vanquished party; and the pope accepted his conditions without demur; during the interval having heard that Trivulce had just recrossed the Alps and re-entered Italy with three thousand Swiss, and fearing lest the Italian general might only be the advance guard of the King of France. So it was settled that the Orsini should pay 70,000 florins for the expenses of the war, and that all the prisoners on both sides should be exchanged without ransom with the single exception of the Duke of Urbino. As a pledge for the future payment of the 70,000 florins, the Orsini handed over to the Cardinals Sforza and San Severino the fortresses of Anguillara and Cervetri; then, when the day came and they had not the necessary money, they gave up their prisoner, the Duke of Urbino, estimating his worth at 40,000 ducats — nearly all the sum required — and handed him over to Alexander on account; he, a rigid observer of engagements, made his own general, taken prisoner in his service, pay, to himself the ransom he owed to the enemy.

Then the pope had the corpse of Virginio sent to Carlo Orsini and Vitellozzo Vitelli, as he could not send him alive. By a strange fatality the prisoner had died, eight days before the treaty was signed, of the same malady — at least, if we may judge by analogy — that had carried off Bajazet's brother.

As soon as the peace was signed, Prospero Calonna and Gonzalvo de Cordova, whom the Pope had demanded from Frederic, arrived at Rome with an army of Spanish and Neapolitan troops. Alexander, as he could not utilize these against the Orsini, set them the work of recapturing Ostia, not desiring to incur the reproach of bringing them to Rome far nothing. Gonzalvo was rewarded for this feat by receiving the Rose of Gold from the pope's hand — that being the highest honor His Holiness can grant. He shared this distinction with the Emperor Maximilian, the King of France, the Doge of Venice, and the Marquis of Mantua.

In the midst of all this occurred the solemn festival of the Assumption; in which Ganzalvo was invited to take part. He accordingly left his palace, proceeded in great pomp in the front of the pontifical cavalry, and took his place on the Duke of Gandia's left hand. The duke attracted all eyes by his personal beauty, set off as it was by all the luxury he thought fit to display at this festival. He had a retinue of pages and servants, clad in sumptuous liveries, incomparable for richness with anything heretofore seen in Rome, that city of religious pomp. All these pages and servants rode magnificent horses, caparisoned in velvet trimmed with silver fringe, and bells of silver hanging down every here and there. He himself was in a robe of gold brocade, and wore at his neck a string of Eastern pearls, perhaps the finest and largest that ever belonged to a Christian prince, while on his cap was a gold chain studded with diamonds of which the smallest was worth more than 20,000 ducats. This magnificence was all the more conspicuous by the contrast it presented to Caesar's dress, whose scarlet robe admitted of no ornaments. The result was that Caesar, doubly jealous of his brother, felt a new hatred rise up within him when he heard all along the way the praises of his fine appearance and noble equipment. From this moment Cardinal Valentino decided in his own mind the fate of this man, this constant obstacle in the path of his pride, his love, and his ambition. Very good reason, says Tommaso, the historian, had the Duke of Gandia to leave behind him an impression on the public mind of his beauty and his grandeur at this fete, for this last display was soon to be followed by the obsequies of the unhappy young man.

Lucrezia also had come to Rome, on the pretext of taking part in the solemnity, but really, as we shall see later, with the view of serving as a new instrument for her father's ambition. As the pope was not satisfied with an empty triumph of vanity and display for his son, and as his war with the Orsini had failed to produce the anticipated results, he decided to increase the fortune of his firstborn by doing the very thing which he had accused Calixtus in his speech of doing for him, viz., alienating from the States of the Church the cities of Benevento, Terracino, and Pontecorvo to form, a duchy as an appanage to his son's house. Accordingly this proposition was put forward in a full consistory, and as the college of cardinals was entirely Alexander's, there was no difficulty about carrying his point. This new favor to his elder brother exasperated Caesar, although he was himself getting a share of the paternal gifts; for he had just been named envoy 'a latere' at Frederic's court, and was appointed to crown him with his own hands as the papal representative. But Lucrezia, when she had spent a few days of pleasure with her father and brothers, had gone into retreat at the convent of San Sisto. No one knew the real motive of her seclusion, and no entreaties of Caesar, whose love for her was strange and unnatural, had induced her to defer this departure from the world even until the day after he left for Naples. His sister's obstinacy wounded him deeply, for ever since the day when the Duke of Gandia had appeared in the procession so magnificently attired, he fancied he had observed a coldness in the mistress of his illicit affection, and so far did this increase his hatred of his rival that he resolved to be rid of him at all costs. So he ordered the chief of his sbirri to come and see him the same night.

Michelotto was accustomed to these mysterious messages, which almost always meant his help was wanted in some love affair or some act of revenge. As in either case his reward was generally a large one, he was careful to keep his engagement, and at the appointed hour was brought into the presence of his patron.

Caesar received him leaning against a tall chimneypiece, no longer wearing his cardinal's robe and hat, but a doublet of black velvet slashed with satin of the same color. One hand toyed mechanically with his gloves, while the other rested an the handle of a poisoned dagger which never left his side. This was the dress he kept for his nocturnal expeditions, so Michelotto felt no surprise at that; but his eyes burned with a flame more gloomy than their want, and his cheeks, generally pale, were now livid. Michelotto had but to cast one look upon his master to see that Caesar and he were about to share some terrible enterprise.

He signed to him to shut the door. Michelotto obeyed. Then, after a moment's silence, during which the eyes of Borgia seemed to burn into the soul of the bravo, who with a careless air stood bareheaded before ham, he said, in a voice whose slightly mocking tone gave the only sign of his emotion.

"Michelotto, how do you think this dress suits me?"

Accustomed as he was to his master's tricks of circumlocution, the bravo was so far from expecting this question, that at first he stood mute, and only after a few moments' pause was able to say

"Admirably, monsignore; thanks to the dress, your Excellency has the appearance as well as the true spirit of a captain."

"I am glad you think so," replied Caesar. "And now let me ask you, do you know who is the cause that, instead of wearing this dress, which I can only put an at night, I am forced to disguise myself in the daytime in a cardinal's robe and hat, and pass my time trotting about from church to church, from consistory to consistory, when I ought properly to be leading a magnificent army in the battlefield, where you would enjoy a captain's rank, instead of being the chief of a few miserable sbirri?"

"Yes, monsignore," replied Michelotto, who had divined Caesar's meaning at his first word; "the man who is the cause of this is Francesco, Duke of Gandia, and Benevento, your elder brother."

"Do you know," Caesar resumed, giving no sign of assent but a nod and a bitter smile, — "do you know who has all the money and none of the genius, who has the helmet and none of the brains, who has the sword and no hand to wield it?"

"That too is the Duke of Gandia," said Michelotto.

"Do you know;" continued Caesar, "who is the man whom I find continually blocking the path of my ambition, my fortune, and my love?"

"It is the same, the Duke of Gandia," said Michelotto.

"And what do you think of it?" asked Caesar.

"I think he must die," replied the man coldly.

"That is my opinion also, Michelotto," said Caesar, stepping towards him and grasping his hand; "and my only regret is that I did not think of it sooner; for if I had carried a sword at my side in stead of a crosier in my hand when the King of France was marching through Italy, I should now have been master of a fine domain. The pope is obviously anxious to aggrandize his family, but he is mistaken in the means he adopts: it is I who ought to have been made duke, and my brother a cardinal. There is no doubt at all that, had he made me duke, I should have contributed a daring and courage to his service that would have made his power far weightier than it is. The man who would make his way to vast dominions and a kingdom ought to trample under foot all the obstacles in his path, and boldly grasp the very sharpest thorns, whatever reluctance his weak flesh may feel; such a man, if he would open out his path to fortune, should seize his dagger or his sword and strike out with his eyes shut; he should not shrink from bathing his hands in the blood of his kindred; he should follow the example offered him by every founder of empire from Romulus to Bajazet, both of whom climbed to the throne by the ladder of fratricide. Yes, Michelotto, as you say, such is my condition, and I am resolved I will not shrink. Now you know why I sent for you: am I wrong in counting upon you?"

As might have been expected, Michelotto, seeing his own fortune in this crime, replied that he was entirely at Caesar's service, and that he had nothing to do but to give his orders as to time, place, and manner of execution. Caesar replied that the time must needs be very soon, since he was on the point of leaving Rome for Naples; as to the place and the mode of execution, they would depend on circumstances, and each of them must look out for an opportunity, and seize the first that seemed favorable.

Two days after this resolution had been taken, Caesar learned that the day of his departure was fixed for Thursday the 15th of June: at the same time he received an invitation from his mother to come to supper with her on the 14th. This was a farewell repast given in his honor. Michelotto received orders to be in readiness at eleven o'clock at night.

The table was set in the open air in a magnificent vineyard, a property of Rosa Vanozza's in the neighborhood of San Piero-in-Vinculis: the guests were Caesar Borgia, the hero of the occasion; the Duke of Gandia; Prince of Squillace; Dona Sancha, his wife; the Cardinal of Monte Reale, Francesco Borgia, son of Calixtus III; Don Roderigo Borgia, captain of the apostolic palace; Don Goffredo, brother of the cardinal; Gian Borgia, at that time ambassador at Perugia; and lastly, Don Alfonso Borgia, the pope's nephew: the whole family therefore was present, except Lucrezia, who was still in retreat, and would not come.

The repast was magnificent: Caesar was quite as cheerful as usual, and the Duke of Gandia seemed more joyous than he had ever been before.

In the middle of supper a man in a mask brought him a letter. The duke unfastened it, coloring up with pleasure; and when he had read it answered in these words, "I will come":

then he quickly hid the letter in the pocket of his doublet; but quick as he was to conceal it from every eye, Caesar had had time to cast a glance that way, and he fancied he recognized the handwriting of his sister Lucrezia. Meanwhile the messenger had gone off with his answer, no one but Caesar paying the slightest attention to him, for at that period it was the custom for have messages to be conveyed by men in domino or by women whose faces were concealed by a veil.

At ten o'clock they rose from the table, and as the air was sweet and mild they walked about a while under the magnificent pine trees that shaded the house of Rosa Vanozza, while Caesar never for an instant let his brother out of his sight. At eleven o'clock the Duke of Gandia bade good-night to his mother. Caesar at once followed suit, alleging his desire to go to the Vatican to bid farewell to the pope, as he would not be able to fulfill this duty an the morrow, his departure being fixed at daybreak. This pretext was all the more plausible since the pope was in the habit of sitting up every night till two or three o'clock in the morning.

The two brothers went out together, mounted their horses, which were waiting for them at the door, and rode side by side as far as the Palazzo Borgia, the present home of Cardinal Ascanio Sforza, who had taken it as a gift from Alexander the night before his election to the papacy. There the Duke of Gandia separated from his brother, saying with a smile that he was not intending to go home, as he had several hours to spend first with a fair lady who was expecting him. Caesar replied that he was no doubt free to make any use he liked best of his opportunities, and wished him a very good night. The duke turned to the right, and Caesar to the left; but Caesar observed that the street the duke had taken led in the direction of the convent of San Sisto, where, as we said, Lucrezia was in retreat; his suspicions were confirmed by this observation, and he directed his horse's steps to the Vatican, found the pope, took his leave of him, and received his benediction.

From this moment all is wrapped in mystery and darkness, like that in which the terrible deed was done that we are now to relate.

This, however, is what is believed.

The Duke of Gandia, when he quitted Caesar, sent away his servants, and in the company of one confidential valet alone pursued his course towards the Piazza della Giudecca. There he found the same man in a mask who had come to speak to him at supper, and forbidding his valet to follow any farther, he bade him wait on the piazza where they then stood, promising to be on his way back in two hours' time at latest, and to take him up as he passed. And at the appointed hour the duke reappeared, took leave this time of the man in the mask, and retraced his steps towards his palace. But scarcely had he turned the corner of the Jewish Ghetto, when four men on foot, led by a fifth who was on horseback, flung themselves upon him. Thinking they were thieves, or else that he was the victim of some mistake, the Duke of Gandia mentioned his name; but instead of the name checking the murderers' daggers, their strokes were redoubled, and the duke very soon fell dead, his valet dying beside him.

Then the man on horseback, who had watched the assassination with no sign of emotion, backed his horse towards the dead body: the four murderers lifted the corpse across the crupper, and walking by the side to support it, then made their way down the lane that leads to the Church of Santa Maria-in-Monticelli. The wretched valet they left for dead upon the pavement. But he, after the lapse of a few seconds, regained some small strength, and his groans were heard by the inhabitants of a poor little house hard by; they came and picked him up, and laid him upon a bed, where he died almost at once, unable to give any evidence as to the assassins or any details of the murder.

All night the duke was expected home, and all the next morning; then expectation was turned into fear, and fear at last into deadly terror. The pope was approached, and told that the Duke of Gandia had never come back to his palace since he left his mother's house. But Alexander tried to deceive himself all through the rest of the day, hoping that his son might have been surprised by the coming of daylight in the midst of an amorous adventure, and was waiting till the next night to get away in that darkness which had aided his coming thither. But the night, like the day, passed and brought no news. On the morrow, the pope, tormented by the gloomiest presentiments and by the raven's croak of the 'vox populi', let himself fall into the depths of despair: amid sighs and sobs of grief, all he could say to any one who came to him was but these words, repeated a thousand times: "Search, search; let us know how my unhappy son has died."

Then everybody joined in the search; for, as we have said, the Duke of Gandia was beloved by all; but nothing could be discovered from scouring the town, except the body of the murdered man, who was recognized as the duke's valet; of his master there was no trace whatever: it was then thought, not without reason, that he had probably been thrown into the Tiber, and they began to follow along its banks, beginning from the Via della Ripetta, questioning every boatman and fisherman who might possibly have seen, either from their houses or from their boats, what had happened on the river banks during the two preceding nights. At first all inquiries were in vain; but when they had gone up as high as the Via del Fantanone, they found a man at last who said he had seen something happen on the night of the 14th which might very possibly have some bearing on the subject of inquiry. He was a Slav named George, who was taking up the river a boat laden with wood to Ripetta. The following are his own words:

"Gentlemen," he said, "last Wednesday evening, when I had set down my load of wood on the bank, I remained in my boat, resting in the cool night air, and watching lest other men should come and take away what I had just unloaded, when, about two o'clock in the morning, I saw coming out of the lane on the left of San Girolamo's Church two men on foot, who came forward into the middle of the street, and looked so carefully all around that they seemed to have come to find out if anybody was going along the street. When they felt sure that it was deserted, they went back along the same lane, whence issued presently two other men, who used similar precautions to make sure that there was nothing fresh; they, when they found all as they wished, gave a sign to their companions to come and join them; next appeared one man on a dapple-grey horse, which was carrying on the crupper the body of a dead man, his head and arms hanging over on one side and his feet on the other. The two fellows I had first seen exploring were holding him up by the arms and legs.

The other three at once went up to the river, while the first two kept a watch on the street, and advancing to the part of the bank where the sewers of the town are discharged into the Tiber, the horseman turned his horse, backing on the river; then the two who were at either side taking the corpse, one by the hands, the other by the feet, swung it three times, and the third time threw it out into the river with all their strength; then at the noise made when the body splashed into the water, the horseman asked, 'Is it done?' and the others answered, 'Yes, sir,' and he at once turned right about face; but seeing the dead man's cloak floating, he asked what was that black thing swimming about. 'Sir,' said one of the men, 'it is his cloak'; and then another man picked up some stones, and running to the place where it was still floating, threw them so as to make it sink under; as soon, as it had quite disappeared, they went off, and after walking a little way along the main road, they went into the lane that leads to San Giacomo. That was all I saw, gentlemen, and so it is all I can answer to the questions you have asked me."

At these words, which robbed of all hope any who might yet entertain it, one of the pope's servants asked the Slav why, when he was witness of such a deed, he had not gone to denounce it to the governor. But the Slav replied that, since he had exercised his present trade on the riverside, he had seen dead men thrown into the Tiber in the same way a hundred times, and had never heard that anybody had been troubled about them; so he supposed it would be the same with this corpse as the others, and had never imagined it was his duty to speak of it, not thinking it would be any more important than it had been before.

Acting on this intelligence, the servants of His Holiness summoned at once all the boatmen and fishermen who were accustomed to go up and down the river, and as a large reward was promised to anyone who should find the duke's body, there were soon mare than a hundred ready for the job; so that before the evening of the same day, which was Friday, two men were drawn out of the water, of whom one was instantly recognized as the hapless duke. At the very first glance at the body there could be no doubt as to the cause of death. It was pierced with nine wounds, the chief one in the throat, whose artery was cut. The clothing had not been touched: his doublet and cloak were there, his gloves in his waistband, gold in his purse; the duke then must have been assassinated not for gain but for revenge.

The ship which carried the corpse went up the Tiber to the Castello Sant' Angelo, where it was set down. At once the magnificent dress was fetched from the duke's palace which he had worn on the day of the procession, and he was clothed in it once more: beside him were placed the insignia of the generalship of the Church. Thus he lay in state all day, but his father in his despair had not the courage to came and look at him. At last, when night had fallen, his most trusty and honored servants carried the body to the church of the Madonna del Papala, with all the pomp and ceremony that Church and State combined could devise for the funeral of the son of the pope.

Meantime the bloodstained hands of Caesar Borgia were placing a royal crown upon the head of Frederic of Aragon.

This blow had pierced Alexander's heart very deeply. As at first he did not know on whom his suspicions should fall, he gave the strictest orders for the pursuit of the murderers; but little by little the infamous truth was forced upon him. He saw that the blow which struck at his house came from that very house itself and then his despair was changed to madness: he ran through the rooms of the Vatican like a maniac, and entering the consistory with torn garments and ashes on his head, he sobbingly avowed all the errors of his past life, owning that the disaster that struck his offspring through his offspring was a just chastisement from God; then he retired to a secret dark chamber of the palace, and there shut himself up, declaring his resolve to die of starvation. And indeed for more than sixty hours he took no nourishment by day nor rest by night, making no answer to those who knocked at his door to bring him food except with the wailings of a woman or a roar as of a wounded lion; even the beautiful Giulia Farnese, his new mistress, could not move him at all, and was obliged to go and seek Lucrezia, that daughter doubly loved to conquer his deadly resolve. Lucrezia came out from the retreat were she was weeping for the Duke of Gandia, that she might console her father. At her voice the door did reaily open, and it was only then that the Duke of Segovia, who had been kneeling almost a whole day at the threshold, begging His Holiness to take heart, could enter with servants bearing wine and food.

The pope remained alone with Lucrezia for three days and nights; then he reappeared in public, outwardly calm, if not resigned; for Guicciardini assures us that his daughter had made him understand how dangerous it would be to himself to show too openly before the assassin, who was coming home, the immoderate love he felt for his victim.

Chapter VIII

Caesar remained at Naples, partly to give time to the paternal grief to cool down, and partly to get on with another business he had lately been charged with, nothing else than a proposition of marriage between Lucrezia and Don Alfonso of Aragon, Duke of Bicelli and Prince of Salerno, natural son of Alfonso II and brother of Dona Sancha. It was true that Lucrezia was already married to the lord of Pesaro, but she was the daughter of an father who had received from heaven the right of uniting and disuniting. There was no need to trouble about so trifling a matter: when the two were ready to marry, the divorce would be effected. Alexander was too good a tactician to leave his daughter married to a son-in-law who was becoming useless to him.

Towards the end of August it was announced that the ambassador was coming back to Rome, having accomplished his mission to the new king to his great satisfaction. And thither he returned an the 5th of September, — that is, nearly three months after the Duke of Gandia's death, — and on the next day, the 6th, from the church of Santa Maria Novella, where, according to custom, the cardinals and the Spanish and Venetian ambassadors were awaiting him on horseback at the door, he proceeded to the Vatican, where His Holiness was sitting; there he entered the consistory, was admitted by the pope, and in accordance with the usual ceremonial received his benediction and kiss; then, accompanied once more in the same fashion by the ambassadors and cardinals, he was escorted to his own apartments. Thence he proceeded to, the pope's, as soon as he was left alone; for at the consis-

tory they had had no speech with one another, and the father
and son had a hundred things to talk about, but of these the
Duke of Gandia was not one, as might have been expected.
His name was not once spoken, and neither on that day nor
afterwards was there ever again any mention of the unhappy
young man: it was as though he had never existed.

It was the fact that Caesar brought good news, King
Frederic gave his consent to the proposed union; so the
marriage of Sforza and Lucrezia was dissolved on a pretext
of nullity. Then Frederic authorized the exhumation of
D'jem's body, which, it will be remembered, was worth
300,000 ducats.

After this, all came about as Caesar had desired; he became
the man who was all-powerful after the pope; but when he
was second in command it was soon evident to the Roman
people that their city was making a new stride in the direction
of ruin. There was nothing but balls, fetes, masquerades; there
were magnificent hunting parties, when Caesar — who had
begun to cast off is cardinal's robe, — weary perhaps of the
color, appeared in a French dress, followed, like a king by
cardinals, envoys. and bodyguard. The whole pontifical town,
given up like a courtesan to orgies and debauchery, had never
been more the home of sedition, luxury, and carnage, according to the Cardinal of Viterba, not even in the days of Nero
and Heliogabalus. Never had she fallen upon days more evil;
never had more traitors done her dishonor or sbirri stained
her streets with blood. The number of thieves was so great,
and their audacity such, that no one could with safety pass
the gates of the town; soon it was not even safe within them.
No house, no castle, availed for defense. Right and justice no
longer existed. Money, farce, pleasure, ruled supreme.

Still, the gold was melting as in a furnace at these Fetes;
and, by Heaven's just punishment, Alexander and Caesar
were beginning to covet the fortunes of those very men who
had risen through their simony to their present elevation.
The first attempt at a new method of coining money was tried
upon the Cardinal Cosenza. The occasion was as follows. A
certain dispensation had been granted some time before to a
nun who had taken the vows: she was the only surviving heir
to the throne of Portugal, and by means of the dispensation

she had been wedded to the natural son of the last king. This marriage was more prejudicial than can easily be imagined to the interests of Ferdinand and Isabella of Spain; so they sent ambassadors to Alexander to lodge a complaint against a proceeding of this nature, especially as it happened at the very moment when an alliance was to be formed between the house of Aragon and the Holy See. Alexander understood the complaint, and resolved that all should be set right. So he denied all knowledge of the papal brief though he had as a fact received 60,000 ducats for signing it — and accused the Archbishop of Cosenza, secretary for apostolic briefs, of having granted a false dispensation. By reason of this accusation, the archbishop was taken to the castle of Sant' Angelo, and a suit was begun.

But as it was no easy task to prove an accusation of this nature, especially if the archbishop should persist in maintaining that the dispensation was really granted by the pope, it was resolved to employ a trick with him which could not fail to succeed. One evening the Archbishop of Cosenza saw Cardinal Valentino come into his prison; with that frank air of affability which he knew well how to assume when it could serve his purpose, he explained to the prisoner the embarrassing situation in which the pope was placed, from which the archbishop alone, whom His Holiness looked upon as his best friend, could save him.

The archbishop replied that he was entirely at the service of His Holiness.

Caesar, on his entrance, found the captive seated, leaning his elbows on a table, and he took a seat opposite him and explained the pope's position: it was an embarrassing one. At the very time of contracting so important an alliance with the house of Aragon as that of Lucrezia and Alfonso, His Holiness could not avow to Ferdinand and Isabella that, for the sake of a few miserable ducats, he had signed a dispensation which would unite in the husband and wife together all the legitimate claims to a throne to which Ferdinand and Isabella had no right at all but that of conquest. This avowal would necessarily put an end to all negotiations, and the pontifical house would fall by the overthrow of that very pedestal which was to have heightened its grandeur. Accord-

ingly the archbishop would understand what the pope expected of his devotion and friendship: it was a simple and
straight avowal that he had supposed he might take it upon
himself to accord the dispensation. Then, as the sentence to
be passed on such an error would be the business of Alexander, the accused could easily imagine beforehand how truly
paternal such a sentence would be. Besides, the reward was in
the same hands, and if the sentence was that of a father, the
recompense would be that of a king. In fact, this recompense
would be no less than the honor of assisting as envoy, with
the title of cardinal, at the marriage of Lucrezia and Alfonso
— a favor which would be very appropriate, since it would be
thanks to his devotion that the marriage could take place.

The Archbishop of Cosenza knew the men he was dealing
with; he knew that to save their own ends they would hesitate
at nothing; he knew they had a poison like sugar to the taste
and to the smell, impossible to discover in food — a poison
that would kill slowly or quickly as the poisoner willed and
would leave no trace behind; he knew the secret of the
poisoned key that lay always on the pope's mantelpiece, so
that when His Holiness wished to destroy some one of his
intimates, he bade him open a certain cupboard: on the
handle of the key there was a little spike, and as the lock of
the cupboard turned stiffly the hand would naturally press,
the lock would yield, and nothing would have come of it but
a trifling scratch: the scratch was mortal. He knew, too, that
Caesar wore a ring made like two lions' heads, and that he
would turn the stone on the inside when he was shaking
hands with a friend. Then the lions' teeth became the teeth
of a viper, and the friend died cursing Borgia. So he yielded,
partly through fear, partly blinded by the thought of the
reward; and Caesar returned to the Vatican armed with a
precious paper, in which the Archbishop of Cosenza admitted that he was the only person responsible for the dispensation granted to the royal nun.

Two days later, by means of the proofs kindly furnished
by the archbishop, the pope; in the presence of the governor
of Rome, the auditor of the apostolic chamber, the advocate,
and the fiscal attorney, pronounced sentence, condemning
the archbishop to the loss of all his benefices and ecclesiastical

offices, degradation from his orders, and confiscation of his goods; his person was to be handed over to the civil arm. Two days later the civil magistrate entered the prison to fulfill his office as received from the pope, and appeared before the archbishop, accompanied by a clerk, two servants, and four guards. The clerk unrolled the paper he carried and read out the sentence; the two servants untied a packet, and, stripping the prisoner of his ecclesiastical garments, they reclothed him in a dress of coarse white cloth which only reached down to his knees, breeches of the same, and a pair of clumsy shoes. Lastly, the guards took him, and led him into one of the deepest dungeons of the castle of Sant' Angelo, where for furniture he found nothing but a wooden crucifix, a table, a chair, and a bed; for occupation, a Bible and a breviary, with a lamp to read by; for nourishment, two pounds of bread and a little cask of water, which were to be renewed every three days, together with a bottle of oil for burning in his lamp.

At the end of a year the poor archbishop died of despair, not before he had gnawed his own arms in his agony.

The very same day that he was taken into the dungeon, Caesar Borgia, who had managed the affair so ably, was presented by the pope with all the belongings of the condemned prisoner.

But the hunting parties, balls, and masquerades were not the only pleasures enjoyed by the pope and his family: from time to time strange spectacles were exhibited. We will only describe two — one of them a case of punishment, the other no more nor less than a matter of the stud farm. But as both of these give details with which we would not have our readers credit our imagination, we will first say that they are literally translated from Burchard's Latin journal.

"About the same time — that is, about the beginning of 1499 — a certain courtesan named La Corsetta was in prison, and had a lover who came to visit her in woman's clothes, a Spanish Moor, called from his disguise 'the Spanish lady from Barbary!' As a punishment, both of them were led through the town, the woman without petticoat or skirt, but wearing only the Moor's dress unbuttoned in front; the man wore his woman's garb; his hands were tied behind his back, and the skirt fastened up to his middle, with a view to complete exposure before the eyes of all. When in this attire they had made the circuit of the town, the Corsetta was sent back to the prison with the Moor. But on the 7th of April following, the Moor was again taken out and escorted in the company of two thieves towards the Campo dei Fiori. The three condemned men were preceded by a constable, who rode backwards on an ass, and held in his hand a long pole, on the end of which were hung, still bleeding, the amputated limbs of a poor Jew who had suffered torture and death for some trifling crime. When the procession reached the place of execution, the thieves were hanged, and the unfortunate Moor was tied to a stake piled round with wood, where he was to have been burnt to death, had not rain fallen in such torrents that the fire would not burn, in spite of all the efforts of the executioner."

This unlooked for accident, taken as a miracle by the people, robbed Lucrezia of the most exciting part of the execution; but her father was holding in reserve another kind of spectacle to console her with later. We inform the reader once more that a few lines we are about to set before him are a translation from the journal of the worthy German Burchard, who saw nothing in the bloodiest or most wanton performances but facts for his journal, which he duly registered with the impassibility of a scribe, appending no remark or moral reflection.

"On the 11th of November a certain peasant was entering Rome with two stallions laden with wood, when the servants of His Holiness, just as he passed the Piazza of St. Peter's, cut their girths, so that their loads fell on the ground with the pack-saddles, and led off the horses to a court between the palace and the gate; then the stable doors were opened, and four stallions, quite free and unbridled, rushed out and in an instant all six animals began kicking, biting and fighting each other until several were killed. Roderigo and Madame Lucrezia, who sat at the window just over the palace gate, took the greatest delight in the struggle and called their courtiers to witness the gallant battle that was being fought below them."

Now Caesar's trick in the matter of the Archbishop of Cosenza had had the desired result, and Isabella and Ferdinand could no longer impute to Alexander the signature of the brief they had complained of: so nothing was now in the way of the marriage of Lucrezia and Alfonso; this certainty gave the pope great joy, for he attached all the more importance to this marriage because he was already cogitating a second, between Caesar and Dona Carlota, Frederic's daughter.

Caesar had shown in all his actions since his brother's death his want of vocation for the ecclesiastical life; so no one was astonished when, a consistory having been summoned one morning by Alexander, Caesar entered, and addressing the pope, began by saying that from his earliest years he had been drawn towards secular pursuits both by natural inclination and ability, and it had only been in obedience to the absolute commands of His Holiness that he entered the Church, accepted the cardinal's scarlet, other dignities, and finally the sacred order of the diaconate; but feeling that in his situation it was improper to follow his passions, and at his age impossible to resist them, he humbly entreated His Holiness graciously to yield to the desire he had failed to overcome, and to permit him to lay aside the dress and dignities of the Church, and enter once more into the world, thereto contract a lawful marriage; also he entreated the lord cardinals to intercede for him with His Holiness, to whom he would freely resign all his churches, abbeys, and benefices, as well as every other ecclesiastical dignity and preferment that had been accorded him. The cardinals, deferring to Caesar's wishes, gave a unanimous vote, and the pope, as we may suppose, like a good father, not wishing to force his son's inclinations, accepted his resignation, and yielded to the petition; thus Caesar put off the scarlet robe, which was suited to him, says his historian Tommaso Tommasi, in one particular only — that it was the color of blood.

In truth, the resignation was a pressing necessity, and there was no time to lose. Charles VIII one day after he had came home late and tired from the hunting-field, had bathed his head in cold water; and going straight to table, had been struck dawn by an apoplectic seizure directly after his supper; and was dead, leaving the throne to the good Louis XII, a man of two conspicuous weaknesses, one as deplorable as the other: the first was the wish to make conquests; the second was the desire to have children. Alexander, who was on the watch far all political changes, had seen in a moment what he could get from Louis XII's accession to the throne, and was prepared to profit by the fact that the new king of France needed his help for the accomplishment of his twofold desire. Louis needed, first, his temporal aid in an expedition against the duchy of Milan, on which, as we explained before, he had inherited claims from Valentina Visconti, his grandmother; and, secondly, his spiritual aid to dissolve his marriage with Jeanne, the daughter of Louis XI; a childless and hideously deformed woman, whom he had only married by reason of the great fear he entertained far her father. Now Alexander was willing to do all this far Louis XII and to give in addition a cardinal's hat to his friend George d'Amboise, provided only that the King of France would use his influence in persuading the young Dona Carlota, who was at his court, to marry his son Caesar.

So, as this business was already far advanced on the day when Caesar doffed his scarlet and donned a secular garb, thus fulfilling the ambition so long cherished, when the lord of Villeneuve, sent by Louis and commissioned to bring Caesar to France, presented himself before the ex-cardinal on his arrival at Rome, the latter, with his usual extravagance of luxury and the kindness he knew well how to bestow on those he needed, entertained his guest for a month, and did all the honors of Rome. After that, they departed, preceded by one of the pope's couriers, who gave orders that every town they passed through was to receive them with marks of honor and respect. The same order had been sent throughout the whole of France, where the illustrious visitors received so numerous a guard, and were welcomed by a populace so eager to behold them, that after they passed through Paris, Caesar's gentlemen-in-waiting wrote to Rome that they had not seen any trees in France, or houses, or walls, but only men, women and sunshine.

The king, on the pretext of going out hunting, went to meet his guest two leagues outside the town. As he knew Caesar was very fond of the name of Valentine, which he had used as cardinal, and still continued to employ with the title of Count, although he had resigned the archbishopric which gave him the name, he there and then bestowed an him the investiture of Valence, in Dauphine, with the title of Duke and a pension of 20,000 francs; then, when he had made this magnificent gift and talked with him for nearly a couple of hours, he took his leave, to enable him to prepare the splendid entry he was proposing to make.

It was Wednesday, the 18th of December 1498, when Caesar Borgia entered the town of Chinon, with pomp worthy of the son of a pope who is about to marry the daughter of a king. The procession began with four-and-twenty mules, caparisoned in red, adorned with escutcheons bearing the duke's arms, laden with carved trunks and chests inlaid with ivory and silver; after them came four-and-twenty mare, also caparisoned, this time in the livery of the King of France, yellow and red; next after these came ten other mules, covered in yellow satin with red crossbars; and lastly another ten, covered with striped cloth of gold, the stripes alternately raised and flat gold.

Behind the seventy mules which led the procession there pranced sixteen handsome battle-horses, led by equerries who marched alongside; these were followed by eighteen hunters ridden by eighteen pages, who were about fourteen or fifteen years of age; sixteen of them were dressed in crimson velvet, and two in raised gold cloth; so elegantly dressed were these two children, who were also the best looking of the little band, that the sight of them gave rise to strange suspicions as to the reason for this preference, if one may believe what Brantome says. Finally, behind these eighteen horses came six beautiful mules, all harnessed with red velvet, and led by six valets, also in velvet to match.

The third group consisted of, first, two mules quite covered with cloth of gold, each carrying two chests in which it was said that the duke's treasure was stored, the precious stones he was bringing to his fiancée, and the relics and papal bulls that his father had charged him to convey for him to Louis XII. These were followed by twenty gentlemen dressed in cloth of gold and silver, among whom rode Paul Giordano Orsino and several barons and knights among the chiefs of the state ecclesiastic.

Next came two drums, one rebeck, and four soldiers blowing trumpets and silver clarions; then, in the midst of a party
of four-and-twenty lackeys, dressed half in crimson velvet and
half in yellow silk, rode Messire George d'Amboise and Monseigneur the Duke of Valentinois. Caesar was mounted on a
handsome tall courser, very richly harnessed, in a robe half
red satin and half cloth of gold, embroidered all over with
pearls and precious stones; in his cap were two rows of rubies,
the size of beans, which reflected so brilliant a light that one
might have fancied they were the famous carbuncles of the
Arabian Nights; he also wore on his neck a collar worth at
least 200,000 livres; indeed, there was no part of him, even
down to his boots, that was not laced with gold and edged
with pearls. His horse was covered with a cuirass in a pattern
of golden foliage of wonderful workmanship, among which
there appeared to grow, like flowers, nosegays of pearls and
clusters of rubies.

Lastly, bringing up the rear of the magnificent cortege,
behind the duke came twenty-four mules with red caparisons
bearing his arms, carrying his silver plate, tents, and baggage.

What gave to all the cavalcade an air of most wonderful
luxury and extravagance was that the horses and mules were
shod with golden shoes, and these were so badly nailed on
that more than three-quarters of their number, were lost on
the road For this extravagance Caesar was greatly blamed, for
it was thought an audacious thing to put on his horses' feet
a metal of which king's crowns are made.

But all this pomp had no effect on the lady for whose sake
it had been displayed; for when Dona Carlota was told that
Caesar Bargia had come to France in the hope of becoming
her husband, she replied simply that she would never take a
priest far her husband, and, moreover, the son of a priest; a
man who was not only an assassin, but a fratricide; not only
a man of infamous birth, but still more infamous in his
morals and his actions.

But, in default of the haughty lady of Aragon, Caesar soon
found another princess of noble blood who consented to be
his wife: this was Mademoiselle d'Albret, daughter of the King
of Navarre. The marriage, arranged on condition that the
pope should pay 200,000 ducats dowry to the bride, and

should make her brother cardinal, was celebrated on the 10th of May; and on the Whitsunday following the Duke of Valentois received the order of St. Michael, an order founded by Louis XI, and esteemed at this period as the highest in the gift of the kings of France. The news of this marriage, which made an alliance with Louis XII certain, was received with great joy by the pope, who at once gave orders far bonfires and illuminations all over the town.

Louis XII was not only grateful to the pope for dissolving his marriage with Jeanne of France and authorizing his union with Anne of Brittany, but he considered it indispensable to his designs in Italy to have the pope as his ally. So he promised the Duke of Valentinois to put three hundred lances at his disposal, as soon as he had made an entry into Milan, to be used to further his own private interests, and against whomsoever he pleased except only the allies of France. The conquest of Milan should be undertaken so soon as Louis felt assured of the support of the Venetians, or at least of their neutrality, and he had sent them ambassadors authorized to promise in his name the restoration of Cremona and Ghiera d'Adda when he had completed the conquest of Lombardy.

Chapter IX

*E*verything from without was favoring Alexander's encroaching policy, when he was compelled to turn his eyes from France towards the center of Italy: in Florence dwelt a man, neither duke, nor king, nor soldier, a man whose power was in his genius, whose armor was his purity, who owned no offensive weapon but his tongue, and who yet began to grow more dangerous for him than all the kings, dukes, princes, in the whole world could ever be; this man was the poor Dominican monk Girolamo Savonarola, the same who had refused absolution to Lorenzo dei Medici because he would not restore the liberty of Florence.

Girolamo Savonarola had prophesied the invasion of a force from beyond the Alps, and Charles VIII had conquered Naples; Girolamo Savonarola had prophesied to Charles VIII that because he had failed to fulfill the mission of liberator entrusted to him by God, he was threatened with a great misfortune as a punishment, and Charles was dead; lastly, Savonarola had prophesied his own fall like the man who paced around the holy city for eight days, crying, "Woe to Jerusalem!" and on the ninth day, "Woe be on my own head!" None the less, the Florentine reformer, who could not recoil from any danger, was determined to attack the colossal abomination that was seated on St. Peter's holy throne; each debauch, each fresh crime that lifted up its brazen face to the light of day or tried to hide its shameful head beneath the veil of night, he had never failed to paint out to the people, denouncing it as the off spring of the pope's luxurious living and lust of power. Thus had he stigmatized Alexander's new amour with the beautiful Giulia Farnese, who in the preceding April a added another son to the pope's family; thus had he cursed the Duke of Gandia's murderer, the lustful, jealous fratricide; lastly, he had pointed out to the Florentines, who were excluded from the league then forming, what sort of future was in store far them when the Borgias should have made themselves masters of the small principalities and should come to attack the duchies and republics. It was clear that in Savonarola, the pope had an enemy at once temporal and spiritual, whose importunate and threatening voice must be silenced at any cost.

*B*ut mighty as the pope's power was, to accomplish a design like this was no easy matter. Savonarola, preaching the stern principles of liberty, had united to his cause, even in the midst of rich, pleasure-loving Florence, a party of some size, known as the 'Piagnoni', or the Penitents: this band was composed of citizens who were anxious for reform in Church and State, who accused the Medici of enslaving the fatherland and the Borgias of upsetting the faith, who demanded two things, that the republic should return to her democratic principles, and religion to a primitive simplicity. Towards the first of these projects considerable progress had been made, since they had successively obtained, first, an amnesty for all crimes and delinquencies committed under other governments; secondly, the abolition of the 'balia', which was an aristocratic magistracy; thirdly, the establishment of a sovereign council, composed of 1800 citizens; and lastly, the substitution of popular elections for drawing by lot and for oligarchical nominations: these changes had been effected in spite of two other factions, the 'Arrabiati', or Madmen, who, consisting of the richest and noblest youths of the Florentine patrician families, desired to have an oligarchical government; and the 'Bigi', or Greys, so called because they always held their meetings in the shade, who desired the return of the Medici.

The first measure Alexander used against the growing power of Savonarola was to declare him heretic, and as such banished from the pulpit; but Savonarola had eluded this prohibition by making his pupil and friend, Domenico Bonvicini di Pescia, preach in his stead. The result was that the master's teachings were issued from other lips, and that was all; the seed, though scattered by another hand, fell none the less on fertile soil, where it would soon burst into flower. Moreover, Savonarola now set an example that was followed to good purpose by Luther, when, twenty-two years later, he burned Leo X's bull of excommunication at Wittenberg; he was weary of silence, so he declared, on the authority of Pope Pelagius, that an unjust excommunication had no efficacy, and that the person excommunicated unjustly did not even need to get absolution. So on Christmas Day, 1497, he declared that by the inspiration of God he renounced his obedience to a corrupt master; and he began to preach once more in the cathedral, with a success that was all the greater for the interruption, and an influence far more formidable than before, because it was strengthened by that sympathy of the masses which an unjust persecution always inspires.

Then Alexander made overtures to Leonardo dei Medici, vicar of the archbishopric of Florence, to obtain the punishment of the rebel: Leonardo, in obedience to the orders he received, from Rome, issued a mandate forbidding the faithful to attend at Savonarola's sermons. After this mandate, any who should hear the discourses of the excommunicated monk would be refused communion and confession; and as when they died they would be contaminated with heresy, in consequence of their spiritual intercourse with a heretic, their dead bodies would be dragged on a hurdle and deprived of the rights of sepulture. Savonarola appealed from the mandate of his superior both to the people and to the Signoria, and the two together gave orders to the episcopal vicar to leave Florence within two hours: this happened at the beginning of the year 1498.

The expulsion of Leonard's dei Medici was a new triumph for Savonarola, so, wishing to turn to good moral account his growing influence, he resolved to convert the last day of the carnival, hitherto given up to worldly pleasures, into a day of religious sacrifice. So actually on Shrove Tuesday a considerable number of boys were collected in front of the cathedral, and there divided into bands, which traversed the whole town, making a house-to-house visitation, claiming all profane books, licentious paintings, lutes, harps, cards and dice, cosmetics and perfumes — in a word, all the hundreds of products of a corrupt society and civilization, by the aid of which Satan at times makes victorious war on God. The inhabitants of Florence obeyed, and came forth to the Piazza of the Duoma, bringing these works of perdition, which were soon piled up in a huge stack, which the youthful reformers set on fire, singing religious psalms and hymns the while. On this pile were burned many copies of Boccaccio and of Margante Maggiore, and pictures by Fro Bartalommeo, who from that day forward renounced the art of this world to consecrate his brush utterly and entirely to the reproduction of religious scenes.

A reform such as this was terrifying to Alexander; so he resolved on fighting Savonarola with his own weapons — that is, by the force of eloquence. He chose as the Dominican's opponent a preacher of recognized talent, called Fra Francesco di Paglia; and he sent him to Florence, where he began to preach in Santa Croce, accusing Savonarola of heresy and impiety. At the same time the pope, in a new brief, announced to the Signaria that unless they forbade the arch-heretic to preach, all the goods of Florentine merchants who lived on the papal territory would be confiscated, and the republic laid under an interdict and declared the spiritual and temporal enemy of the Church. The Signoria, abandoned by France, and aware that the material power of Rome was increasing in a frightful manner, was forced this time to yield, and to issue to Savonarola an order to leave off preaching. He obeyed, and bade farewell to his congregation in a sermon full of strength and eloquence.

But the withdrawal of Savonarola, so far from calming the ferment, had increased it: there was talk about his prophecies being fulfilled; and some zealots, more ardent than their mastery added miracle to inspiration, and loudly proclaimed that Savonarola had offered to go down into the vaults of the cathedral with his antagonist, and there bring a dead man to life again, to prove that his doctrine was true, promising to declare himself vanquished if the miracle were performed by his adversary. These rumors reached the ears of Fra Francesco, and as he was a man of warm blood, who counted his own life as nothing if it might be spent to help his cause, he declared in all humility that he felt he was too great a sinner for God to work a miracle in his behalf; but he proposed another challenge: he would try with Savonarola the ordeal of fire. He knew, he said, that he must perish, but at least he should perish avenging the cause of religion, since he was certain to involve in his destruction the tempter who plunged so many souls beside his own into eternal damnation.

The proposition made by Fra Francesco was taken to Savanarola; but as he had never proposed the earlier challenge, he hesitated to accept the second; hereupon his disciple, Fra Domenico Bonvicini, more confident than his master in his own power, declared himself ready to accept the trial by fire in his stead; so certain was he that God would perform a miracle by the intercession of Savonarola, His prophet.

Instantly the report spread through Florence that the mortal challenge was accepted; Savonarola's partisans, all men of the strongest convictions, felt no doubt as to the success of their cause. His enemies were enchanted at the thought of the heretic giving himself to the flames; and the indifferent saw in the ordeal a spectacle of real and terrible interest.

But the devotion of Fra Bonvicini of Pescia was not what Fra Francesco was reckoning with. He was willing, no doubt, to die a terrible death, but on condition that Savanarola died with him. What mattered to him the death of an obscure disciple like Fra Bonvicini? It was the master he would strike, the great teacher who must be involved in his own ruin. So he refused to enter the fire except with Savonarola himself, and, playing this terrible game in his own person, would not allow his adversary to play it by proxy.

Then a thing happened which certainly no one could have anticipated. In the place of Fra Francesco, who would not tilt with any but the master, two Franciscan monks appeared to tilt with the disciple. These were Fra Nicholas de Pilly and Fra Andrea Rondinelli. Immediately the partisans of Savonarala, seeing this arrival of reinforcements for their antagonist, came forward in a crowd to try the ordeal. The Franciscans were unwilling to be behindhand, and everybody took sides with equal ardor for one or other party. All Florence was like a den of madmen; everyone wanted the ordeal, everyone wanted to go into the fire; not only did men challenge one another, but women and even children were clamoring to be allowed to try. At last the Signoria, reserving this privilege for the first applicants, ordered that the strange duel should take place only between Fra Domenico Bonvicini and Fra Andrea Rondinelli; ten of the citizens were to arrange all details; the day was fixed for the 7th of April, 1498, and the place the Piazza del Palazzo.

The judges of the field made their arrangements conscientiously. By their orders scaffolding was erected at the appointed place, five feet in height, ten in width, and eighty feet long. This scaffolding was covered with faggots and heath, supported by cross-bars of the very driest wood that could be found. Two narrow paths were made, two feet wide at most, their entrance giving an the Loggia dei Lanzi, their exit exactly opposite. The loggia was itself divided into two by a partition, so that each champion had a kind of room to make his preparations in, just as in the theater every actor has his dressing-room; but in this instance the tragedy that was about to be played was not a fictitious one.

The Franciscans arrived on the piazza and entered the compartment reserved for them without making any religious demonstration; while Savonarola, on the contrary, advanced to his own place in the procession, wearing the sacerdotal robes in which he had just celebrated the Holy Eucharist, and holding in his hand the sacred host for all the world to see, as it was enclosed in a crystal tabernacle. Fra Domenico di Pescia, the hero of the occasion, followed, bearing a crucifix, and all the Dominican monks, their red crosses in their hands, marched behind singing a psalm; while behind them again followed the most considerable of the citizens of their party, bearing torches, for, sure as they were of the triumph of their cause, they wished to fire the faggots themselves. The piazza was so crowded that the people overflowed into all the streets around. In every door and window there was nothing to be seen but heads ranged one above the other; the terraces were covered with people, and curious spectators were observed an the roof of the Duomo and on the tap of the

Campanile.

But, brought face to face with the ordeal, the Franciscans raised such difficulties that it was very plain the heart of their champion was failing him. The first fear they expressed was that Fra Bonvicini was an enchanter, and so carried about him some talisman or charm which would save him from the fire. So they insisted that he should be stripped of all has clothes and put on others to be inspected by witnesses. Fra Bonvicini made no objection, though the suspicion was humiliating; he changed shirt, dress, and cowl. Then, when the Franciscans observed that Savanarola was placing the tabernacle in his hands, they protested that it was profanation to expose the sacred host to the risk of burning, that this was not in the bond, and if Bonvicini would not give up this supernatural aid, they far their part would give up the trial altogether. Savonarola replied that it was not astonishing that the champion of religion who put his faith in God should bear in his hands that very God to whom he entrusted his salvation. But this reply did not satisfy the Franciscans, who were unwilling to let go their contention. Savonarola remained inflexible, supporting his own right, and thus nearly four hours passed in the discussion of points which neither party would give up, and affairs remained in 'statu quo'. Meanwhile the people, jammed together in the streets, on the terraces, on the roofs, since break of day, were suffering from hunger and thirst and beginning to get impatient: their impatience soon developed into loud murmurs, which reached even the champions' ears, so that the partisans of Savonarala, who felt such faith in him that they were confident of a miracle, entreated him to yield to all the conditions suggested. To this Savonarola replied that if it were himself making the trial he would be less inexorable; but since another man was incurring the danger; he could not take too many precautions. Two more hours passed, while his partisans tried in vain to combat his refusals. At last, as night was coming on and the people grew ever more and more impatient and their murmurs began to assume a threatening tone, Bonvicini declared that he was ready to walk through the fire, holding nothing in his hand but a crucifix. No one could refuse him this; so Fra Rondinelli was compelled to accept

his proposition. The announcement was made to the populace that the champions had come to terms and the trial was
about to take place. At this news the people calmed down, in
the hope of being compensated at last for their long wait; but
at that very moment a storm which had long been threatening
brake over Florence with such fury that the faggots which had
just been lighted were extinguished by the rain, leaving no
possibility of their rekindling. From the moment when the
people suspected that they had been fooled, their enthusiasm
was changed into derision. They were ignorant from which
side the difficulties had arisen that had hindered the trial, so
they laid the responsibility on both champions without distinction. The Signoria, foreseeing the disorder that was now
imminent, ordered the assembly to retire; but the assembly
thought otherwise, and stayed on the piazza, waiting for the
departure of the two champions, in spite of the fearful rain
that still fell in torrents. Rondinelli was taken back amid
shouts and hootings, and pursued with showers of stones.
Savonarola, thanks to his sacred garments and the host which
he still carried, passed calmly enough through the midst of
the mob — a miracle quite as remarkable as if he had passed
through the fire unscathed.

But it was only the sacred majesty of the host that had
protected this man, who was indeed from this moment regarded as a false prophet: the crowd allowed Savonarola to
return to his convent, but they regretted the necessity, so
excited were they by the Arrabbiati party, who had always
denounced him as a liar and a hypocrite. So when the next
morning, Palm Sunday, he stood up in the pulpit to explain
his conduct, he could not obtain a moment's silence for
insults, hooting, and loud laughter. Then the outcry, at first
derisive, became menacing: Savonarola, whose voice was too
weak to subdue the tumult, descended from his pulpit, retired
into the sacristy, and thence to his convent, where he shut
himself up in his cell. At that moment a cry was heard, and
was repeated by everybody present:

"To San Marco, to San Marco!" The rioters, few at first,
were recruited by all the populace as they swept along the
streets, and at last reached the convent, dashing like an angry
sea against the wall.

The doors, closed on Savonarala's entrance, soon crashed before the vehement onset of the powerful multitude, which struck down on the instant every obstacle it met: the whole convent was quickly flooded with people, and Savonarola, with his two confederates, Domenico Bonvicini and Silvestro Maruffi, was arrested in his cell, and conducted to prison amid the insults of the crowd, who, always in extremes, whether of enthusiasm or hatred, would have liked to tear them to pieces, and would not be quieted till they had exacted a promise that the prisoners should be forcibly compelled to make the trial of fire which they had refused to make of their own free will.

Alexander VI, as we may suppose, had not been without influence in bringing about this sudden and astonishing reaction, although he was not present in person; and had scarcely learned the news of Savonarola's fall and arrest when he claimed him as subject to ecclesiastical jurisdiction. But in spite of the grant of indulgences wherewith this demand was accompanied, the Signoria insisted that Savonarola's trial should take place at Florence, adding a request so as not to appear to withdraw the accused completely from the pontifi- cal authority — that the pope would send two ecclesiastical judges to sit in the Florentine tribunal. Alexander, seeing that he would get nothing better from the magnificent republic, sent as deputies Gioacchino Turriano of Venice, General of the Dominicans, and Francesco Ramolini, doctor in law: they practically brought the sentence with them, declaring Savon- arola and his accomplices heretics, schismatics, persecutors of the Church and seducers of the people.

The firmness shown by the Florentines in claiming their rights of jurisdiction were nothing but an empty show to save appearances; the tribunal, as a fact, was composed of eight members, all known to be fervent haters of Savonarola, whose trial began with the torture. The result was that, feeble in body constitutionally nervous and irritable, he had not been able to endure the rack, and, overcome by agony just at the moment when the executioner had lifted him up by the wrists and then dropped him a distance of two feet to the ground, he had confessed, in order to get some respite, that his prophecies were nothing mare than conjectures. If is true that,

so soon as he went back to prison, he protested against the
confession, saying that it was the weakness of his bodily
organs and his want of firmness that had wrested the lie from
him, but that the truth really was that the Lord had several
times appeared to him in his ecstasies and revealed the things
that he had spoken. This protestation led to a new application
of the torture, during which Savonarola succumbed once
more to the dreadful pain, and once more retracted. But
scarcely was he unbound, and was still lying on the bed of
torture, when he declared that his confessions were the fault
of his torturers, and the vengeance would recoil upon their
heads; and he protested yet once mare against all he had
confessed and might confess again. A third time the torture
produced the same avowals, and the relief that followed it the
same retractions. The judges therefore, when they condemned
him and his two disciples to the flames, decided that his
confession should not be read aloud at the stake, according
to custom, feeling certain that an this occasion also he would
give it the lie, and that publicly, which, as anyone must see
who knew the versatile spirit of the public, would be a most
dangerous proceeding.

On the 23rd of May, the fire which had been promised to
the people before was a second time prepared on the Piazza
del Palazzo, and this time the crowd assembled quite certain
that they would not be disappointed of a spectacle so long
anticipated. And towards eleven o'clock in the morning,
Girolamo Savonarola, Domenico Bonvicini, and Silvestro
Maruffi were led to the place of execution, degraded of their
orders by the ecclesiastical judges, and bound all three to the
same stake in the center of an immense pile of wood. Then
the bishop Pagnanoli told the condemned men that he cut
them off from the Church. "Aye, from the Church militant,"
said Savonarola, who from that very hour, thanks to his
martyrdom, was entering into the Church triumphant. No
other words were spoken by the condemned men, for at this
moment one of the Arrabbiati, a personal enemy of Savonarola, breaking through the hedge of guards around the
scaffold, snatched the torch from the executioner's hand and
himself set fire to the four corners of the pile. Savonarola and
his disciples, from the moment when they saw the smoke

arise, began to sing a psalm, and the flames enwrapped them on all sides with a glowing veil, while their religious song was yet heard mounting upward to the gates of heaven.

Pope Alexander VI was thus set free from perhaps the most formidable enemy who had ever risen against him, and the pontifical vengeance pursued the victims even after their death: the Signoria, yielding to his wishes, gave orders that the ashes of the prophet and his disciples should be thrown into the Arno. But certain half-burned fragments were picked up by the very soldiers whose business it was to keep the people back from approaching the fire, and the holy relics are even now shown, blackened by the flames, to the faithful, who if they no longer regard Savonarola as a prophet, revere him none the less as a martyr.

Chapter X

*T*he French army was now preparing to cross the Alps a second time, under the command of Trivulce. Louis XII had come as far as Lyons in the company of Caesar Borgia and Giuliano della Rovere, on whom he had forced a reconciliation, and towards the beginning of the month of May had sent his vanguard before him, soon to be followed by the main body of the army. The forces he was employing in this second campaign of conquest were 1600, lances, 5000 Swiss, 9000 Gascons, and 3500 infantry, raised from all parts of France. On the 13th of August this whole body, amounting to nearly 15,000 men, who were to combine their forces with the Venetians, arrived beneath the walls of Arezzo, and immediately laid siege to the town.

Ludovico Sforza's position was a terrible one: he was now suffering from his imprudence in calling the French into Italy; all the allies he had thought he might count upon were abandoning him at the same moment, either because they were busy about their own affairs, or because they were afraid of the powerful enemy that the Duke of Milan had made for himself. Maximilian, who had promised him a contribution of 400 lances, to make up for not renewing the hostilities with Louis XII that had been interrupted, had just made a league with the circle of Swabia to war against the Swiss, whom he had declared rebels against the Empire. The Florentines, who had engaged to furnish him with 300 men-at-arms and 2000 infantry, if he would help them to retake Pisa, had just retracted their promise because of Louis XII's threats, and had undertaken to remain neutral. Frederic, who was holding back his troops for the defense of his own States, because he supposed, not without reason, that, Milan once conquered, he would again have to defend Naples, sent him no help, no men, no money, in spite of his promises. Ludovico Sforza was therefore reduced to his own proper forces.

But as he was a man powerful in arms and clever in artifice, he did not allow himself to succumb at the first blow, and in all haste fortified Annona, Novarro, and Alessandria, sent off Cajazzo with troops to that part of the Milanese territory which borders on the states of Venice, and collected on the Po as many troops as he could. But these precautions availed him nothing against the impetuous onslaught of the French, who in a few days had taken Annona, Arezzo, Novarro, Voghiera, Castelnuovo, Ponte Corona, Tartone, and Alessandria, while Trivulce was on the march to Milan.

Seeing the rapidity of this conquest and their numerous victories, Ludovico Sforza, despairing of holding out in his capital, resolved to retire to Germany, with his children, his brother, Cardinal Ascanio Sforza, and his treasure, which had been reduced in the course of eight years from 1,500,000 to 200,000 ducats. But before he went he left Bernardino da Carte in charge of the castle of Milan. In vain did his friends warn him to distrust this man, in vain did his brother Ascanio offer to hold the fortress himself, and offer to hold it to the very last; Ludovico refused to make any change in his arrangements, and started on the 2nd of September, leaving in the citadel three thousand foot and enough provisions, ammunition, and money to sustain a siege of several months.

Two days after Ludovico's departure, the French entered Milan. Ten days later Bernardino da Come gave up the castle before a single gun had been fired. Twenty-one days had sufficed for the French to get possession of the various towns, the capital, and all the territories of their enemy.

Louis XII received the news of this success while he was at Lyons, and he at once started for Milan, where he was received with demonstrations of joy that were really sincere. Citizens of every rank had come out three miles' distance from the gates to receive him, and forty boys, dressed in cloth of gold and silk, marched before him singing hymns of victory composed by poets of the period, in which the king was styled their liberator and the envoy of freedom. The great joy of the Milanese people was due to the fact that friends of Louis had been spreading reports beforehand that the King of France was rich enough to abolish all taxes. And so soon as the second day from his arrival at Milan the conqueror made some slight reduction, granted important favors to certain Milanese gentlemen, and bestowed the town of Vigavano on Trivulce as a reward for his swift and glorious campaign. But Caesar Borgia, who had followed Louis XII with a view to playing his part in the great hunting-ground of Italy, scarcely waited for him to attain his end when he claimed the fulfillment of his promise, which the king with his accustomed loyalty hastened to perform. He instantly put at the disposal of Caesar three hundred lances under the command of Yves d'Alegre, and four thousand Swiss under the command of the bailiff of Dijon, as a help in his work of reducing the Vicars of the Church.

We must now explain to our readers who these new personages were whom we introduce upon the scene by the above name.

During the eternal wars of Guelphs and Ghibelines and the long exile of the popes at Avignon, most of the towns and fortresses of the Romagna had been usurped by petty tyrants, who for the most part hard received from the Empire the investiture of their new possessions; but ever since German influence had retired beyond the Alps, and the popes had again made Rome the center of the Christian world, all the small princes, robbed of their original protector, had rallied round the papal see, and received at the hands of the pope a new investiture, and now they paid annual dues, for which they received the particular title of duke, count, or lord, and the general name of Vicar of the Church.

It had been no difficult matter for Alexander, scrupulously examining the actions and behavior of these gentlemen during the seven years that had elapsed since he was exalted to St. Peter's throne, to find in the conduct of each one of them something that could be called an infraction of the treaty made between vassals and suzerain; accordingly he brought forward his complaints at a tribunal established for the purpose, and obtained sentence from the judges to the effect that the vicars of the Church, having failed to fulfill the conditions of their investiture, were despoiled of their domains, which would again become the property of the Holy See. As the pope was now dealing with men against whom it was easier to pass a sentence than to get it carried out, he had nominated as captain-general the new Duke of Valentinois, who was commissioned to recover the territories for his own benefit. The lords in question were the Malatesti of Rimini, the Sforza of Pesaro, the Manfredi of Faenza, the Riarii of Imola and Farli, the Variani of Camerina, the Montefeltri of Urbino, and the Caetani of Sermoneta.

But the Duke of Valentinois, eager to keep as warm as possible his great friendship with his ally and relative Louis XII, was, as we know, staying with him at Milan so long as he remained there, where, after a month's occupation, the king retraced his steps to his own capital, the Duke of Valentinois ordered his men-at-arms and his Swiss to await him between Parma and Modena, and departed posthaste for Rome, to explain his plans to his father viva voce and to receive his final instructions. When he arrived, he found that the fortune of his sister Lucrezia had been greatly augmented in his absence, not from the side of her husband Alfonso, whose future was very uncertain now in consequence of Louis's successes, which had caused some coolness between Alfonso and the pope, but from her father's side, upon whom at this time she exercised an influence mare astonishing than ever. The pope had declared Lucrezia Borgia of Aragon life-governor of Spoleto and its duchy, with all emoluments, rights, and revenues accruing thereunto. This had so greatly increased her power and improved her position, that in these days she never showed herself in public without a company of two hundred horses ridden by the most illustrious ladies and noblest knights of Rome. Moreover, as the twofold affection of her father was a secret to nobody, the first prelates in the Church, the frequenters of the Vatican, the friends of His Holiness, were all her most humble servants; cardinals gave her their hands when she stepped from her litter or her horse, archbishops disputed the honor of celebrating mass in her private apartments.

But Lucrezia had been obliged to quit Rome in order to take possession of her new estates; and as her father could not spend much time away from his beloved daughter, he resolved to take into his hands the town of Nepi, which on a former occasion, as the reader will doubtless remember, he had bestowed on Ascanio Sforza in exchange for his suffrage. Ascanio had naturally lost this town when he attached himself to the fortunes of the Duke of Milan, his brother; and when the pope was about to take it again, he invited his daughter Lucrezia to join him there and be present at the rejoicings held in honor of his resuming its possession.

Lucrezia's readiness in giving way to her father's wishes brought her a new gift from him: this was the town and territory of Sermoneta, which belonged to the Caetani. Of course the gift was as yet a secret, because the two owners of the seigneury, had first to be disposed of, one being Monsignore Giacomo Caetano, apostolic protonotary, the other Prospero Caetano, a young cavalier of great promise; but as both lived at Rome, and entertained no suspicion, but indeed supposed themselves to be in high favor with His Holiness, the one by virtue of his position, the other of his courage, the matter seemed to present no great difficulty. So directly after the return of Alexander to Rome, Giacomo Caetano was arrested, on what pretext we know not, was taken to the castle of Sant' Angelo, and there died shortly after, of poison: Prospero Caetano was strangled in his own house. After these two deaths, which both occurred so suddenly as to give no time for either to make a will, the pope declared that Sermoneta and all of her property appertaining to the Caetani devolved upon the apostolic chamber; and they were sold to Lucrezia for the cum of 80,000 crowns, which her father refunded to her the day after. Though Caesar hurried to Rome, he found when he arrived that his father had been beforehand with him, and had made a beginning of his conquests.

Another fortune also had been making prodigious strides during Caesar's stay in France, viz. the fortune of Gian Borgia, the pope's nephew, who had been one of the most devoted friends of the Duke of Gandia up to the time of his death. It was said in Rome, and not in a whisper, that the

young cardinal owed the favors heaped upon him by His
Holiness less to the memory of the brother than to the
protection of the sister. Both these reasons made Gian Borgia
a special object of suspicion to Caesar, and it was with an
inward vow that he should not enjoy his new dignities very
long that the Duke of Valentinois heard that his cousin Gian
had just been nominated cardinal 'a latere' of all the Christian
world, and had quitted Rome to make a circuit through all
the pontifical states with a suite of archbishops, bishops,
prelates, and gentlemen, such as would have done honor to
the pope himself.

Caesar had only come to Rome to get news; so he only
stayed three days, and then, with all the troops His Holiness
could supply, rejoined his forces on the borders of the Euza,
and marched at once to Imola. This town, abandoned by its
chiefs, who had retired to Forli, was forced to capitulate.
Imola taken, Caesar marched straight upon Forli. There he
met with a serious check; a check, moreover, which came from
a woman. Caterina Sforza, widow of Girolamo and mother
of Ottaviano Riario, had retired to this town, and stirred up
the courage of the garrison by putting herself, her goods and
her person, under their protection. Caesar saw that it was no
longer a question of a sudden capture, but of a regular siege;
so he began to make all his arrangements with a view to it,
and placing a battery of cannon in front of the place where
the walls seemed to him weakest, he ordered an uninterrupted
fire, to be continued until the breach was practicable.

When he returned to the camp after giving this order, he
found there Gian Borgia, who had gone to Rome from Ferrara
and was unwilling to be so near Caesar without paying him
a visit: he was received with effusion and apparently the
greatest joy, and stayed three days; on the fourth day all the
officers and members of the court were invited to a grand
farewell supper, and Caesar bade farewell to his cousin, charging him with dispatches for the pope, and lavishing upon
him all the tokens of affection he had shown on his arrival.

Cardinal Gian Bargia posted off as soon as he left the
supper-table, but on arriving at Urbino he was seized with
such a sudden and strange indisposition that he was forced
to stop; but after a few minutes, feeling rather better, he went

an; scarcely, however, had he entered Rocca Cantrada when he again felt so extremely ill that he resolved to go no farther, and stayed a couple of days in the town. Then, as he thought he was a little better again, and as he had heard the news of the taking of Forli and also that Caterina Sforza had been taken prisoner while she was making an attempt to retire into the castle, he resolved to go back to Caesar and congratulate him on his victory; but at Fassambrane he was forced to stop a third time, although he had given up his carriage for a litter. This was his last halt: the same day he sought his bed, never to rise from it again; three days later he was dead.

His body was taken to Rome and buried without any ceremony in the church of Santa Maria del Populo, where lay awaiting him the corpse of his friend the Duke of Gandia; and there was now no more talk of the young cardinal, high as his rank had been, than if he had never existed. Thus in gloom and silence passed away all those who were swept to destruction by the ambition of that terrible trio, Alexander, Lucrezia, and Caesar.

Almost at the same time Rome was terrified by another murder. Don Giovanni Cerviglione, a gentleman by birth and a brave soldier, captain of the pope's men-at-arms, was attacked one evening by the sbirri, as he was on his way home from supping with Dan Elisio Pignatelli. One of the men asked his name, and as he pronounced it, seeing that there was no mistake, plunged a dagger into his breast, while a second man with a back stroke of his sword cut off his head, which lay actually at his feet before his body had time to fall.

The governor of Rome lodged a complaint against this assassination with the pope; but quickly perceiving, by the way his intimation was received, that he would have done better to say nothing, he stopped the inquiries he had started, so that neither of the murderers was ever arrested. But the rumor was circulated that Caesar, in the short stay he had made at Rome, had had a rendezvous with Cerviglione's wife, who was a Borgia by birth, and that her husband when he heard of this infringement of conjugal duty had been angry enough to threaten her and her lover, too: the threat had reached Caesar's ears, who, making a long arm of Michelotto, had, himself at Forli, struck down Cerviglione in the streets of Rome.

Another unexpected death followed so quickly on that of Don Giovanni Cerviglione that it could not but be attributed to the same originator, if not to the same cause. Monsignore Agnelli of Mantua, archbishop of Cosenza, clerk of the chamber and vice-legate of Viterbo, having fallen into disgrace with His Holiness, how it is not known, was poisoned at his own table, at which he had passed a good part of the night in cheerful conversation with three or four guests, the poison gliding meanwhile through his veins; then going to bed in perfect health, he was found dead in the morning. His possessions were at once divided into three portions: the land and houses were given to the Duke of Valentinois; the bishopric went to Francesco Borgia, son of Calixtus III; and the office of clerk of the chamber was sold for 5000 ducats to Ventura Bonnassai, a merchant of Siena, who produced this sum for Alexander, and settled down the very same day in the Vatican.

This last death served the purpose of determining a point of law hitherto uncertain: as Monsignore Agnelli's natural heirs had made some difficulty about being disinherited, Alexander issued a brief; whereby he took from every cardinal and every priest the right of making a will, and declared that all their property should henceforth devolve upon him.

But Caesar was stopped short in the midst of his victories. Thanks to the 200,000 ducats that yet remained in his treasury, Ludovico Sforza had levied 500 men-at-arms from Burgundy and 8000 Swiss infantry, with whom he had entered Lombardy. So Trivulce, to face this enemy, had been compelled to call back Yves d'Alegre and the troops that Louis XII had lent to Caesar; consequently Caesar, leaving behind a body of pontifical soldiery as garrison at Forli and Imola, betook himself with the rest of his force to Rome.

It was Alexander's wish that his entry should be a triumph; so when he learned that the quartermasters of the army were only a few leagues from the town, he sent out runners to invite the royal ambassadors, the cardinals, the prelates, the Roman barons, and municipal dignitaries to make procession with all their suite to meet the Duke of Valentinois; and as it always happens that the pride of those who command is surpassed by the baseness of those who obey, the orders were not only fulfilled to the letter, but beyond it.

The entry of Caesar took place on the 26th of February, 1500. Although this was the great Jubilee year, the festivals of the carnival began none the less for that, and were conducted in a manner even more extravagant and licentious than usual; and the conqueror after the first day prepared a new display of ostentation, which he concealed under the veil of a masquerade. As he was pleased to identify himself with the glory, genius, and fortune of the great man whose name he bore, he resolved on a representation of the triumph of Julius Caesar, to be given on the Piazzi di Navona, the ordinary place for holding the carnival fetes. The next day, therefore, he and his retinue started from that square, and traversed all the streets of Rome, wearing classical costumes and riding in antique cars, on one of which Caesar stood, clad in the robe of an emperor of old, his brow crowned with a golden laurel wreath, surrounded by lictors, soldiers, and ensign-bearers, who carried banners whereon was inscribed the motto, 'Aut Caesar aut nihil'.

Finally, an the fourth Sunday, in Lent, the pope conferred upon Caesar the dignity he had so long coveted, and appointed him general and gonfaloniere of the Holy Church.

In the meanwhile Sforza had crossed the Alps and passed the Lake of Como, amid acclamations of joy from his former subjects, who had quickly lost the enthusiasm that the French army and Louis's promises had inspired. These demonstrations were so noisy at Milan, that Trivulce, judging that there was no safety for a French garrison in remaining there, made his way to Navarra. Experience proved that he was not deceived; for scarcely had the Milanese observed his preparations for departure when a suppressed excitement began to spread through the town, and soon the streets were filled with armed men. This murmuring crowd had to be passed through, sword in hand and lance in rest; and scarcely had the French got outside the gates when the mob rushed out after the army into the country, pursuing them with shouts and hooting as far as the banks of the Tesino. Trivulce left 400 lances at Novarra as well as the 3000 Swiss that Yves d'Alegre had brought from the Romagna, and directed his course with the rest of the army towards Mortara, where he stopped at last to await the help he had demanded from the King of France. Behind him Cardinal Ascanio and Ludovico entered Milan amid the acclamations of the whole town.

Neither of them lost any time, and wishing to profit by this enthusiasm, Ascanio undertook to besiege the castle of Milan while Ludovico should cross the Tesino and attack Novarra.

There besiegers and besieged were sons of the same nation; for Yves d'Alegre had scarcely as many as 300 French with him, and Ludovico 500 Italians. In fact, for the last sixteen years the Swiss had been practically the only infantry in Europe, and all the Powers came, purse in hand, to draw from the mighty reservoir of their mountains. The consequence was that these rude children of William Tell, put up to auction by the nations, and carried away from the humble, hardy life of a mountain people into cities of wealth and pleasure, had lost, not their ancient courage, but that rigidity of principle for which they had been distinguished before their inter-course with other nations. From being models of honor and good faith they had become a kind of marketable ware, always ready for sale to the highest bidder. The French were the first to experience this venality, which later-on proved so fatal to Ludovico Sforza.

Now the Swiss in the garrison at Novarra had been in communication with their compatriots in the vanguard of the ducal army, and when they found that they, who as a fact were unaware that Ludavico's treasure was nearly exhausted, were better fed as well as better paid than themselves, they offered to give up the town and go over to the Milanese, if they could be certain of the same pay. Ludovico, as we may well suppose, closed with this bargain. The whole of Novarra was given up to him except the citadel, which was defended by Frenchmen: thus the enemy's army was recruited by 3000 men. Then Ludovico made the mistake of stopping to besiege the castle instead of marching on to Mortara with the new reinforcement. The result of this was that Louis XII, to whom runners had been sent by Trivulce, understanding his perilous position, hastened the departure of the French gendarmerie who were already collected to cross into Italy, sent off the bailiff of Dijon to levy new Swiss forces, and ordered Cardinal Amboise, his prime minister, to cross the Alps and take up a position at Asti, to hurry on the work of collecting the troops. There the cardinal found a nest-egg of 3000 men. La Trimouille added 1500 lances and 6000 French infantry; finally, the bailiff of Dijon arrived with 10,000 Swiss; so that, counting the troops which Trivulce had at Mortara, Louis XII found himself master on the other side of the Alps of the first army any French king had ever led out to battle. Soon, by good marching, and before Ludovico knew the strength or even the existence of this army, it took up a position between Novarra and Milan, cutting off all communication between the duke and his capital. He was therefore compelled, in spite of his inferior numbers, to prepare for a pitched battle.

But it so happened that just when the preparations for a decisive engagement were being made on both sides, the Swiss Diet, learning that the sons of Helvetia were on the paint of cutting one another's throats, sent orders to all the Swiss serving in either army to break their engagements and return to the fatherland. But during the two months that had passed between the surrender of Novarra and the arrival of the French army before the town, there had been a very great change in the face of things, because Ludovico Sforza's treasure was now exhausted. New confabulations had gone on between the outposts, and this time, thanks to the money sent by Louis XII, it was the Swiss in the service of France who were found to be the better fed and better paid. The worthy Helvetians, since they no longer fought far their own liberty, knew the value of their blood too well to allow a single drop of it to be spilled for less than its weight in gold: the result was that, as they had, betrayed Yves d'Alegre, they resolved to betray Ludovico Sforza too; and while the recruits brought in by the bailiff of Dijon were standing firmly by the French flag, careless of the order of the Diet, Ludovico's auxiliaries declared that in fighting against their Swiss brethren they would be acting in disobedience to the Diet, and would risk capital punishment in the end — a danger that nothing would induce them to incur unless they immediately received the arrears of their pay. The duke, who a spent the last ducat he had with him, and was entirely cut off from his capital, knew that he could not get money till he had fought his way through to it, and therefore invited the Swiss to make one last effort, promising them not only the pay that was in arrears but a double hire. But unluckily the fulfillment of this promise was dependent on the doubtful issue of a battle, and the Swiss replied that they had far too much respect for their country to disobey its decree, and that they loved their brothers far too well to consent to shed their blood without reward; and therefore Sforza would do well not to count upon them, since indeed the very next day they proposed to return to their homes. The duke then saw that all was lost, but he made a last appeal to their honor, adjuring them at least to ensure his personal safety by making it a condition of capitulation. But they replied that even if a condition of such a kind, would not make capitulation impossible, it would certainly deprive them of advantages which they had aright to expect, and on which they counted as indemnification for the arrears of their pay. They pretended, however, at last that they were touched by the prayers of the man whose orders they had obeyed so long, and offered to conceal him dressed in their clothes among their ranks. This proposition was barely plausible; far Sforza was short and, by this time an old man, and he could not possibly escape recognition in the midst of an army where the oldest was not past thirty and the shortest not less than five foot six. Still, this was his last chance, and he did not reject it at once, but tried to modify it so that it might help him in his straits. His plan was to disguise himself as a Franciscan monk, so that mounted an a shabby horse he might pass for their chaplain; the others, Galeazzo di San Severing, who commanded under him, and his two brothers, were all tall men, so, adopting the dress of common soldiers, they hoped they might escape detection in the Swiss ranks.

Scarcely were these plans settled when the duke heard that the capitulation was signed between Trivulce and the Swiss, who had made no stipulation in favor of him and his generals. They were to go over the next day with arms and baggage right into the French army; so the last hope of the wretched Ludovico and his generals must needs be in their disguise. And so it was. San Severino and his brothers took their place in the ranks of the infantry, and Sforza took his among the baggage, clad in a monk's frock, with the hood pulled over his eyes.

The army marched off; but the Swiss, who had first trafficked in their blood, now trafficked in their honor. The French were warned of the disguise of Sforza and his generals, and thus they were all four recognized, and Sforza was arrested by Trimouille himself. It is said that the price paid for this treason was the town of Bellinzona; far it then belonged to the French, and when the Swiss returned to their mountains and took possession of it, Louis XII took no steps to get it back again.

When Ascanio Sforza, who, as we know, had stayed at Milan, learned the news of this cowardly desertion, he supposed that his cause was lost and that it would be the best plan for him to fly, before he found himself a prisoner in the hand's of his brother's old subjects: such a change of face on the people's part would be very natural, and they might propose perhaps to purchase their own pardon at the price of his liberty; so he fled by night with the chief nobles of the Ghibelline party, taking the road to Piacenza, an his way to the kingdom of Naples. But when he arrived at Rivolta, he remembered that there was living in that town an old friend of his childhood, by name Conrad Lando, whom he had helped to much wealth in his days of power; and as Ascanio and his companions were extremely; tired, he resolved to beg his hospitality for a single night. Conrad received them with every sign of joy, putting all his house and servants at their disposal. But scarcely had they retired to bed when he sent a runner to Piacenza, to inform Carlo Orsini, at that time commanding the Venetian garrison, that he was prepared to deliver up Cardinal Ascanio and the chief men of the Milanese army. Carlo Orsini did not care to resign to another so important an expedition, and mounting hurriedly with twenty-five men, he first surrounded Conrads house, and then entered sword in hand the chamber wherein Ascanio and his companions lay, and being surprised in the middle of their sleep, they yielded without resistance. The prisoners were taken to Venice, but Louis XII claimed them, and they were given up. Thus the King of France found himself master

of Ludovico Sforza and of Ascania, of a legitimate nephew
of the great Francesco Sforza named Hermes, of two bastards
named Alessandro and Cortino, and of Francesco, son of the
unhappy Gian Galeazza who had been poisoned by his uncle.

Louis XII, wishing to make an end of the whole family at
a blow, forced Francesco to enter a cloister, shut up Cardinal
Ascanio in the tower of Baurges, threw into prison Alessandro, Cartino, and Hermes, and finally, after transferring the
wretched Ludovico from the fortress of Pierre-Eucise to Lys-
Saint-George he relegated him for good and all to the castle
of Loches, where he lived for ten years in solitude and utter
destitution, and there died, cursing the day when the idea
first came into his head of enticing the French into Italy.

The news of the catastrophe of Ludovica and his family
caused the greatest joy at Rome, for, while the French were
consolidating their power in Milanese territory, the Holy See
was gaining ground in the Romagna, where no further opposition was offered to Caesar's conquest. So the runners who
brought the news were rewarded with valuable presents, and
it was published throughout the whole town of Rome to the
sound of the trumpet and drum. The war-cry of Louis, France,
France, and that of the Orsini, Orso, Orso, rang through all
the streets, which in the evening were illuminated, as though
Constantinople or Jerusalem had been taken. And the pope
gave the people fetes and fireworks, without troubling his
head the least in the world either about its being Holy Week,
or because the Jubilee had attracted more than 200,000 people
to Rome; the temporal interests of his family seeming to him
far more important than the spiritual interests of his subjects.

Chapter XI

One thing alone was wanting to assure the success of the vast projects that the pope and his son were founding upon the friendship of Louis and an alliance with him — that is, — money. But Alexander was not the man to be troubled about a paltry worry of that kind; true, the sale of benefices was by now exhausted, the ordinary and extraordinary taxes had already been collected for the whole year, and the prospect of inheritance from cardinals and priests was a poor thing now that the richest of them had been poisoned; but Alexander had other means at his disposal, which were none the less efficacious because they were less often used.

The first he employed was to spread a, report that the Turks were threatening an invasion of Christendom, and that he knew for a positive fact that before the end of the summer Bajazet would land two considerable armies, one in Romagna, the other in Calabria; he therefore published two bulls, one to levy tithes of all ecclesiastical revenues in Europe of whatever nature they might be, the other to force the Jews into paying an equivalent sum: both bulls contained the severest sentences of excommunication against those who refused to submit, or attempted opposition.

The second plan was the selling of indulgences, a thing which had never been done before: these indulgences affected the people who had been prevented by reasons of health or business from coming to Rome for the Jubilee; the journey by this expedient was rendered unnecessary, and sins were pardoned for a third of what it would have cost, and just as completely as if the faithful had fulfilled every condition of the pilgrimage. For gathering in this tax a veritable army of collectors was instituted, a certain Ludovico delta Torre at their head. The sum that Alexander brought into the pontifical treasury is incalculable, and same idea of it may be gathered from the fact that 799,000 livres in gold was paid in from the territory of Venice alone.

But as the Turks did as a fact make some sort of demonstration from the Hungarian side, and the Venetians began to fear that they might be coming in their direction, they asked for help from the pope, who gave orders that at twelve o'clock in the day in all his States an Ave Maria should be said, to pray God to avert the danger which was threatening the most serene republic. This was the only help the Venetians got from His Holiness in exchange for the 799,000 livres in gold that he had got from them.

But it seemed as though God wished to show His strange vicar on earth that He was angered by the mockery of sacred things, and on the Eve of St. Peter's Day, just as the pope was passing the Capanile on his way to the tribune of benedictions, a enormous piece of iron broke off and fell at his feet; and then, as though one warning had not been enough, on the next day, St. Peter's, when the pope happened to be in one of the rooms of his ordinary dwelling with Cardinal Capuano and Monsignare Poto, his private chamberlain, he saw through the open windows that a very black cloud was coming up. Foreseeing a thunderstorm, he ordered the cardinal and the chamberlain to shut the windows. He had not been mistaken; for even as they were obeying his command, there came up such a furious gust of wind that the highest chimney of the Vatican was overturned, just as a tree is rooted up, and was dashed upon the roof, breaking it in; smashing the upper flooring, it fell into the very room where they were. Terrified by the noise of this catastrophe, which made the whole palace tremble, the cardinal and Monsignore Poto turned round, and seeing the room full of dust and debris, sprang out upon the parapet and shouted to the guards at the gate, "The pope is dead, the pope is dead!" At this cry, the guards ran up and discovered three persons lying in the rubbish on the floor, one dead and the other two dying. The dead man was a gentleman of Siena ailed Lorenzo Chigi, and the dying were two resident officials of the Vatican. They had been walking across the floor above, and had been flung down with the debris. But Alexander was not to be found; and as he gave no answer, though they kept on calling to him, the belief that he had perished was confirmed, and very soon spread about the town. But he had only fainted, and at the end of a certain time he began to come to himself, and moaned, whereupon he was discovered, dazed with the blow, and injured, though not seriously, in several parts of his body. He had been saved by little short of a miracle: a beam had broken in half and had left each of its two ends in the side walls; and one of these had formed a sort of roof aver the pontifical throne; the pope, who was sitting there at the time, was protected by this overarching beam, and had received only a few contusions.

The two contradictory reports of the sudden death and the miraculous preservation of the pope spread rapidly through Rome; and the Duke of Valentinois, terrified at the thought of what a change might be wrought in his own fortunes by any slight accident to the Holy Father, hurried to the Vatican, unable to assure himself by anything less than the evidence of his own eyes. Alexander desired to render public thanks to Heaven for the protection that had been granted him; and on the very same day was carried to the church of Santa Maria del Popalo, escorted by a numerous procession of prelates and men-at arms, his pontifical seat borne by two valets, two equerries, and two grooms. In this church were buried the Duke of Gandia and Gian Borgia, and perhaps Alexander was drawn thither by same relics of devotion, or may be by the recollection of his love for his former mistress, Rosa Vanazza, whose image, in the guise of the Madonna, was exposed for the veneration of the faithful in a chapel on the left of the high altar. Stopping before this altar, the pope offered to the church the gift of a magnificent chalice in which were three hundred gold crowns, which the Cardinal of Siena poured out into a silver paten before the eyes of all, much to the gratification of the pontifical vanity.

But before he left Rome to complete the conquest of the Romagna, the Duke of Valentinois had been reflecting that the marriage, once so ardently desired, between Lucrezia and

Alfonso had been quite useless to himself and his father. There was more than this to be considered: Louis XII's rest in Lombardy was only a halt, and Milan was evidently but the stage before Naples. It was very possible that Louis was annoyed about the marriage which converted his enemy's nephew into the son-in-law of his ally. Whereas, if Alfonso were dead, Lucrezia would be the position to marry some powerful lord of Ferrara or Brescia, who would be able to help his brother-in-law in the conquest of Romagna. Alfonso was now not only useless but dangerous, which to anyone with the character of the Borgias perhaps seemed worse, the death of Alfonso was resolved upon. But Lucrezia's husband, who had understand for a long time past what danger he incurred by living near his terrible father-in-law, had retired to Naples. Since, however, neither Alexander nor Caesar had changed in their perpetual dissimulation towards him, he was beginning to lose his fear, when he received an invitation from the pope and his son to take part in a bull-fight which was to be held in the Spanish fashion in honor of the duke before his departure: In the present precarious position of Naples it would not have been good policy far Alfonso to afford Alexander any sort of pretext for a rupture, so he could not refuse without a motive, and betook himself to Rome. It was thought of no use to consult Lucrezia in this affair, for she had two or three times displayed an absurd attachment for her husband, and they left her undisturbed in her government of Spoleto.

Alfonso was received by the pope and the duke with every demonstration of sincere friendship, and rooms in the Vatican were assigned to him that he had inhabited before with Lucrezia, in that part of the building which is known as the Torre Nuova.

Great lists were prepared on the Piazza of St. Peter's; the streets about it were barricaded, and the windows of the surrounding houses served as boxes for the spectators. The pope and his court took their places on the balconies of the Vatican.

The fete was started by professional toreadors: after they had exhibited their strength and skill, Alfonso and Caesar in their turn descended to the arena, and to offer a proof of their mutual kindness, settled that the bull which pursued Caesar should be killed by Alfonso, and the bull that pursued Alfonso by Caesar.

Then Caesar remained alone an horseback within the lists, Alfonso going out by an improvised door which was kept ajar, in order that he might go back on the instant if he judged that his presence was necessary. At the same time, from the opposite side of the lists the bull was introduced, and was at the same moment pierced all over with darts and arrows, some of them containing explosives, which took fire, and irritated the bull to such a paint that he rolled about with pain, and then got up in a fury, and perceiving a man on horseback, rushed instantly upon him. It was now, in this narrow arena, pursued by his swift enemy, that Caesar displayed all that skill which made him one of the finest horsemen of the period. Still, clever as he was, he could not have remained safe long in that restricted area from an adversary against whom he had no other resource than flight, had not Alfonso appeared suddenly, just when the bull was beginning to gain upon him, waving a red cloak in his left hand, and holding in his right a long delicate Aragon sword. It was high time: the bull was only a few paces distant from Caesar, and the risk he was running appeared so imminent that a woman's scream was heard from one of the windows. But at the sight of a man on foot the bull stopped short, and judging that he would do better business with the new enemy than the old one, he turned upon him instead. For a moment he stood motionless, roaring, kicking up the dust with his hind feet, and lashing his sides with his tail. Then he rushed upon Alfonso, his eyes all bloodshot, his horns tearing up the ground. Alfonso awaited him with a tranquil air; then, when he was only three paces away, he made a bound to one sides and presented instead of his body his sword, which disappeared at once to the hilt; the bull, checked in the middle of his onslaught, stopped one instant motionless and trembling, then fell upon his knees, uttered one dull roar, and lying down on the very spot where his course had been checked, breathed his last without moving a single step forward.

Applause resounded an all sides, so rapid and clever had been the blow. Caesar had remained on horseback, seeking to discover the fair spectator who had given so lively a proof of her interest in him, without troubling himself about what was going on: his search had not been unrewarded, far he had recognized one of the maids of honor to Elizabeth, Duchess of Urbino, who was betrothed to Gian Battista Carraciualo, captain-general of the republic of Venice.

It was now Alfonso's turn to run from the bull, Caesar's to fight him: the young men changed parts, and when four mules had reluctantly dragged the dead bull from the arena, and the valets and other servants of His Holiness had scattered sand over the places that were stained with blood, Alfonso mounted a magnificent Andalusian steed of Arab origin, light as the wind of Sahara that had wedded with his mother, while Caesar, dismounting, retired in his turn, to reappear at the moment when Alfonso should be meeting the same danger from which he had just now rescued him.

Then a second bull was introduced upon the scene, excited in the same manner with steeled darts and flaming arrows. Like his predecessor, when he perceived a man on horseback he rushed upon him, and then began a marvelous race, in which it was impossible to see, so quickly did they fly over the ground, whether the horse was pursuing the bull or the bull the horse. But after five or six rounds, the bull began to gain upon the son of Araby, for all his speed, and it was plain to see who fled and who pursued; in another moment there was only the length of two lances between them, and then suddenly Caesar appeared, armed with one of those long two handed swords which the French are accustomed to use, and just when the bull, almost close upon Don Alfonso, came in front of Caesar he brandished the sword, which flashed like lightning, and cut off his head, while his body, impelled by the speed of the run, fell to the ground ten paces farther on. This blow was so unexpected, and had been performed with such dexterity, that it was received not with mere clapping but with wild enthusiasm and frantic outcry. Caesar, apparently remembering nothing else in his hour of triumph but the scream that had been caused by his former danger, picked up the bull's head, and, giving it to one of his equerries, ordered him to lay it as an act of homage at the feet of the fair Venetian who had bestowed upon him so lively a sign of interest. This fete, besides affording a triumph to each of the young men, had another end as well; it was meant to prove to the populace that perfect goodwill existed between the two, since each had saved the life of the other. The result was that, if any accident should happen to Caesar, nobody would dream of accusing Alfanso; and also if any accident should happen to Alfonso, nobody would dream, of accusing Caesar.

There was a supper at the Vatican. Alfonso made an elegant toilet, and about ten o'clock at night prepared to go from the quarters he inhabited into those where the pope lived; but the door which separated the two courts of the building was shut, and knock as he would, no one came to open it. Alfonso then thought that it was a simple matter for him to go round by the Piazza of St. Peter's; so he went out unaccompanied through one of the garden gates of the Vatican and made his way across the gloomy streets which led to the stairway which gave on the piazza. But scarcely had he set his foot on the first step when he was attacked by a band of armed men. Alfonso would have drawn his sword; but before it was out of the scabbard he had received two blows from a halberd, one on his head, the other on his shoulder; he was stabbed in the side, and wounded both in the leg and in the temple. Struck down by these five blows, he lost his footing and fell to the ground unconscious; his assassins, supposing he was dead, at once remounted the stairway, and found on the piazza forty horsemen waiting for them: by them they were calmly escorted from the city by the Porta Portesa. Alfonso was found at the point of death, but not actually dead, by some passers-by, some of whom recognized him, and instantly conveyed the news of his assassination to the Vatican, while the others, lifting the wounded man in their arms, carried him to his quarters in the Torre Nuova. The pope and Caesar, who learned this news just as they were sitting down to table, showed great distress, and leaving their companions, at once went to see Alfonso, to be quite certain whether his wounds were fatal or not; and an the next morning, to divert any suspicion that might be turned towards themselves, they arrested Alfonso's maternal uncle, Francesco Gazella, who had come to Rome in his nephew's company. Gazella was found guilty on the evidence of false witnesses, and was consequently beheaded.

But they had only accomplished half of what they wanted. By some means, fair or foul, suspicion had been sufficiently diverted from the true assassins; but Alfonso was not dead, and, thanks to the strength of his constitution and the skill of his doctors, who had taken the lamentations of the pope and Caesar quite seriously, and thought to please them by curing Alexander's son-in-law, the wounded man was making progress towards convalescence: news arrived at the same time that Lucrezia had heard of her husband's accident, and was starting to come and nurse him herself. There was no time to lose, and Caesar summoned Michelotto.

"The same night," says Burcardus, "Don Alfonso, who would not die of his wounds, was found strangled in his bed."

The funeral took place the next day with a ceremony not unbecoming in itself, though, unsuited to his high rank. Dan Francesca Bargia, Archbishop of Cosenza, acted as chief mourner at St. Peter's, where the body was buried in the chapel of Santa Maria delle Febbre.

Lucrezia arrived the same evening: she knew her father and brother too well to be put on the wrong scent; and although, immediately after Alfonso's death, the Duke of Valentinois had arrested the doctors, the surgeons, and a poor deformed wretch who had been acting as valet, she knew perfectly well from what quarter the blow had proceeded. In fear, therefore, that the manifestation of a grief she felt this time too well might alienate the confidence of her father and brother, she retired to Nepi with her whole household, her whole court, and more than six hundred cavaliers, there to spend the period of her mourning.

This important family business was now settled, and Lucrezia was again a widow, and in consequence ready to be utilized in the pope's new political machinations. Caesar only stayed at Rome to receive the ambassadors from France and Venice; but as their arrival was somewhat delayed, and consider able inroads had been made upon the pope's treasury by the recent festivities, the creation of twelve new cardinals was arranged: this scheme was to have two effects, viz., to bring 600,000 ducats into the pontifical chest, each hat having been priced at 50,000 ducats, and to assure the pope of a constant majority m the sacred council.

The ambassadors at last arrived: the first was M. de Ville-neuve, the same who had come before to see the Duke of Valentinois in the name of France. Just as he entered Rome, he met on the road a masked man, who, without removing his domino, expressed the joy he felt at his arrival. This man was Caesar himself, who did not wish to be recognized, and who took his departure after a short conference without uncovering his face. M. de Villeneuve then entered the city after him, and at the Porta del Populo found the ambassadors of the various Powers, and among them those of Spain and Naples, whose sovereigns were not yet, it is true, in declared hostility to France, though there was already some coolness. The last-named, fearing to compromise themselves, merely said to their colleague of France, by way of complimentary address, "Sir, you are welcome"; whereupon the master of the ceremonies, surprised at the brevity of the greeting, asked if they had nothing else to say. When they replied that they had not, M. de Villeneuve turned his back upon them, remarking that those who had nothing to say required no answer; he then took his place between the Archbishop of Reggia, governor of Rome, and the Archbishop of Ragusa, and made his way to the palace of the Holy Apostles, which had been, got ready far his reception.

Same days later, Maria Giorgi, ambassador extraordinary of Venice, made his arrival. He was commissioned not only to arrange the business on hand with the pope, but also to convey to Alexander and Caesar the title of Venetian nobles, and to inform them that their names were inscribed in the Golden Book — a favor that both of them had long coveted, less far the empty honor's sake than for the new influence that this title might confer. Then the pope went on to bestow the twelve cardinals' hats that had been sold. The new princes of the Church were Don Diego de Mendoza, archbishop of Seville; Jacques, archbishop of Oristagny, the Pope's vicar-general; Thomas, archbishop of Strigania; Piero, archbishop of Reggio, governor of Rome; Francesco Bargia, archbishop of Cosenza, treasurer-general; Gian, archbishop of Salerno, vice-chamberlain; Luigi Bargia, archbishop of Valencia, secretary to His Holiness, and brother of the Gian Borgia whom

Caesar had poisoned; Antonio, bishop of Coma; Gian Battista Ferraro, bishop of Modem; Amedee d'Albret, son of the King of Navarre, brother-in-law of the Duke of Valentinois; and Marco Cornaro, a Venetian noble, in whose person His Holiness rendered back to the most serene republic the favor he had just received.

Then, as there was nothing further to detain the Duke of Valentinois at Rome, he only waited to effect a loan from a rich banker named Agostino Chigi, brother of the Lorenzo Chigi who had perished on the day when the pope had been nearly killed by the fall of a chimney, and departed far the Romagna, accompanied by Vitellozzo Vitelli, Gian Paolo Baglione, and Jacopo di Santa Croce, at that time his friends, but later on his victims.

His first enterprise was against Pesaro: this was the polite attention of a brother-in-law, and Gian Sforza very well knew what would be its consequences; for instead of attempting to defend his possessions by taking up arms, or to venture an negotiations, unwilling moreover to expose the fair lands he had ruled so long to the vengeance of an irritated foe, he begged his subjects, to preserve their former affection towards himself, in the hope of better days to come; and he fled into Dalmatia. Malatesta, lord of Rimini, followed his example; thus the Duke of Valentinois entered both these towns without striking a single blow. Caesar left a sufficient garrison behind him, and marched on to Faenza.

But there the face of things was changed: Faenza at that time was under the rule of Astor Manfredi, a brave and handsome young man of eighteen, who, relying on the love of his subjects towards his family, had resolved on defending himself to the uttermost, although he had been forsaken by the Bentivagli, his near relatives, and by his allies, the Venetian and Florentines, who had not dared to send him any aid because of the affection felt towards Caesar by the King of France. Accordingly, when he perceived that the Duke of Valentinois was marching against him, he assembled in hot haste all those of his vassals who were capable of bearing arms, together with the few foreign soldiers who were willing to come into his pay, and collecting victual and ammunition, he took up his position with them inside the town.

By these defensive preparations Caesar was not greatly, disconcerted; he commanded a magnificent army, composed of the finest troops of France and Italy; led by such men as Paolo and Giulio Orsini, Vitellozzo Vitelli and Paolo Baglione, not to steak of himself — that is to say, by the first captains of the period. So, after he had reconnoitered, he at once began the siege, pitching his camp between the two rivers, Amana and Marziano, placing his artillery on the side which faces on Forli, at which point the besieged party had erected a powerful bastion.

At the end of a few days busy with entrenchments, the breach became practicable, and the Duke of Valentinois ordered an assault, and gave the example to his soldiers by being the first to march against the enemy. But in spite of his courage and that of his captains beside him, Astor Manfredi made so good a defense that the besiegers were repulsed with great loss of men, while one of their bravest leaders, Honario Savella; was left behind in the trenches.

But Faenza, in spite of the courage and devotion of her defenders, could not have held out long against so formidable an army, had not winter come to her aid. Surprised by the rigor of the season, with no houses for protection and no trees for fuel, as the peasants had destroyed both beforehand, the Duke of Valentinois was forced to raise the siege and take up his winter quarters in the neighboring towns, in order to be quite ready for a return next spring; for Caesar could not forgive the insult of being held in check by a little town which had enjoyed a long time of peace, was governed by a mere boy, and deprived of all outside aid, and had sworn to take his revenge. He therefore broke up his army into three sections, sent one-third to Imola, the second to Forli, and himself took the third to Cesena, a third-rate town, which was thus suddenly transformed into a city of pleasure and luxury.

Indeed, for Caesar's active spirit there must needs be no cessation of warfare or festivities. So, when war was interrupted, fetes began, as magnificent and as exciting as he knew how to make them: the days were passed in games and displays of horsemanship, the nights in dancing and gallantry; for the loveliest women of the Romagna — and that is to say of the whole world had come hither to make a seraglio for the victor which might have been envied by the Sultan of Egypt or the Emperor of Constantinople.

While the Duke of Valentinois was making one of his excursions in the neighborhood of the town with his retinue of flattering nobles and titled courtesans, who were always about him, he noticed a cortege an the Rimini road so numerous that it must surely indicate the approach of someone of importance. Caesar, soon perceiving that the principal person was a woman, approached, and recognized the very same lady-in-waiting to the Duchess of Urbino who, on the day of the bull-fight, had screamed when Caesar was all but touched by the infuriated beast. At this time she was betrothed, as we mentioned, to Gian Carracciuola, general of the Venetians. Elizabeth of Gonzaga, her protectress and godmother, was now sending her with a suitable retinue to Venice, where the marriage was to take place.

Caesar had already been struck by the beauty of this young girl, when at Rome; but when he saw her again she appeared more lovely than on the first occasion, so he resolved on the instant that he would keep this fair flower of love for himself: having often before reproached himself for his indifference in passing her by. Therefore he saluted her as an old acquaintance, inquired whether she were staying any time at Cesena, and ascertained that she was only passing through, traveling by long stages, as she was awaited with much impatience, and that she would spend the coming night at Forli. This was all that Caesar cared to knew; he summoned Michelotto, and in a low voice said a few wards to him, which were heard by no one else.

The cortege only made a halt at the neighboring town, as the fair bride had said, and started at once for Forli, although the day was already far advanced; but scarcely had a league been revered when a troop of horsemen from Cesena overtook and surrounded them. Although the soldiers in the escort were far from being in sufficient force, they were eager to defend their general's bride; but soon same fell dead, and ethers, terrified, took to flight; and when the lady came dawn from her litter to try to escape, the chief seized her in his arms and set her in front of him on his horse; then, ordering his men to return to Cesena without him, he put his horse to the gallop in a cross direction, and as the shades of evening were now beginning to fall, he soon disappeared into the darkness.

Carracciuolo learned the news through one of the fugitives, who declared that he had recognized among the ravishers the Duke of Valentinois' soldiers. At first he thought his ears had deceived him, so hard was it to believe this terrible intelligence; but it was repeated, and he stood for one instant motionless, and, as it were, thunderstruck; then suddenly, with a cry of vengeance, he threw off his stupor and dashed away to the ducal palace, where sat the Doge Barberigo and the Council of Ten; unannounced, he rushed into their midst, the very moment after they had heard of Caesar's outrage.

"Most serene lords," he cried, "I am come to bid you farewell, for I am resolved to sacrifice my life to my private vengeance, though indeed I had hoped to devote it to the service of the republic. I have been wounded in the soul's noblest part — in my honor. The dearest thing I possessed, my wife, has been stolen from me, and the thief is the most treacherous, the most impious, the most infamous of men, it is Valentinois! My lords, I beg you will not be offended if I speak thus of a man whose boast it is to be a member of your noble ranks and to enjoy your protection: it is not so; he lies, and his loose and criminal life has made him unworthy of such honors, even as he is unworthy of the life whereof my sword shall deprive him. In truth, his very birth was a sacrilege; he is a fratricide, an usurper of the goods of other men, an oppressor of the innocent, and a highway assassin; he is a man who will violate every law, even, the law of hospitality respected by the veriest barbarian, a man who will do violence to a virgin who is passing through his own country, where she had every right to expect from him not only the consideration due to her sex and condition, but also that which is due to the most serene republic, whose condottiere I am, and which is insulted in my person and in the dishonoring of my bride; this man, I say, merits indeed to die by another hand than mine. Yet, since he who ought to punish him is not for him a prince and judge, but only a father quite as guilty as the son, I myself will seek him out, and I will sacrifice my own life, not only in avenging my own injury and the blood of so many innocent beings, but also in promoting the welfare of the most serene republic, on which it is his ambition to trample when he has accomplished the ruin of the other princes of Italy."

The doge and the senators, who, as we said, were already apprised of the event that had brought Carracciuolo before them, listened with great interest and profound indignation; for they, as he told them, were themselves insulted in the person of their general: they all swore, on their honor, that if he would put the matter in their hands, and not yield to his rage, which could only work his own undoing, either his bride should be rendered up to him without a smirch upon her bridal veil, or else a punishment should be dealt out proportioned to the affront. And without delay, as a proof of the energy wherewith the noble tribunal would take action in the affair, Luigi Manenti, secretary to the Ten, was sent to Imola, where the duke was reported to be, that he might explain to him the great displeasure with which the most serene republic viewed the outrage perpetrated upon their candottiere. At the same time the Council of Ten and the doge sought out the French ambassador, entreating him to join with them and repair in person with Manenti to the Duke of Valentinois, and summon him, in the name of King Louis XII, immediately to send back to Venice the lady he had carried off.

The two messengers arrived at Imola, where they found Caesar, who listened to their complaint with every mark of utter astonishment, denying that he had been in any way connected with the crime, nay, authorizing Manenti and the French ambassador to pursue the culprits and promising that he would himself have the most active search carried on. The duke appeared to act in such complete good faith that the envoys were for the moment hoodwinked, and themselves undertook a search of the most careful nature. They accordingly repaired to the exact spot and began to procure information. On the highroad there had been found dead and wounded. A man had been seen going by at a gallop, carrying a woman in distress on his saddle; he had soon left the beaten track and plunged across country. A peasant coming home from working in the fields had seen him appear and vanish again like a shadow, taking the direction of a lonely house. An old woman declared that she had seen him go into this house. But the next night the house was gone, as though by enchantment, and the ploughshare had passed over where it stood; so that none could say, what had become of her whom they sought, far those who had dwelt in the house, and even the house itself, were there no longer.

Manenti and the French ambassador returned to Venice, and related what the duke had said, what they had done, and how all search had been in vain. No one doubted that Caesar was the culprit, but no one could prove it. So the most serene republic, which could not, considering their war with the Turks, be embroiled with the pope, forbade Caracciuala to take any sort of private vengeance, and so the talk grew gradually less, and at last the occurrence was no more mentioned.

But the pleasures of the winter had not diverted Caesar's mind from his plans about Faenza. Scarcely did the spring season allow him to go into the country than he marched anew upon the town, camped opposite the castle, and making a new breach, ordered a general assault, himself going up first of all; but in spite of the courage he personally displayed, and the able seconding of his soldiers, they were repulsed by Astor, who, at the head of his men, defended the breach, while even the women, at the top of the rampart, rolled down stones and trunks of trees upon the besiegers. After an hour's struggle man to man, Caesar was forced to retire, leaving two thousand men in the trenches about the town, and among the two thousand one of his bravest condottieri, Valentino Farnese.

Then, seeing that neither excommunications nor assaults could help him, Caesar converted the siege into a blockade: all the roads leading to Faenza were cut off, all communications stopped; and further, as various signs of revolt had been remarked at Cesena, a governor was installed there whose powerful will was well known to Caesar, Ramiro d'Orco, with powers of life and death over the inhabitants; he then waited quietly before Faenza, till hunger should drive out the citizens from those walls they defended with such vehement enthusiasm. At the end of a month, during which the people of

Faenza had suffered all the horrors of famine, delegates came out to parley with Caesar with a view to capitulation. Caesar, who still had plenty to do in the Romagna, was less hard to satisfy than might have been expected, and the town yielded an condition that he should not touch either the persons or the belongings of the inhabitants, that Astor Manfredi, the youthful ruler, should have the privilege of retiring whenever he pleased, and should enjoy the revenue of his patrimony wherever he might be.

The conditions were faithfully kept so far as the inhabitants were concerned; but Caesar, when he had seen Astor, whom he did not know before, was seized by a strange passion for this beautiful youth, who was like a woman: he kept him by his side in his own army, showing him honors befitting a young prince, and evincing before the eyes of all the strongest affection for him: one day Astor disappeared, just as Caracciuolo's bride had disappeared, and no one knew what had become of him; Caesar himself appeared very uneasy, saying that he had no doubt made his escape somewhere, and in order to give credence to this story, he sent out couriers to seek him in all directions.

A year after this double disappearance, there was picked up in the Tiber, a little below the Castle Sant' Angelo, the body of a beautiful young woman, her hands bound together behind her back, and also the corpse of a handsome youth with the bowstring he had been strangled with tied round his neck. The girl was Caracciuolo's bride, the young man was Astor.

During the last year both had been the slaves of Caesar's pleasures; now, tired of them, he had had them thrown into the Tiber.

The capture of Faenza had brought Caesar the title of Duke of Romagna, which was first bestowed on him by the pope in full consistory, and afterwards ratified by the King of Hungary, the republic of Venice, and the Kings of Castile and Portugal. The news of the ratification arrived at Rome on the eve of the day on which the people are accustomed to keep the anniversary of the foundation of the Eternal City; this fete, which went back to the days of Pomponius Laetus, acquired a new splendor in their eyes from the joyful events that had just happened to their sovereign: as a sign of joy cannon were fired all day long; in the evening there were illuminations and bonfires, and during part of the night the Prince of Squillace, with the chief lords of the Roman nobility, marched about the streets, bearing torches, and exclaiming, "Long live Alexander! Long live Caesar! Long live the Borgias! Long live the Orsini! Long live the Duke of Romagna!"

Chapter XII

Caesar's ambition was only fed by victories: scarcely was he master of Faenza before, excited by the Mariscotti, old enemies of the Bentivoglio family, he cast his eyes upon Bologna; but Gian di Bentivoglio, whose ancestors had possessed this town from time immemorial, had not only made all preparations necessary for a long resistance, but he had also put himself under the protection of France; so, scarcely had he learned that Caesar was crossing the frontier of the Bolognese territory with his army, than he sent a courier to Louis XII to claim the fulfillment of his promise. Louis kept it with his accustomed good faith; and when Caesar arrived before Bologna, he received an intimation from the King of France that he was not to enter on any undertaking against his ally Bentivoglio; Caesar, not being the man to have his plans upset for nothing, made conditions for his retreat, to which Bentivoglio consented, only too happy to be quit of him at this price: the conditions were the cession of Castello Bolognese, a fortress between Imola and Faenza, the payment of a tribute of 9000 ducats, and the keeping for his service of a hundred men-at-arms and two thousand infantry. In exchange for these favors, Caesar confided to Bentivoglio that his visit had been due to the counsels of the Mariscotti; then, reinforced by his new ally's contingent, he took the road for Tuscany. But he was scarcely out of sight when Bentivoglio shut the gates of Bologna, and commanded his son Hermes to assassinate with his own hand Agamemnon Mariscotti, the head of the family, and ordered the massacre of four-and-thirty of his near relatives, brothers, sons, daughters, and

nephews, and two hundred other of his kindred and friends.
The butchery was carried out by the noblest youths of Bologna; whom Bentivoglio forced to bathe their hands in this
blood, so that he might attach them to himself through their
fear of reprisals.

Caesar's plans with regard to Florence were now no longer
a mystery: since the month of January he had sent to Pisa ten
or twelve hundred men under the Command of Regniero
della Sassetta and Piero di Gamba Corti, and as soon as the
conquest of the Romagna was complete, he had further
dispatched Oliverotto di Fermo with new detachments. His
own army he had reinforced, as we have seen, by a hundred
men-at-arms and two thousand infantry; he had just been
joined by Vitellozzo Vitelli, lord of Citta, di Castello, and by
the Orsini, who had brought him another two or three
thousand men; so, without counting the troops sent to Pisa,
he had under his control seven hundred men-at-arms and five
thousand infantry.

Still, in spite of this formidable company, he entered
Tuscany declaring that his intentions were only pacific, pro-
testing that he only desired to pass through the territories of
the republic on his way to Rome, and offering to pay in ready
money for any victual his army might require. But when he
had passed the defiles of the mountains and arrived at Bar-
berino, feeling that the town was in his power and nothing
could now hinder his approach, he began to put a price on
the friendship he had at first offered freely, and to impose
his own conditions instead of accepting those of others. These
were that Piero dei Medici, kinsman and ally of the Orsini,
should be reinstated in his ancient power; that six Florentine
citizens, to be chosen by Vitellozzo, should be put into his
hands that they might by their death expiate that of Paolo
Vitelli, unjustly executed by the Florentines; that the Signoria
should engage to give no aid to the lord of Piombino, whom
Caesar intended to dispossess of his estates without delay;
and further, that he himself should be taken into the service
of the republic, for a pay proportionate to his deserts. But
just as Caesar had reached this point in his negotiations with
Florence, he received orders from Louis XII to get ready, so
soon as he conveniently could, to follow him with his army

and help in the conquest of Naples, which he was at last in a position to undertake. Caesar dared not break his word to so powerful an ally; he therefore replied that he was at the king's orders, and as the Florentines were not aware that he was quitting them on compulsion, he sold his retreat for the sum of 36,000 ducats per annum, in exchange for which sum he was to hold three hundred men-at-arms always in readiness to go to the aid of the republic at her earliest call and in any circumstances of need.

But, hurried as he was, Caesar still hoped that he might find time to conquer the territory of Piombino as he went by, and take the capital by a single vigorous stroke; so he made his entry into the lands of Jacopo IV of Appiano. The latter, he found, however, had been beforehand with him, and, to rob him of all resource, had laid waste his own country, burned his fodder, felled his trees, torn down his vines, and destroyed a few fountains that produced salubrious waters. This did not hinder Caesar from seizing in the space of a few days Severeto, Scarlino, the isle of Elba, and La Pianosa; but he was obliged to stop short at the castle, which opposed a serious resistance. As Louis XII's army was continuing its way towards Rome, and he received a fresh order to join it, he took his departure the next day, leaving behind him, Vitellozzo and Gian Paolo Bagliani to prosecute the siege in his absence.

Louis XII was this time advancing upon Naples, not with the incautious ardor of Charles VIII, but, on the contrary, with that prudence and circumspection which characterized him. Besides his alliance with Florence and Rome, he had also signed a secret treaty with Ferdinand the Catholic, who had similar pretensions, through the house of Duras, to the throne of Naples to those Louis himself had through the house of Anjou. By this treaty the two kings were sharing their conquests beforehand: Louis would be master of Naples, of the town of Lavore and the Abruzzi, and would bear the title of King of Naples and Jerusalem; Ferdinand reserved for his own share Apulia and Calabria, with the title of Duke of these provinces; both were to receive the investiture from the pope and to hold them of him. This partition was all the more likely to be made, in fact, because Frederic, supposing all the time that Ferdinand was his good and faithful friend, would open the gates of his towns, only to receive into his fortresses conquerors and masters instead of allies. All this perhaps was not very loyal conduct on the part of a king who had so long desired and had just now received the surname of Catholic, but it mattered little to Louis, who profited by treasonable acts he did not have to share.

The French army, which the Duke of Valentinois had just joined, consisted of 1000 lances, 4000 Swiss, and 6000 Gascons and adventurers; further, Philip of Rabenstein was bringing by sea six Breton and Provencal vessels, and three Genoese caracks, carrying 6500 invaders.

Against this mighty host the King of Naples had. only 700 men-at-arms, 600 light horse, and 6000 infantry under the command of the Colonna, whom he had taken into his pay after they were exiled by the pope from the States of the Church; but he was counting on Gonsalvo of Cordova, who was to join him at Gaeta, and to whom he had confidingly opened all his fortresses in Calabria.

But the feeling of safety inspired by Frederic's faithless ally was not destined to endure long: on their arrival at Rome, the French and Spanish ambassadors presented to the pope the treaty signed at Grenada on the 11th of November, 1500, between Louis XII and Ferdinand the Catholic, a treaty which up, to that time had been secret. Alexander, foreseeing the probable future, had, by the death of Alfonso, loosened all the bonds that attached him to the house of Aragon, and then began by making some difficulty about it. It was demonstrated that the arrangement had only been undertaken to provide the Christian princes with another weapon for attacking the Ottoman Empire, and before this consideration, one may readily suppose, all the pope's scruples vanished; on the 25th of June, therefore, it was decided to call a consistory which was to declare Frederic deposed from the throne of Naples. When Frederic heard all at once that the French army had arrived at Rome, that his ally Ferdinand had deceived him, and that Alexander had pronounced the sentence of his downfall, he understood that all was lost; but he did not wish it to be said that he had abandoned his kingdom without even attempting to save it. So he charged his two new condottieri, Fabrizio Calonna and Ranuzia di Marciano, to check the French before Capua with 300 men-at-arms, some light horse, and 3000 infantry; in person he occupied Aversa with another division of his army, while Prospero Colonna was sent to defend Naples with the rest, and make a stand against the Spaniards on the side of Calabria.

These dispositions were scarcely made when d'Aubigny, having passed the Volturno, approached to lay siege to Capua, and invested the town on both sides of the river. Scarcely were the French encamped before the ramparts than they began to set up their batteries, which were soon in play, much to the terror of the besieged, who, poor creatures, were almost all strangers to the town, and had fled thither from every side, expecting to find protection beneath the walls. So, although bravely repulsed by Fabrizio Colonna, the French, from the moment of their first assault, inspired so great and blind a terror that everyone began to talk of opening the gates, and it was only with great difficulty that Calonna made this multitude understand that at least they ought to reap some benefit from the check the besiegers had received and obtain good terms of capitulation. When he had brought them round to his view, he sent out to demand a parley with d'Aubigny, and a conference was fixed for the next day but one, in which they were to treat of the surrender of the town.

But this was not Caesar Borgia's idea at all: he had stayed behind to confer with the pope, and had joined the French army with some of his troops on the very day on which the conference had been arranged for two days later: and a capitulation of any nature would rob him of his share of the booty and the promise of such pleasure as would come from the capture of a city so rich and populous as Capua. So he opened up negotiations on his own account with a captain who was on guard at one of the gates such negotiations, made with cunning supported by bribery, proved as usual more prompt and efficacious than any others. At the very moment when Fabrizio Colonna in a fortified outpost was discussing the conditions of capitulation with the French captains, suddenly great cries of distress were heard. These were caused by Borgia, who without a word to anyone had entered the town with his faithful army from Romagna, and was begin-

ning to cut the throats of the garrison, which had naturally
somewhat relaxed their vigilance in the belief that the capitulation was all but signed. The French, when they saw that the
town was half taken, rushed on the gates with such impetuosity that the besieged did not even attempt to defend themselves any longer, and forced their way into Capua by three
separate sides: nothing more could be done then to stop the
issue. Butchery and pillage had begun, and the work of
destruction must needs be completed: in vain did Fabrizio
Colonna, Ranuzio di Marciano, and Don Ugo di Cardona
attempt to make head against the French and Spaniards with
such men as they could get together. Fabrizia Calonna and
Don Ugo were made prisoners; Ranuzia, wounded by an
arrow, fell into the hands of the Duke of Valentinois; seven
thousand inhabitants were massacred in the streets among
them the traitor who had given up the gate; the churches were
pillaged, the convents of nuns forced open; and then might
be seen the spectacle of some of these holy virgins casting
themselves into pits or into the river to escape the soldiers.
Three hundred of the noblest ladies of the town took refuge
in a tower. The Duke of Valentinois broke in the doors, chased
out for himself forty of the most beautiful, and handed over
the rest to his army.

The pillage continued for three days.

Capua once taken, Frederic saw that it was useless any
longer to attempt defense. So he shut himself up in Castel
Nuovo and gave permission to Gaeta and to Naples to treat
with the conqueror. Gaeta bought immunity from pillage
with 60,000 ducats; and Naples with the surrender of the
castle. This surrender was made to d'Aubigny by Frederic
himself, an condition that he should be allowed to take to
the island of Ischia his money, jewels, and furniture, and there
remain with his family for six months secure from all hostile
attack. The terms of this capitulation were faithfully adhered
to on both sides: d'Aubigny entered Naples, and Frederic
retired to Ischia.

Thus, by a last terrible blow, never to rise again, fell this
branch of the house of Aragon, which had now reigned for
sixty-five years. Frederic, its head, demanded and obtained a
safe-conduct to pass into France, where Louis XII gave him

the duchy of Anjou and 30,000 ducats a year, an condition that he should never quit the kingdom; and there, in fact, he died, an the 9th of September 1504. His eldest son, Dan Ferdinand, Duke of Calabria, retired to Spain, where he was permitted to marry twice, but each time with a woman who was known to be barren; and there he died in 1550. Alfonso, the second son, who had followed his father to France, died, it is said, of poison, at Grenoble, at the age of twenty-two; lastly Caesar, the third son, died at Ferrara, before he had attained his eighteenth birthday.

Frederic's daughter Charlotte married in France Nicholas, Count of Laval, governor and admiral of Brittany; a daughter was born of this marriage, Anne de Laval, who married Francois de la Trimauille. Through her those rights were transmitted to the house of La Trimouille which were used later on as a claim upon the kingdom of the Two Sicilies.

The capture of Naples gave the Duke of Valentinois his liberty again; so he left the French army, after he had received fresh assurances on his own account of the king's friendliness, and returned to the siege of Piombino, which he had been forced to interrupt. During this interval Alexander had been visiting the scenes of his son's conquests, and traversing all the Romagna with Lucrezia, who was now consoled for her husband's death, and had never before enjoyed quite so much favor with His Holiness; so, when she returned to Rome. She no longer had separate rooms from him. The result of this recrudescence of affection was the appearance of two pontifical bulls, converting the towns of Nepi and Sermoneta into duchies: one was bestowed on Gian Bargia, an illegitimate child of the pope, who was not the son of either of his mistresses, Rosa Vanozza or Giulia Farnese, the other an Don Roderigo of Aragon, son of Lucrezia and Alfonso: the lands of the Colonna were in appanage to the two duchies.

But Alexander was dreaming of yet another addition to his fortune; this was to came from a marriage between Lucrezia and Don Alfonso d'Este, son of Duke Hercules of Ferrara, in favor of which alliance Louis XII had negotiated.

His Holiness was now having a run of good fortune, and he learned on the same day that Piombino was taken and that Duke Hercules had given the King of France his assent to the marriage. Both of these pieces of news were good for Alexander, but the one could not compare in importance with the other; and the intimation that Lucrezia was to marry the heir presumptive to the duchy of Ferrara was received with a joy so great that it smacked of the humble beginnings of the Borgian house. The Duke of Valentinois was invited to return to Rome, to take his share in the family rejoicing, and on the day when the news was made public the governor of St. Angelo received orders that cannon should be fired every quarter of an hour from noon to midnight. At two o'clock, Lucrezia, attired as a fiancée, and accompanied by her two brothers, the Dukes of Valentinois and Squillace, issued from the Vatican, followed by all the nobility of Rome, and proceeded to the church of the Madonna del Papalo, where the Duke of Gandia and Cardinal Gian Borgia were buried, to render thanks for this new favor accorded to her house by God; and in the evening, accompanied by the same cavalcade, which shone the more brightly under the torchlight and brilliant illuminations, she made procession through the whale town, greeted by cries of "Long live Pope Alexander VI! Lang live the Duchess of Ferrara!" which were shouted aloud by heralds clad in cloth of gold.

The next day an announcement was made in the town that a racecourse for women was opened between the castle of Sant' Angelo and the Piazza of St. Peter's; that on every third day there would be a bull-fight in the Spanish fashion; and that from the end of the present month, which was October, until the first day of Lent, masquerades would be permitted in the streets of Rome.

Such was the nature of the fetes outside; the program of those going on within the Vatican was not presented to the people; for by the account of Bucciardo, an eye-witness, this is what happened —

"On the last Sunday of the month of October, fifty courtesans supped in the apostolic palace in the Duke of Valentinois' rooms, and after supper danced with the equerries and servants, first wearing their usual garments, afterwards in dazzling draperies; when supper was over, the table was removed, candlesticks were set on the floor in a symmetrical pattern, and a great quantity of chestnuts was scattered on the ground: these the fifty women skillfully picked up, running about gracefully, in and out between the burning lights; the pope, the Duke of Valentinois, and his sister Lucrezia, who were looking on at this spectacle from a gallery, encouraged the most agile and industrious with their applause, and they received prizes of embroidered garters, velvet boots, golden caps, and laces; then new diversions took the place of these."

We humbly ask forgiveness of our readers, and especially of our lady readers; but though we have found words to describe the first part of the spectacle, we have sought them in vain for the second; suffice it to say that just as there had been prizes for feats of adroitness, others were given now to the dancers who were most daring and brazen.

Some days after this strange night, which calls to mind the Roman evenings in the days of Tiberius, Nero, and Heliogabalus, Lucrezia, clad in a robe of golden brocade, her train carried by young girls dressed in white and crowned with roses, issued from her palace to the sound of trumpets and clarions, and made her way over carpets that were laid down in the streets through which she had to pass. Accompanied by the noblest cavaliers and the loveliest women in Rome, she betook herself to the Vatican, where in the Pauline hall the pope awaited her, with the Duke of Valentinois, Don Ferdinand, acting as proxy for Duke Alfonso, and his cousin, Cardinal d'Este. The pope sat on one side of the table, while the envoys from Ferrara stood on the other: into their midst came Lucrezia, and Don Ferdinand placed on her finger the nuptial ring; this ceremony over, Cardinal d'Este approached and presented to the bride four magnificent rings set with precious stones; then a casket was placed on the table, richly inlaid with ivory, whence the cardinal drew forth a great many trinkets, chains, necklaces of pearls and diamonds, of workmanship as costly as their material; these he also begged Lucrezia to accept, before she received those the bridegroom was hoping to offer himself, which would be more worthy of her. Lucrezia showed the utmost delight in accepting these gifts; then she retired into the next room, leaning on the pope's arm, and followed by the ladies of her suite, leaving the Duke of Valentinois to do the honors of the Vatican to

the men. That evening the guests met again, and spent half
the night in dancing, while a magnificent display of fireworks
lighted up the Piazza of San Paolo.

The ceremony of betrothal over, the pope and the Duke
busied themselves with making preparations for the departure. The pope, who wished the journey to be made with a
great degree of splendor, sent in his daughter's company, in
addition to the two brothers-in-law and the gentlemen in their
suite, the Senate of Rome and all the lords who, by virtue of
their wealth, could display most magnificence in their costumes and liveries. Among this brilliant throng might be seen
Olivero and Ramiro Mattei, sons of Piero Mattel, chancellor
of the town, and a daughter of the pope whose mother was
not Rosa Vanozza; besides these, the pope nominated in
consistory Francesco Borgia, Cardinal of Sosenza, legate a
latere, to accompany his daughter to the frontiers of the
Ecclesiastical States.

Also the Duke of Valentinois sent out messengers into all
the cities of Romagna to order that Lucrezia should be
received as sovereign lady and mistress: grand preparations
were at once set on foot for the fulfillment of his orders. But
the messengers reported that they greatly feared that there
would be some grumbling at Cesena, where it will be remembered that Caesar had left Ramiro d'Orco as governor with
plenary powers, to calm the agitation of the town. Now
Ramiro d'Orco had accomplished his task so well that there
was nothing more to fear in the way of rebellion; for one-sixth
of the inhabitants had perished on the scaffold, and the result
of this situation was that it was improbable that the same
demonstrations of joy could be expected from a town
plunged in mourning that were looked for from Imala,
Faenza, and Pesaro. The Duke of Valentinais averted this
inconvenience in the prompt and efficacious fashion charac-
teristic of him alone. One morning the inhabitants of Cesena
awoke to find a scaffold set up in the square, and upon it the
four quarters of a man, his head, severed from the trunk,
stuck up on the end of a pike.

This man was Ramiro d'Orco.

No one ever knew by whose hands the scaffold had been
raised by night, nor by what executioners the terrible deed

had been carried out; but when the Florentine Republic sent to ask Macchiavelli, their ambassador at Cesena, what he thought of it, he replied:

"Magnificent Lords, —
"I can tell you nothing concerning the execution of Ramiro d'Orco, except that Caesar Borgia is the prince who best knows how to make and unmake men according to their deserts.
"Niccolo Macchiavelli"

The Duke of Valentinois was not disappointed, and the future Duchess of Ferrara was admirably received in every town along her route, and particularly at Cesena.

While Lucrezia was on her way to Ferrara to meet her fourth husband, Alexander and the Duke of Valentinois resolved to make a progress in the region of their last conquest, the duchy of Piombino. The apparent object of this journey was that the new subjects might take their oath to Caesar, and the real object was to form an arsenal in Jacopo d'Appiano's capital within reach of Tuscany, a plan which neither the pope nor his son had ever seriously abandoned. The two accordingly started from the port of Corneto with six ships, accompanied by a great number of cardinals and prelates, and arrived the same evening at Piombina. The pontifical court made a stay there of several days, partly with a view of making the duke known to the inhabitants, and also in order to be present at certain ecclesiastical functions, of which the most important was a service held on the third Sunday in Lent, in which the Cardinal of Cosenza sang a mass and the pope officiated in state with the duke and the cardinals. After these solemn functions the customary pleasures followed, and the pope summoned the prettiest girls of the country and ordered them to dance their national dances before him.

Following on these dances came feasts of unheard of magnificence, during which the pope in the sight of all men completely ignored Lent and did not fast. The abject of all these fetes was to scatter abroad a great deal of money, and so to make the Duke of Valentinois popular, while poor

Jacopo d'Appiano was forgotten.

When they left Piombino, the pope and his son visited the
island of Elba, where they only stayed long enough to visit
the old fortifications and issue orders for the building of new
ones.

Then the illustrious travelers embarked on their return
journey to Rome; but scarcely had they put out to sea when
the weather became adverse, and the pope not wishing to put
in at Porto Ferrajo, they remained five days on board, though
they had only two days' provisions. During the last three days
the pope lived on fried fish that were caught under great
difficulties because of the heavy weather. At last they arrived
in sight of Corneto, and there the duke, who was not on the
same vessel as the pope, seeing that his ship could not get in,
had a boat put out, and so was taken ashore. The pope was
obliged to continue on his way towards Pontercole, where at
last he arrived, after encountering so violent a tempest that
all who were with him were utterly subdued either by sickness
or by the terror of death. The pope alone did not show one
instant's fear, but remained on the bridge during the storm,
sitting on his armchair, invoking the name of Jesus and
making the sign of the cross. At last his ship entered the roads
of Pontercole, where he landed, and after sending to Corneto
to fetch horses, he rejoined the duke, who was there awaiting
him. They then returned by slow stages, by way of Civita
Vecchia and Palo, and reached Rome after an absence of a
month. Almost at the same time d'Albret arrived in quest of
his cardinal's hat. He was accompanied by two princes of the
house of Navarre, who were received with not only those
honors which beseemed their rank, but also as brothers-in-law
to whom the, duke was eager to show in what spirit he was
contracting this alliance.

Chapter XIII

The time had now come for the Duke of Valentinois to
continue the pursuit of his conquests. So, since on the 1st of
May in the preceding year the pope had pronounced sentence
of forfeiture in full consistory against Julius Caesar of Varano,
as punishment for the murder of his brother Rudolph and
for the harboring of the pope's enemies, and he had accordingly been mulcted of his fief of Camerino, which was to be
handed over to the apostolic chamber, Caesar left Rome to
put the sentence in execution. Consequently, when he arrived
on the frontiers of Perugia, which belonged to his lieutenant,
Gian Paolo Baglioni, he sent Oliverotta da Fermo and Orsini
of Gravina to lay waste the March of Camerino, at the same
time petitioning Guido d'Ubaldo di Montefeltro, Duke of
Urbino, to lend his soldiers and artillery to help him in this
enterprise. This the unlucky Duke of Urbino, who enjoyed
the best possible relations with the pope, and who had no
reason for distrusting Caesar, did not dare refuse. But on the
very same day that the Duke of Urbina's troops started for
Camerino, Caesar's troops entered the duchy of Urbino, and
took possession of Cagli, one of the four towns of the little
State. The Duke of Urbino knew what awaited him if he tried
to resist, and fled incontinently, disguised as a peasant; thus
in less than eight days Caesar was master of his whole duchy,
except the fortresses of Maiolo and San Leone.

The Duke of Valentinois forthwith returned to Camerino,
where the inhabitants still held out, encouraged by the presence of Julius Caesar di Varano, their lord, and his two sons,
Venantio and Hannibal; the eldest son, Gian Maria, had been

sent by his father to Venice.

The presence of Caesar was the occasion of parleying between the besiegers and besieged. A capitulation was arranged whereby Varano engaged to give up the town, on condition that he and his sons were allowed to retire safe and sound, taking with them their furniture, treasure, and carriages. But this was by no means Caesar's intention; so, profiting by the relaxation in vigilance that had naturally come about in the garrison when the news of the capitulation had been announced, he surprised the town in the night preceding the surrender, and seized Caesar di Varano and his two sons, who were strangled a short time after, the father at La Pergola and the sons at Pesaro, by Don Michele Correglio, who, though he had left the position of sbirro for that of a captain, every now and then returned to his first business.

Meanwhile Vitellozzo Vitelli, who had assumed the title of General of the Church, and had under him 800 men-at-arms and 3,000 infantry, was following the secret instructions that he had received from Caesar by word of mouth, and was carrying forward that system of invasion which was to encircle Florence in a network of iron, and in the end make her defense an impossibility. A worthy pupil of his master, in whose school he had learned to use in turn the cunning of a fox and the strength of a lion, he had established an understanding between himself and certain young gentlemen of Arezzo to get that town delivered into his hands. But the plot had been discovered by Guglielma dei Pazzi, commissary of the Florentine Republic, and he had arrested two of the conspirators, whereupon the others, who were much more numerous than was supposed; had instantly dispersed about the town summoning the citizens to arms. All the republican faction, who saw in any sort of revolution the means of subjugating Florence, joined their party, set the captives at liberty, and seized Guglielmo; then proclaiming the establishment of the ancient constitution, they besieged the citadel, whither Cosimo dei Pazzi, Bishop of Arezzo, the son of Guglielmo, had fled for refuge; he, finding himself invested on every side, sent a messenger in hot haste to Florence to ask for help.

Unfortunately for the cardinal, Vitellozzo's troops were

nearer to the besiegers than were the soldiers of the most serene republic to the besieged, and instead of help — the whole army of the enemy came down upon him. This army was under the command of Vitellozzo, of Gian Paolo Baglioni, and of Fabio Orsino, and with them were the two Medici, ever ready to go wherever there was a league against Florence, and ever ready at the command of Borgia, on any conditions whatever, to re-enter the town whence they had been banished. The next day more help in the form of money and artillery arrived, sent by Pandolfo Petrucci, and on the 18th of June the citadel of Arezzo, which had received no news from Florence, was obliged to surrender.

Vitellozzo left the men of Arezzo to look after their town themselves, leaving also Fabio Orsina to garrison the citadel with a thousand men. Then, profiting by the terror that had been spread throughout all this part of Italy by the successive captures of the duchy of Urbino, of Camerino, and of Arezzo, he marched upon Monte San Severino, Castiglione, Aretino, Cortone, and the other towns of the valley of Chiana, which submitted one after the other almost without a struggle. When he was only ten or twelve leagues from Florence, and dared not an his own account attempt anything against her, he made known the state of affairs to the Duke of Valentinois. He, fancying the hour had came at last far striking the blow so long delayed, started off at once to deliver his answer in person to his faithful lieutenants.

But the Florentines, though they had sent no help to Guglielmo dei Pazzi, had demanded aid from Chaumont dumbest, governor of the Milanese, an behalf of Louis XII, not only explaining the danger they themselves were in but also Caesar's ambitious projects, namely that after first overcoming the small principalities and then the states of the second order, he had now, it seemed, reached such a height of pride that he would attack the King of France himself. The news from Naples was disquieting; serious differences had already occurred between the Count of Armagnac and Gonzalva di Cordova, and Louis might any day need Florence, whom he had always found loyal and faithful. He therefore resolved to check Caesar's progress, and not only sent him orders to advance no further step forwards, but also sent off, to give effect to his injunction, the captain Imbaut with 400 lances. The Duke of Valentinais on the frontier of Tuscany received a copy of the treaty signed between the republic and the King of France, a treaty in which the king engaged to help his ally against any enemy whatsoever, and at the same moment the formal prohibition from Louis to advance any further. Caesar also learned that beside the 400 lances with the captain Imbaut, which were on the road to Florence, Louis XII had as soon as he reached Asti sent off to Parma Louis de la Trimouille and 200 men-at-arms, 3000 Swiss, and a considerable train of artillery. In these two movements combined he saw hostile intentions towards himself, and turning right about face with his usual agility, he profited by the fact that he had given nothing but verbal instructions to all his lieutenants, and wrote a furious letter to Vitellozzo, reproaching him for compromising his master with a view to his own private interest, and ordering the instant surrender to the Florentines of the towns and fortresses he had taken, threatening to march down with his own troops and take them if he hesitated for a moment.

As soon as this letter was written, Caesar departed for Milan, where Louis XII had just arrived, bringing with him proof positive that he had been calumniated in the evacuation of the conquered towns. He also was entrusted with the pope's mission to renew for another eighteen months the title of legate 'a latere' in France to Cardinal dumbest, the friend rather than the minister of Louis XII. Thus, thanks to the public proof of his innocence and the private use of his influence, Caesar soon made his peace with the King of France.

But this was not all. It was in the nature of Caesar's genius to divert an impending calamity that threatened his destruction so as to come out of it better than before, and he suddenly saw the advantage he might take from the pretended disobedience of his lieutenants. Already he had been disturbed now and again by their growing power, and coveted their towns, now he thought the hour had perhaps came for suppressing them also, and in the usurpation of their private possessions striking a blow at Florence, who always escaped him at the very moment when he thought to take her. It was indeed an annoying thing to have these fortresses and towns displaying another banner than his own in the midst of the beautiful Romagna which he desired far his own kingdom. For Vitellozzo possessed Citta di Castello, Bentivoglio Bologna, Gian Paolo Baglioni was in command of Perugia, Oliverotto had just taken Fermo, and Pandolfo Petrucci was lord of Siena; it was high time that all these returned: into his own hands. The lieutenants of the Duke of Valentinois, like Alexander's, were becoming too powerful, and Borgia must inherit from them, unless he were willing to let them become his own heirs. He obtained from Louis XII three hundred lances wherewith to march against them. As soon as Vitellozzo Vitelli received Caesar's letter he perceived that he was being sacrificed to the fear that the King of France inspired; but he was not one of those victims who suffer their throats to be cut in the expiation of a mistake: he was a buffalo of Romagna who opposed his horns to the knife of the butcher; besides, he had the example of Varano and the Manfredi before him, and, death for death, he preferred to perish in arms.

So Vitellozzo convoked at Maggione all whose lives or lands were threatened by this new reversal of Caesar's policy. These were Paolo Orsino, Gian Paolo Baglioni, Hermes Bentivoglio, representing his father Gian, Antonio di Venafro, the envoy of Pandolfo Petrucci, Olivertoxo da Fermo, and the Duke of Urbino: the first six had everything to lose, and the last had already lost everything.

A treaty of alliance was signed between the confederates: they engaged to resist whether he attacked them severally or all together.

Caesar learned the existence of this league by its first effects: the Duke of Urbino, who was adored by his subjects, had come with a handful of soldiers to the fortress of San Leone, and it had yielded at once. In less than a week towns and fortresses followed this example, and all the duchy was once more in the hands of the Duke of Urbino.

At the same time, each member of the confederacy openly proclaimed his revolt against the common enemy, and took up a hostile attitude.

Caesar was at Imola, awaiting the French troops, but with

scarcely any men; so that Bentivoglio, who held part of the
country, and the Duke of Urbino, who had just reconquered
the rest of it, could probably have either taken him or forced
him to fly and quit the Romagna, had they marched against
him; all the more since the two men on whom he counted,
viz., Don Ugo di Cardona, who had entered his service after
Capua was taken, and Michelotto had mistaken his intention,
and were all at once separated from him. He had really
ordered them to fall back upon Rimini, and bring 200 light
horse and 500 infantry of which they had the command; but,
unaware of the urgency of his situation, at the very moment
when they were attempting to surprise La Pergola and Fossombrone, they were surrounded by Orsino of Gravina and
Vitellozzo. Ugo di Cardona and Michelotto defended themselves like lions; but in spite of their utmost efforts their little
band was cut to pieces, and Ugo di Cardona taken prisoner,
while Michelotto only escaped the same fate by lying down
among the dead; when night came on, he escaped to Fano.

But even alone as he was, almost without troops at Imola,
the confederates dared attempt nothing against Caesar,
whether because of the personal fear he inspired, or because
in him they respected the ally of the King of France; they
contented themselves with taking the towns and fortresses in
the neighborhood. Vitellozzo had retaken the fortresses of
Fossombrone, Urbino, Cagli, and Aggobbio; Orsino of Gravina had reconquered Fano and the whole province; while
Gian Maria de Varano, the same who by his absence had
escaped being massacred with the rest of his family, had
re-entered Camerino, borne in triumph by his people. Not
even all this could destroy Caesar's confidence in his own
good fortune, and while he was on the one hand urging on
the arrival of the French troops and calling into his pay all
those gentlemen known as "broken lances," because they went
about the country in parties of five or six only, and attached
themselves to anyone who wanted them, he had opened up
negotiations with his enemies, certain that from that very day
when he should persuade them to a conference they were
undone. Indeed, Caesar had the power of persuasion as a gift
from heaven; and though they perfectly well knew his duplicity, they had no power of resisting, not so much his actual

eloquence as that air of frank good-nature which Macchiavelli so greatly admired, and which indeed more than once deceived even him, wily politician as he was. In order to get Paolo Orsino to treat with him at Imola, Caesar sent Cardinal Borgia to the confederates as a hostage; and on this Paolo Orsino hesitated no longer, and on the 25th of October, 1502, arrived at Imola.

Caesar received him as an old friend from whom one might have been estranged a few days because of some slight passing differences; he frankly avowed that all the fault was no doubt on his side, since he had contrived to alienate men who were such loyal lords and also such brave captains; but with men of their nature, he added, an honest, honorable explanation such as he would give must put everything once more in statu quo. To prove that it was goodwill, not fear, that brought him back to them, he showed Orsino the letters from Cardinal Amboise which announced the speedy arrival of French troops; he showed him those he had collected about him, in the wish, he declared, that they might be thoroughly convinced that what he chiefly regretted in the whole matter was not so much the loss of the distinguished captains who were the very soul of his vast enterprise, as that he had led the world to believe, in a way so fatal to his own interest, that he could for a single instant fail to recognize their merit; adding that he consequently relied upon him, Paolo Orsino, whom he had always cared for most, to bring back the confederates by a peace which would be as much for the profit of all as a war was hurtful to all, and that he was ready to sign a treaty in consonance with their wishes so long as it should not prejudice his own honor.

Orsino was the man Caesar wanted: full of pride and confidence in himself, he was convinced of the truth of the old proverb that says, "A pope cannot reign eight days, if he has hath the Colonnas and the Orsini against him." He believed, therefore, if not in Caesar's good faith, at any rate in the necessity he must feel for making peace; accordingly he signed with him the following conventions — which only needed ratification — on the 18th of October, 1502, which we reproduce here as Macchiavelli sent them to the magnificent republic of Florence.

"Agreement between the Duke of Valentinois and the Confederates.

"Let it be known to the parties mentioned below, and to all who shall see these presents, that His Excellency the Duke of Romagna of the one part and the Orsini of the other part, together with their confederates, desiring to put an end to differences, enmities, misunderstandings, and suspicions which have arisen between them, have resolved as follows:

"There shall be between them peace and alliance true and perpetual, with a complete obliteration of wrongs and injuries which may have taken place up to this day, both parties engaging to preserve no resentment of the same; and in conformity with the aforesaid peace and union, His Excellency the Duke of Romagna shall receive into perpetual confederation, league, and alliance all the lords aforesaid; and each of them shall promise to defend the estates of all in general and of each in particular against any power that may annoy or attack them for any cause whatsoever, excepting always nevertheless the Pope Alexander VI and his Very Christian Majesty Louis XII, King of France: the lords above named promising on the other part to unite in the defense of the person and estates of His Excellency, as also those of the most illustrious lards, Don Gaffredo Bargia, Prince of Squillace, Don Roderigo Bargia, Duke of Sermaneta and Biselli, and Don Gian Borgia, Duke of Camerino and Negi, all brothers or nephews of the Duke of Romagna.

"Moreover, since the rebellion and usurpation of Urbino have occurred during the above-mentioned misunderstandings, all the confederates aforesaid and each of them shall bind themselves to unite all their forces for the recovery of the estates aforesaid and of such other places as have revolted and been usurped.

"His Excellency the Duke of Romagna shall undertake to continue to the Orsini and Vitelli their ancient engagements in the way of military service and an the same conditions.

"His Excellency promises further not to insist on the service in person of more than one of them, as they may choose: the service that the others may render shall be voluntary.

"He also promises that the second treaty shall be ratified by the sovereign pontiff, who shall not compel Cardinal Orsino to reside in Rome longer than shall seem convenient to this prelate.

"Furthermore, since there are certain differences between the Pope and the lord Gian Bentivoglio, the confederates aforesaid agree that they shall be put to the arbitration of Cardinal Orsino, of His Excellency the Duke of Romagna, and of the lord Pandolfo Petrucci, without appeal.

"Thus the confederates engage, each and all, so soon as they may be required by the Duke of Romagna, to put into his hands as a hostage one of the legitimate sons of each of them, in that place and at that time which he may be pleased to indicate.

"The same confederates promising moreover, all and each, that if any project directed against any one of them come to their knowledge, to give warning thereof, and all to prevent such project reciprocally.

"It is agreed, over and above, between the Duke of Romagna and the confederates aforesaid, to regard as a common enemy any who shall fail to keep the present stipulations, and to unite in the destruction of any States not conforming thereto.

"(Signed)
"CAESAR, PAOLO ORSINO
"AGAPIT, SECRETARY"

At the same time, while Orsino was carrying to the confederates the treaty drawn up between him and the duke, Bentivoglio, not willing to submit to the arbitration indicated, made an offer to Caesar of settling their differences by a private treaty, and sent his son to arrange the conditions: after some parleying, they were settled as follows: —

Bentivaglio should separate his fortunes from the Vitelli and Orsini;

He should furnish the Duke of Valentinois with a hundred men-at-arms and a hundred mounted archers for eight years;

He should pay 12,000 ducats per annum to Caesar, for the support of a hundred lances;

In return for this, his son Hannibal was to marry the sister of the Archbishop of Enna, who was Caesar's niece, and the pope was to recognize his sovereignty in Bologna;

The King of France, the Duke of Ferrara, and the republic of Florence were to be the guarantors of this treaty.

But the convention brought to the confederates by Orsino was the cause of great difficulties on their part. Vitellozza Vitelli in particular, who knew Caesar the best, never ceased to tell the other condottieri that so prompt and easy a peace must needs be the cover to some trap; but since Caesar had meanwhile collected a considerable army at Imala, and the four hundred lances lent him by Louis XII had arrived at last, Vitellozzo and Oliverotto decided to sign the treaty that Orsino brought, and to let the Duke of Urbino and the lord of Camerino know of it; they, seeing plainly that it was henceforth impassible to make a defense unaided, had retired, the one to Citta di Castello and the other into the kingdom of Naples.

But Caesar, saying nothing of his intentions, started on the 10th of December, and made his way to Cesena with a powerful army once more under his command. Fear began to spread on all sides, not only in Romagna but in the whole of Northern Italy; Florence, seeing him move away from her, only thought it a blind to conceal his intentions; while Venice, seeing him approach her frontiers, dispatched all her troops to the banks of the Po. Caesar perceived their fear, and lest harm should be done to himself by the mistrust it might inspire, he sent away all French troops in his service as soon as he reached Cesena, except a hundred men with M. de Candale, his brother-in-law; it was then seen that he only had 2000 cavalry and 2000 infantry with him. Several days were spent in parleying, for at Cesena Caesar found the envoys of the Vitelli and Orsini, who themselves were with their army in the duchy of Urbino; but after the preliminary discussions as to the right course to follow in carrying on the plan of conquest, there arose such difficulties between the general-in-chief and these agents, that they could not but see the impossibility of getting anything settled by intermediaries, and the urgent necessity of a conference between Caesar and one of the chiefs. So Oliverotto ran the risk of joining the duke in order to make proposals to him, either to march an Tuscany or to take Sinigaglia, which was the only place in the duchy of Urbino that had not again fallen into Caesar's power. Caesar's reply was that he did not desire to war upon Tuscany, because the Tuscans were his friends; but that he approved of the lieutenants' plan with regard to Sinigaglia, and therefore was marching towards Fano.

But the daughter of Frederic, the former Duke of Urbino, who held the town of Sinigaglia, and who was called the lady-prefect, because she had married Gian delta Rovere, whom his uncle, Sixtus IV, had made prefect of Rome, judging that it would be impossible to defend herself against the forces the Duke of Valentinais was bringing, left the citadel in the hands of a captain, recommending him to get the best terms he could for the town, and took boat for Venice.

Caesar learned this news at Rimini, through a messenger from Vitelli and the Orsini, who said that the governor of the citadel, though refusing to yield to them, was quite ready to make terms with him, and consequently they would engage to go to the town and finish the business there. Caesar's reply was that in consequence of this information he was sending some of his troops to Cesena and Imola, for they would be useless to him, as he should now have theirs, which together with the escort he retained would be sufficient, since his only object was the complete pacification of the duchy of Urbino. He added that this pacification would not be possible if his old friends continued to distrust him, and to discuss through intermediaries alone plans in which their own fortunes were interested as well as his. The messenger returned with this answer, and the confederates, though feeling, it is true, the justice of Caesar's remarks, none the less hesitated to comply with his demand. Vitellozzo Vitelli in particular showed a want of confidence in him which nothing seemed able to subdue; but, pressed by Oliverotto, Gravina, and Orsino, he consented at last to await the duke's coming; making concession rather because he could not bear to appear more timid

than his companions, than because of any confidence he felt
in the return of friendship that Borgia was displaying.

The duke learned the news of this decision, so much
desired, when he arrived at Fano on the 20th of December
1502. At once he summoned eight of his most faithful
friends, among whom were d'Enna, his nephew, Michelotto,
and Ugo di Cardona, and ordered them, as soon as they
arrived at Sinigaglia, and had seen Vitellozzo, Gravina,
Oliveratta, and Orsino come out to meet them, on a pretext
of doing them honor, to place themselves on the right and
left hand of the four generals, two beside each, so that at a
given signal they might either stab or arrest them; next he
assigned to each of them his particular man, bidding them
not quit his side until he had reentered Sinigaglia and arrived
at the quarters prepared far him; then he sent orders to such
of the soldiers as were in cantonments in the neighborhood
to assemble to the number of 8000 on the banks of the
Metaurus, a little river of Umbria which runs into the Adriatic and has been made famous by the defeat of Hannibal.

The duke arrived at the rendezvous given to his army on
the 31st of December, and instantly sent out in front two
hundred horse, and immediately behind them his infantry;
following close in the midst of his men-at-arms, following
the coast of the Adriatic, with the mountains on his right
and the sea on his left, which in part of the way left only
space for the army to march ten abreast.

After four hours' march, the duke at a turn of the path
perceived Sinigaglia, nearly a mile distant from the sea, and
a bowshot from the mountains; between the army and the
town ran a little river, whose banks he had to follow far some
distance. At last he found a bridge opposite a suburb of the
town, and here Caesar ordered his cavalry to stop: it was
drawn up in two lines, one between the road and the river,
the other on the side of the country, leaving the whole width
of the road to the infantry: which latter defiled, crossed the
bridge, and entering the town, drew themselves up in battle
array in the great square.

On their side, Vitellazzo, Gravina, Orsino, and Oliverotto,
to make room for the duke's army, had quartered their
soldiers in little towns or villages in the neighborhood of

Sinigaglia; Oliverotto alone had kept nearly 1000 infantry and 150 horse, who were in barracks in the suburb through which the duke entered.

Caesar had made only a few steps towards the town when he perceived Vitellozzo at the gate, with the Duke of Gravina and Orsina, who all came out to meet him; the last two quite gay and confident, but the first so gloomy and dejected that you would have thought he foresaw the fate that was in store for him; and doubtless he had not been without same pre-sentiments; for when he left his army to came to Sinigaglia, he had bidden them farewell as though never to meet again, had commended the care of his family to the captains, and embraced his children with tears — a weakness which appeared strange to all who knew him as a brave condottiere.

The duke marched up to them holding out his hand, as a sign that all was over and forgotten, and did it with an air at once so loyal and so smiling that Gravina and Orsina could no longer doubt the genuine return of his friendship, and it was only Vitellozza still appeared sad. At the same moment, exactly as they had been commanded, the duke's accomplices took their pasts on the right and left of those they were to watch, who were all there except Oliverotto, whom the duke could not see, and began to seek with uneasy looks; but as he crossed the suburb he perceived him exercising his troops on the square. Caesar at once dispatched Michelotto and d'Enna, with a message that it was a rash thing to have his troops out, when they might easily start some quarrel with the duke's men and bring about an affray: it would be much better to settle them in barracks and then come to join his compan-ions, who were with Caesar. Oliverotto, drawn by the same fate as his friends, made no abjection, ordered his soldiers indoors, and put his horse to the gallop to join the duke, escorted on either side by d'Enna and Michelotto. Caesar, on seeing him, called him, took him by the hand, and continued his march to the palace that had been prepared for him, his four victims following after.

Arrived on the threshold, Caesar dismounted, and signing to the leader of the men-at-arms to, await his orders, he went in first, followed by Oliverotto, Gravina, Vitellozzo Vitelli, and Orsino, each accompanied by his two satellites; but scarcely had they gone upstairs and into the first room when the door was shut behind them, and Caesar turned round, saying, "The hour has come!" This was the signal agreed upon. Instantly the former confederates were seized, thrown down, and forced to surrender with a dagger at their throat. Then, while they were being carried to a dungeon, Caesar opened the window, went out on the balcony and cried out to the leader of his men-at-arms, "Go forward!" The man was in the secret, he rushed on with his band towards the barracks where Oliverotto's soldiers had just been consigned, and they, suddenly surprised and off their guard, were at once made prisoners; then the duke's troops began to pillage the town, and he summoned Macchiavelli.

Caesar and the Florentine envoy were nearly two hours shut up together, and since Macchiavelli himself recounts the history of this interview, we will give his own words.

"He summoned me," says the Florentine ambassador, "and in the calmest manner showed me his joy at the success of this enterprise, which he assured me he had spoken of to me the evening before; I remember that he did, but I did not at that time understand what he meant; next he explained, in terms of much feeling and lively affection for our city, the different motives which had made him desire your alliance, a desire to which he hopes you will respond. He ended with charging me to lay three proposals before your lordships: first, that you rejoice with him in the destruction at a single blow of the mortal enemies of the king, himself, and you, and the consequent disappearance of all seeds of trouble and dissension likely to waste Italy: this service of his, together with his refusal to allow the prisoners to march against you, ought, he thinks, to excite your gratitude towards him; secondly, he begs that you will at this juncture give him a striking proof of your friendliness, by urging your cavalry's advance towards Borgo, and there assembling some infantry also, in order that they may march with him, should need arise, on Castello or on Perugia. Lastly, he desires — and this is his third condition — that you arrest the Duke of Urbino, if he should flee from Castello into your territories, when he learns that Vitellozzo is a prisoner.

"When I objected that to give him up would not beseem

the dignity of the republic, and that you would never consent, he approved of my words, and said that it would be enough for you to keep the duke, and not give him his liberty without His Excellency's permission. I have promised to give you all this information, to which he awaits your reply."

*T*he same night eight masked men descended to the dungeon where the prisoners lay: they believed at that moment that the fatal hour had arrived for all. But this time the executioners had to do with Vitellozzo and Oliverotto alone. When these two captains heard that they were condemned, Oliverotto burst forth into reproaches against Vitellozzo, saying that it was all his fault that they had taken up arms against the duke: not a word Vitellozzo answered except a prayer that the pope might grant him plenary indulgence for all his sins. Then the masked men took them away, leaving Orsino and Gravina to await a similar fate, and led away the two chosen out to die to a secluded spot outside the ramparts of the town, where they were strangled and buried at once in two trenches that had been dug beforehand.

The two others were kept alive until it should be known if the pope had arrested Cardinal Orsino, archbishop of Florence and lord of Santa Croce; and when the answer was received in the affirmative from His Holiness, Gravina and Orsina, who had been transferred to a castle, were likewise strangled.

The duke, leaving instructions with Michelotto, set off for Sinigaglia as soon as the first execution was over, assuring Macchiavelli that he had never had any other thought than that of giving tranquility to the Romagna and to Tuscany, and also that he thought he had succeeded by taking and putting to death the men who had been the cause of all the trouble; also that any other revolt that might take place in the future would be nothing but sparks that a drop of water could extinguish.

The pope had barely learned that Caesar had his enemies in his power, when, eager to play the same winning game himself, he announced to Cardinal Orsino, though it was then midnight, that his son had taken Sinigaglia, and gave him an invitation to come the next morning and talk over the good news. The cardinal, delighted at this increase of favor, did not miss his appointment. So, in the morning, he started an horseback for the Vatican; but at a turn of the first street he met the governor of Rome with a detachment of cavalry, who congratulated himself on the happy chance that they were taking the same road, and accompanied him to the threshold of the Vatican. There the cardinal dismounted, and began to ascend the stairs; scarcely, however, had he reached the first landing before his mules and carriages were seized and shut in the palace stables. When he entered the hall of the Perropont, he found that he and all his suite were surrounded by armed men, who led him into another apartment, called the Vicar's Hall, where he found the Abbate Alviano, the protonotary Orsino, Jacopo Santa Croce, and Rinaldo Orsino, who were all prisoners like himself; at the same time the governor received orders to seize the castle of Monte Giardino, which belonged to the Orsini, and take away all the jewels, all the hangings, all the furniture, and all the silver that he might find.

The governor carried out his orders conscientiously, and brought to the Vatican everything he seized, down to the cardinal's account-book. On consulting this book, the pope found out two things: first, that a sum of 2000 ducats was due to the cardinal, no debtor's name being mentioned; secondly, that the cardinal had bought three months before, for 1500 Roman crowns, a magnificent pearl which could not be found among the objects belonging to him: on which Alexander ordered that from that very moment until the negligence in the cardinal's accounts was repaired, the men who were in the habit of bringing him food twice a day on behalf of his mother should not be admitted into the Castle Sant' Angelo. The same day, the cardinal's mother sent the pope the 2000 ducats, and the next day his mistress, in man's attire, came in person to bring the missing pearl. His Holiness, however, was so struck with her beauty in this costume, that, we are told, he let her keep the pearl for the same price she had paid for it.

Then the pope allowed the cardinal to have his food

brought as before, and he died of poison on the 22nd of February — that is, two days after his accounts had been set right.

That same night the Prince of Squillace set off to take possession, in the pope's name, of the lands of the deceased.

Chapter XIV

*T*he Duke of Valentinois had continued, his road towards Citta di Castello and Perugia, and had seized these two towns without striking a blow; for the Vitelli had fled from the former, and the latter had been abandoned by Gian Paolo Baglione with no attempt whatever at resistance. There still remained Siena, where Pandolfo Petrucci was shut up, the only man remaining of all who had joined the league against Caesar.

But Siena was under the protection of the French. Besides, Siena was not one of the States of the Church, and Caesar had no rights there. Therefore he was content with insisting upon Pandolfo Petrucci's leaving the town and retiring to Lucca, which he accordingly did.

Then all on this side being peaceful and the whole of Romagna in subjection, Caesar resolved to return to Rome and help the pope to destroy all that was left of the Orsini.

This was all the easier because Louis XII, having suffered reverses in the kingdom of Naples, had since then been much concerned with his own affairs to disturb himself about his allies. So Caesar, doing for the neighborhood of the Holy See the same thing that he had done far the Romagna, seized in succession Vicovaro, Cera, Palombera, Lanzano, and Cervetti ; when these conquests were achieved, having nothing else to do now that he had brought the pontifical States into subjection from the frontiers of Naples to those of Venice, he returned to Rome to concert with his father as to the means of converting his duchy into a kingdom.

Caesar arrived at the right moment to share with Alexander

the property of Cardinal Gian Michele, who had just died, having received a poisoned cup from the hands of the pope.

The future King of Italy found his father preoccupied with a grand project: he had resolved, for the Feast of St. Peter's, to create nine cardinals. What he had to gain from these nominations is as follows:

First, the cardinals elected would leave all their offices vacant; these offices would fall into the hands of the pope, and he would sell them;

Secondly, each of them would buy his election, more or less dear according to his fortune; the price, left to be settled at the pope's fancy, would vary from 10,000 to 40,000 ducats;

Lastly, since as cardinals they would by law lose the right of making a will, the pope, in order to inherit from them, had only to poison them: this put him in the position of a butcher who, if he needs money, has only to cut the throat of the fattest sheep in the flock.

The nomination came to pass: the new cardinals were Giovanni Castellaro Valentine, archbishop of Trani; Francesco Remolini, ambassador from the King of Aragon; Francesco Soderini, bishop of Volterra; Melchiore Copis, bishop of Brissina; Nicolas Fiesque, bishop of Frejus; Francesco di Sprate, bishop of Leome; Adriano Castellense, clerk of the chamber, treasurer-general, and secretary of the briefs; Francesco Boris, bishop of Elva, patriarch of Constantinople, and secretary to the pope; and Giacomo Casanova, protonotary and private chamberlain to His Holiness.

The price of their simony paid and their vacated offices sold, the pope made his choice of those he was to poison: the number was fixed at three, one old and two new; the old one was Cardinal Casanova, and the new ones Melchiore Copis and Adriano Castellense, who had taken the name of Adrian of Carneta from that town where he had been born, and where, in the capacity of clerk of the chamber, treasurer-general, and secretary of briefs, he had amassed an immense fortune.

So, when all was settled between Caesar and the pope, they invited their chosen guests to supper in a vineyard situated near the Vatican, belonging to the Cardinal of Corneto. In the morning of this day, the 2nd of August, they sent their servants and the steward to make all preparations, and Caesar himself gave the pope's butler two bottles of wine prepared with the white powder resembling sugar whose mortal properties he had so often proved, and gave orders that he was to serve this wine only when he was told, and only to persons specially indicated; the butler accordingly put the wine an a sideboard apart, bidding the waiters on no account to touch it, as it was reserved for the pope's drinking.*

Towards evening Alexander VI walked from the Vatican leaning on Caesar's arm, and turned his steps towards the vineyard, accompanied by Cardinal Caraffa; but as the heat was great and the climb rather steep, the pope, when he reached the top, stopped to take breath; then putting his hand on his breast, he found that he had left in his bedroom a chain that he always wore round his neck, which suspended a gold medallion that enclosed the sacred host. He owed this habit to a prophecy that an astrologer had made, that so long as he carried about a consecrated wafer, neither steel nor poison could take hold upon him. Now, finding himself without his talisman, he ordered Monsignors Caraffa to hurry back at once to the Vatican, and told him in which part of his room he had left it, so that he might get it and bring it him without delay. Then, as the walk had made him thirsty, he turned to a valet, giving signs with his hand as he did so that his messenger should make haste, and asked for something to drink. Caesar, who was also thirsty, ordered the man

---

* The poison of the Borgias, say contemporary writers, was of two kinds, powder and liquid. The poison in the form of powder was a sort of white flour, almost impalpable, with the taste of sugar, and called Contarella. Its composition is unknown.

The liquid poison was prepared, we are told in so strange a fashion that we cannot pass it by in silence. We repeat here what we read, and vouch for nothing ourselves, lest science should give us the lie.

A strong dose of arsenic was administered to a boar; as soon as the poison began to take effect, he was hung up by his heels; convulsions supervened, and a froth deadly and abundant ran out from his jaws; it was this froth, collected into a silver vessel and transferred into a bottle hermetically sealed, that made the liquid poison.

to bring two glasses. By a curious coincidence, the butler had just gone back to the Vatican to fetch some magnificent peaches that had been sent that very day to the pope, but which had been forgotten when he came here; so the valet went to the under butler, saying that His Holiness and Monsignors the Duke of Romagna were thirsty and asking for a drink. The under butler, seeing two bottles of wine set apart, and having heard that this wine was reserved for the pope, took one, and telling the valet to bring two glasses on a tray, poured out this wine, which both drank, little thinking that it was what they had themselves prepared to poison their guests.

Meanwhile Caraffa hurried to the Vatican, and, as he knew the palace well, went up to the pope's bedroom, a light in his hand and attended by no servant. As he turned round a corridor a puff of wind blew out his lamp; still, as he knew the way, he went on, thinking there was no need of seeing to find the object he was in search of; but as he entered the room he recoiled a step, with a cry of terror: he beheld a ghastly apparition; it seemed that there before his eyes, in the middle of the room, between the door and the cabinet which held the medallion, Alexander VI, motionless and livid, was lying on a bier at whose four corners there burned four torches. The cardinal stood still for a moment, his eyes fixed, and his hair standing on end, without strength to move either backward or forward; then thinking it was all a trick of fancy or an apparition of the devil's making, he made the sign of the cross, invoking God's holy name; all instantly vanished, torches, bier, and corpse, and the seeming mortuary, chamber was once more in darkness.

Then Cardinal Caraffa, who has himself recorded this strange event, and who was afterwards Pope Paul IV, entered baldly, and though an icy sweat ran dawn his brow, he went straight to the cabinet, and in the drawer indicated found the gold chain and the medallion, took them, and hastily went out to give them to the pope. He found supper served, the guests arrived, and His Holiness ready to take his 317 place at table; as soon as the cardinal was in sight, His Holiness, who was very pale, made one step towards him; Caraffa doubled his pace, and handed the medallion to him; but as the pope stretched forth his arm to take it, he fell back with a cry, instantly followed by violent convulsions: an instant later, as he advanced to render his father assistance, Caesar was similarly seized; the effect of the poison had been more rapid than usual, for Caesar had doubled the dose, and there is little doubt that their heated condition increased its activity.

The two stricken men were carried side by side to the Vatican, where each was taken to his own rooms: from that moment they never met again.

As soon as he reached his bed, the pope was seized with a violent fever, which did not give way to emetics or to bleeding; almost immediately it became necessary to administer the last sacraments of the Church; but his admirable bodily constitution, which seemed to have defied old age, was strong enough to fight eight days with death; at last, after a week of mortal agony, he died, without once uttering the name of Caesar or Lucrezia, who were the two poles around which had turned all his affections and all his crimes. His age was seventy-two, and he had reigned eleven years.

Caesar, perhaps because he had taken less of the fatal beverage, perhaps because the strength of his youth overcame the strength of the poison, or maybe, as some say, because when he reached his own rooms he had swallowed an antidote known only to himself, was not so prostrated as to lose sight for a moment of the terrible position he was in: he summoned his faithful Michelotto, with those he could best count on among his men, and disposed this band in the various rooms that led to his own, ordering the chief never to leave the foot of his bed, but to sleep lying on a rug, his hand upon the handle of his sward.

The treatment had been the same for Caesar as for the pope, but in addition to bleeding and emetics strange baths were added, which Caesar had himself asked for, having heard that in a similar case they had once cured Ladislaus, King of Naples. Four posts, strongly welded to the floor and ceiling, were set up in his room, like the machines at which farriers shoe horses; every day a bull was brought in, turned over on his back and tied by his four legs to the four posts; then, when he was thus fixed, a cut was made in his belly a foot and a half long, through which the intestines were drawn out; then Caesar slipped into this living bath of blood: when the bull was dead, Caesar was taken out and rolled up in burning hot blankets, where, after copious perspirations, he almost always felt some sort of relief.

Every two hours Caesar sent to ask news of his father: he hardly waited to hear that he was dead before, though still at death's door himself, he summoned up all the force of character and presence of mind that naturally belonged to him. He ordered Michelotto to shut the doors of the Vatican before the report of Alexander's decease could spread about the town, and forbade anyone whatsoever to enter the pope's apartments until the money and papers had been removed. Michelotto obeyed at once, went to find Cardinal Casanova, held a dagger at his throat, and made him deliver up the keys of the pope's rooms and cabinets; then, under his guidance, took away two chests full of gold, which perhaps contained 100,000 Roman crowns in specie, several boxes full of jewels, much silver and many precious vases; all these were carried to Caesar's chamber; the guards of the room were doubled; then the doors of the Vatican were once more thrown open, and the death of the pope was proclaimed.

Although the news was expected, it produced none the less a terrible effect in Rome; for although Caesar was still alive, his condition left everyone in suspense: had the mighty Duke of Romagna, the powerful condottiere who had taken thirty towns and fifteen fortresses in five years, been seated, sword in hand, upon his charger, nothing would have been uncertain of fluctuating even for a moment; far, as Caesar afterwards told Macchiavelli, his ambitious soul had provided for all things that could occur on the day of the pope's death, except the one that he should be dying himself; but being nailed down to his bed, sweating off the effects the poison had wrought; so, though he had kept his power of thinking he could no longer act, but must needs wait and suffer the course of events, instead of marching on in front and controlling them.

Thus he was forced to regulate his actions no longer by his own plans but according to circumstances. His most bitter enemies, who could press him hardest, were the Orsini and the Colonnas: from the one family he had taken their blood, from the other their goods.

So he addressed himself to those to whom he could return what he had taken, and opened negotiations with the Colonnas.

Meanwhile the obsequies of the pope were going forward: the vice-chancellor had sent out orders to the highest among the clergy, the superiors of convents, and the secular orders, not to fail to appear, according to regular custom, on pain of being despoiled of their office and dignities, each bringing his own company to the Vatican, to be present at the pope's funeral; each therefore appeared on the day and at the hour appointed at the pontifical palace, whence the body was to be conveyed to the church of St. Peter's, and there buried. The corpse was found to be abandoned and alone in the mortuary chamber; for everyone of the name of Borgia, except Caesar, lay hidden, not knowing what might come to pass. This was indeed well justified; for Fabio Orsino, meeting one member of the family, stabbed him, and as a sign of the hatred they had sworn to one another, bathed his mouth and hands in the blood.

The agitation in Rome was so great, that when the corpse of Alexander VI was about to enter the church there occurred a kind of panic, such as will suddenly arise in times of popular agitation, instantly causing so great a disturbance in the funeral cortege that the guards drew up in battle array, the clergy fled into the sacristy, and the bearers dropped the bier.

The people, tearing off the pall which covered it, disclosed the corpse, and everyone could see with impunity and close at hand the man who, fifteen days before, had made princes, kings and emperors tremble, from one end of the world to the other.

But in accordance with that religious feeling towards death which all men instinctively feel, and which alone survives every other, even in the heart of the atheist, the bier was taken up again and carried to the foot of the great altar in St. Peter's, where, set on trestles, it was exposed to public view; but the body had become so black, so deformed and swollen, that it was horrible to behold; from its nose a bloody matter escaped, the mouth gaped hideously, and the tongue was so mon-

strously enlarged that it filled the whole cavity; to this frightful appearance was added a decomposition so great that,
although at the pope's funeral it is customary to kiss the hand
which bore the Fisherman's ring, not one approached to offer
this mark of respect and religious reverence to the representative of God on earth.

Towards seven o'clock in the evening, when the declining
day adds so deep a melancholy to the silence of a church,
four porters and two working carpenters carried the corpse
into the chapel where it was to be interred, and, lifting it off
the catafalque, where it lay in state, put it in the coffin which
was to be its last abode; but it was found that the coffin was
too short, and the body could not be got in till the legs were
bent and thrust in with violent blows; then the carpenters
put on the lid, and while one of them sat on the top to force
the knees to bend, the others hammered in the nails: amid
those Shakespearian pleasantries that sound as the last orison
in the ear of the mighty; then, says Tommaso Tommasi, he
was placed on the right of the great altar of St. Peter's, beneath
a very ugly tomb.

The next morning this epitaph was found inscribed upon
the tomb:

"VENDIT ALEXANDER CLAVES, ALTARIA, CHRISTUM:
EMERAT ILLE PRIUS, VENDERE JUKE POTEST";

that is,

"POPE ALEXANDER SOLD THE CHRIST, THE ALTARS, AND THE KEYS:
BUT ANYONE WHO BUYS A THING MAY SELL IT IF HE PLEASE."

Chapter XV

*F*rom the effect produced at Rome by Alexander's death, one may imagine what happened not only in the whole of Italy but also in the rest of the world: for a moment Europe swayed, for the column which supported the vault of the political edifice had given way, and the star with eyes of flame and rays of blood, round which all things had revolved for the last eleven years, was now extinguished, and for a moment the world, on a sudden struck motionless, remained in silence and darkness.

After the first moment of stupefaction, all who had an injury to avenge arose and hurried to the chase. Sforza retook Pesaro, Bagloine Perugia, Guido and Ubaldo Urbino, and La Rovere Sinigaglia; the Vitelli entered Citta di Castello, the Appiani Piombino, the Orsini Monte Giordano and their other territories; Romagna alone remained impassive and loyal, for the people, who have no concern with the quarrels of the great, provided they do not affect themselves, had never been so happy as under the government of Caesar.

The Colonnas were pledged to maintain a neutrality, and had been consequently restored to the possession of their castles and the cities of Chiuzano, Capo d'Anno, Frascati, Rocca di Papa, and Nettuno, which they found in a better condition than when they had left them, as the pope had had them embellished and fortified.

Caesar was still in the Vatican with his troops, who, loyal to him in his misfortune, kept watch about the palace, where he was writhing on his bed of pain and roaring like a wounded lion. The cardinals, who had in their first terror fled, each his own way, instead of attending the pope's obsequies, began to assemble once more, some at the Minerva, others around Cardinal Caraffa. Frightened by the troops that Caesar still had, especially since the command was entrusted to Michelotto, they collected all the money they could to levy an army of 2000 soldiers with. Charles Taneo at their head, with the title of Captain of the Sacred College. It was then hoped that peace was re-established, when it was heard that Prospero Colonna was coming with 3000 men from the side of Naples, and Fabio Orsino from the side of Viterbo with 200 horse and more than 1000 infantry. Indeed, they entered Rome at only one day's interval one from another, by so similar an ardor were they inspired.

Thus there were five armies in Rome: Caesar's army, holding the Vatican and the Borgo; the army of the Bishop of Nicastro, who had received from Alexander the guardianship of the Castle Sant' Angelo and had shut himself up there, refusing to yield; the army of the Sacred College, which was stationed round about the Minerva; the army of Prospero Colonna, which was encamped at the Capitol; and the army of Fabio Orsino, in barracks at the Ripetta.

On their side, the Spaniards had advanced to Terracino, and the French to Nepi. The cardinals saw that Rome now stood upon a mine which the least spark might cause to explode: they summoned the ambassadors of the Emperor of Germany, the Kings of France and Spain, and the republic of Venice to raise their voice in the name of their masters. The ambassadors, impressed with the urgency of the situation, began by declaring the Sacred College inviolable: they then ordered the Orsini, the Colonnas, and the Duke of Valentinois to leave Rome and go each his own, way.

The Orsini were the first to submit: the next morning their example was followed by the Colonnas. No one was left but Caesar, who said he was willing to go, but desired to make his conditions beforehand: the Vatican was undermined, he declared, and if his demands were refused he and those who came to take him should be blown up together.

It was known that his were never empty threats they came to terms with him.*

---

* Caesar promised to remain ten miles away from Rome the

At the day and hour appointed Caesar sent out his artillery, which consisted of eighteen pieces of cannon, and 400 infantry of the Sacred College, on each of whom he bestowed a ducat: behind the artillery came a hundred chariots escorted by his advance guard.

The duke was carried out of the gate of the Vatican: he lay on a bed covered with a scarlet canopy, supported by twelve halberdiers, leaning forward on his cushions so that no one might see his face with its purple lips and bloodshot eyes: beside him was his naked sword, to show that, feeble as he was, he could use it at need: his finest charger, caparisoned in black velvet embroidered with his arms, walked beside the bed, led by a page, so that Caesar could mount in case of surprise or attack: before him and behind, both right and left, marched his army, their arms in rest, but without beating of drums or blowing of trumpets: this gave a somber, funereal air to the whole procession, which at the gate of the city met Prospero Colonna awaiting it with a considerable band of men.

Caesar thought at first that, breaking his word as he had so often done himself, Prospero Colonna was going to attack him. He ordered a halt, and prepared to mount his horse; but Prospera Colonna, seeing the state he was in, advanced to his bedside alone: he came, against expectation, to offer him an escort, fearing an ambuscade on the part of Fabio Orsino, who had loudly sworn that he would lose his honor or avenge the death of Paolo Orsina, his father. Caesar thanked Colanna, and replied that from the moment that Orsini stood alone he ceased to fear him. Then Colonna saluted the duke, and rejoined his men, directing them towards Albano, while

whole time the Conclave lasted, and not to take any action against the town or any other of the Ecclesiastical States: Fabio Orsino and Prospero Colonna had made the same promises.

It was agreed that Caesar should quit Rome with his army, artillery, and baggage; and to ensure his not being attacked or molested in the streets, the Sacred College should add to his numbers 400 infantry, who, in case of attack or insult, would fight for him. The Venetian ambassador answered for the Orsini, the Spanish ambassador for the Colonnas, the ambassador of France for Caesar.

Caesar took the road to Citta Castellana, which had remained loyal.

When there, Caesar found himself not only master of his own fate but of others as well: of the twenty-two votes he owned in the Sacred College twelve had remained faithful, and as the Conclave was composed in all of thirty-seven cardinals, he with his twelve votes could make the majority incline to whichever side he chose. Accordingly he was courted both by the Spanish and the French party, each desiring the election of a pope of their own nation. Caesar listened, promising nothing and refusing nothing: he gave his twelve votes to Francesco Piccolomini, Cardinal of Siena, one of his father's creatures who had remained his friend, and the latter was elected on the 8th of October and took the name of Pius III.

Caesar's hopes did not deceive him: Pius III was hardly elected before he sent him a safe-conduct to Rome: the duke came back with 250 men-at-arms, 250 light horse, and 800 infantry, and lodged in his palace, the soldiers camping round about.

Meanwhile the Orsini, pursuing their projects of vengeance against Caesar, had been levying many troops at Perugia and the neighborhood to bring against him to Rome, and as they fancied that France, in whose service they were engaged, was humoring the duke for the sake of the twelve votes which were wanted to secure the election of Cardinal Amboise at the next Conclave, they went over to the service of Spain.

Meanwhile Caesar was signing a new treaty with Louis XII, by which he engaged to support him with all his forces, and even with his person, so soon as he could ride, in maintaining his conquest of Naples: Louis, on his side, guaranteed that he should retain possession of the States he still held, and promised his help in recovering those he had lost.

The day when this treaty was made known, Gonzalvo di Cordovo proclaimed to the sound of a trumpet in all the streets of Rome that every Spanish subject serving in a foreign army was at once to break his engagement on pain of being found guilty of high treason.

This measure robbed Caesar of ten or twelve of his best officers and of nearly 300 men.

Then the Orsini, seeing his army thus reduced, entered Rome, supported by the Spanish ambassador, and summoned Caesar to appear before the pope and the Sacred College and give an account of his crimes.

Faithful to his engagements, Pius III replied that in his quality of sovereign prince the duke in his temporal administration was quite independent and was answerable for his actions to God alone.

But as the pope felt he could not much longer support Caesar against his enemies for all his goodwill, he advised him to try to join the French army, which was still advancing on Naples, in the midst of which he would alone find safety. Caesar resolved to retire to Bracciano, where Gian Giordano Orsino, who had once gone with him to France, and who was the only member of the family who had not declared against him, offered him an asylum in the name of Cardinal dumbest: so one morning he ordered his troops to march for this town, and, taking his place in their midst, he left Rome.

But though Caesar had kept his intentions quiet, the Orsini had been forewarned, and, taking out all the troops they had by the gate of San Pancracio, they had made along detour and blocked Caesar's way; so, when the latter arrived at Storta, he found the Orsini's army drawn up awaiting him in numbers exceeding his own by at least one-half.

Caesar saw that to come to blows in his then feeble state was to rush on certain destruction; so he ordered his troops to retire, and, being a first-rate strategist, echeloned his retreat so skillfully that his enemies, though they followed, dared not attack him, and he re-entered the pontifical town without the loss of a single man.

This time Caesar went straight to the Vatican, to put himself more directly under the pope's protection; he distributed his soldiers about the palace, so as to guard all its exits. Now the Orsini, resolved to make an end of Caesar, had determined to attack him wheresoever he might be, with no regard to the sanctity of the place: this they attempted, but without success, as Caesar's men kept a good guard on every side, and offered a strong defense.

Then the Orsini, not being able to force the guard of the Castle Sant' Angelo, hoped to succeed better with the duke by leaving Rome and then returning by the Torione gate; but Caesar anticipated this move, and they found the gate guarded and barricaded. None the less, they pursued their design, seeking by open violence the vengeance that they had hoped to obtain by craft; and, having surprised the approaches to the gate, set fire to it: a passage gained, they made their way into the gardens of the castle, where they found Caesar awaiting them at the head of his cavalry.

Face to face with danger, the duke had found his old strength: and he was the first to rush upon his enemies, loudly challenging Orsino in the hope of killing him should they meet; but either Orsino did not hear him or dared not fight; and after an exciting contest, Caesar, who was numerically two-thirds weaker than his enemy, saw his cavalry cut to pieces; and after performing miracles of personal strength and courage, was obliged to return to the Vatican. There he found the pope in mortal agony: the Orsini, tired of contending against the old man's word of honor pledged to the duke, had by the interposition of Pandolfo Petrucci, gained the ear of the pope's surgeon, who placed a poisoned plaster upon a wound in his leg.

The pope then was actually dying when Caesar, covered with dust and blood, entered his room, pursued by his enemies, who knew no check till they reached the palace walls, behind which the remnant of his army still held their ground.

Pius III, who knew he was about to die, sat up in his bed, gave Caesar the key of the corridor which led to the Castle of Sant' Angelo, and an order addressed to the governor to admit him and his family, to defend him to the last extremity, and to let him go wherever he thought fit; and then fell fainting on his bed.

Caesar took his two daughters by the hand, and, followed by the little dukes of Sermaneta and Nepi, took refuge in the last asylum open to him.

The same night the pope died: he had reigned only twenty-six days.

After his death, Caesar, who had cast himself fully dressed upon his bed, heard his door open at two o'clock in the morning: not knowing what anyone might want of him at such an hour, he raised himself on one elbow and felt for the handle of his sword with his other hand; but at the first glance he recognized in his nocturnal visitor Giuliano della Rovere.

Utterly exhausted by the poison, abandoned by his troops, fallen as he was from the height of his power, Caesar, who could now do nothing for himself, could yet make a pope: Giuliano delta Rovere had come to buy the votes of his twelve cardinals.

Caesar imposed his conditions, which were accepted.

If elected, Giuliano delta Ravere was to help Caesar to recover his territories in Romagna; Caesar was to remain general of the Church; and Francesco Maria delta Rovere, prefect of Rome, was to marry one of Caesar's daughters.

On these conditions Caesar sold his twelve cardinals to Giuliano.

The next day, at Giuliano's request, the Sacred College ordered the Orsini to leave Rome for the whole time occupied by the Conclave.

On the 31st of October 1503, at the first scrutiny, Giuliano delta Rovere was elected pope, and took the name of Julius II.

He was scarcely installed in the Vatican when he made it his first care to summon Caesar and give him his former rooms there; then, since the duke was fully restored to health, he began to busy himself with the re-establishment of his affairs, which had suffered sadly of late.

The defeat of his army and his own escape to Sant' Angelo, where he was supposed to be a prisoner, had brought about great changes in Romagna. Sesena was once more in the power of the Church, as formerly it had been; Gian Sforza had again entered Pesaro; Ordelafi had seized Forli; Malatesta was laying claim to Rimini; the inhabitants of Imola had assassinated their governor, and the town was divided between two opinions, one that it should be put into the hands of the Riani, the other, into the hands of the Church; Faenza had remained loyal longer than any other place; but at last, losing hope of seeing Caesar recover his power, it had summoned Francesco, a natural son of Galeotto Manfredi, the last surviving heir of this unhappy family, all whose legitimate descendants had been massacred by Borgia.

It is true that the fortresses of these different places had taken no part in these revolutions, and had remained immutably faithful to the Duke of Valentinois.

So it was not precisely the defection of these towns, which, thanks to their fortresses, might be reconquered, that was the cause of uneasiness to Caesar and Julius II, it was the difficult situation that Venice had thrust upon them. Venice, in the spring of the same year, had signed a treaty of peace with the Turks: thus set free from her eternal enemy, she had just led her forces to the Romagna, which she had always coveted: these troops had been led towards Ravenna, the farthermost limit of the Papal estates, and put under the command of Giacopo Venieri, who had failed to capture Cesena, and had only failed through the courage of its inhabitants; but this check had been amply compensated by the surrender of the fortresses of Val di Lamane and Faenza, by the capture of Farlimpopoli, and the surrender of Rimini, which Pandolfo Malatesta, its lard, exchanged for the seigniory of Cittadella, in the State of Padua, and far the rank of gentleman of Venice.

Then Caesar made a proposition to Julius II: this was to make a momentary cession to the Church of his own estates in Romagna, so that the respect felt by the Venetians for the Church might save these towns from their aggressors; but, says Guicciardini, Julius II, whose ambition, so natural in sovereign rulers, had not yet extinguished the remains of rectitude, refused to accept the places, afraid of exposing himself to the temptation of keeping them later on, against his promises.

But as the case was urgent, he proposed to Caesar that he should leave Rome, embark at Ostia, and cross over to Spezia, where Michelotto was to meet him at the head of 100 men-at-arms and 100 light horse, the only remnant of his magnificent army, thence by land to Ferrara, and from Ferrara to Imala, where, once arrived, he could utter his war-cry so loud that it would be heard through the length and breadth of Romagna.

This advice being after Caesar's own heart, he accepted it at once.

The resolution submitted to the Sacred College was approved, and Caesar left for Ostia, accompanied by Bartolommeo della Rovere, nephew of His Holiness.

Caesar at last felt he was free, and fancied himself already on his good charger, a second time carrying war into all the places where he had formerly fought. When he reached Ostia, he was met by the cardinals of Sorrento and Volterra, who came in the name of Julius II to ask him to give up the very same citadels which he had refused three days before: the fact was that the pope had learned in the interim that the Venetians had made fresh aggressions, and recognized that the method proposed by Caesar was the only one that would check them. But this time it was Caesar's turn, to refuse, for he was weary of these tergiversations, and feared a trap; so he said that the surrender asked for would be useless, since by God's help he should be in Romagna before eight days were past. So the cardinals of Sorrento and Volterra returned to Rome with a refusal.

The next morning, just as Caesar was setting foot on his vessel, he was arrested in the name of Julius II.

He thought at first that this was the end; he was used to this mode of action, and knew how short was the space between a prison and a tomb; the matter was all the easier in his case, because the pope, if he chose, would have plenty of pretext for making a case against him. But the heart of Julius was of another kind from his; swift to anger, but open to clemency; so, when the duke came back to Rome guarded, the momentary irritation his refusal had caused was already calmed, and the pope received him in his usual fashion at his palace, and with his ordinary courtesy, although from the beginning it was easy for the duke to see that he was being watched. In return for this kind reception, Caesar consented to yield the fortress of Cesena to the pope, as being a town which had once belonged to the Church, and now should return; giving the deed, signed by Caesar, to one of his captains, called Pietro d'Oviedo, he ordered him to take possession of the fortress in the name of the Holy See. Pietro obeyed, and starting at once for Cesena, presented himself armed with his warrant before Don Diego Chinon; a noble condottiere of Spain, who was holding the fortress in Caesar's name. But when he had read over the paper that Pietro d'Oviedo brought, Don Diego replied that as he knew his lord and master was a prisoner, it would be disgraceful in him to obey an order that had probably been wrested from him by violence, and that the bearer deserved to die for undertaking such a cowardly office. He therefore bade his soldiers seize d'Oviedo and fling him down from the top of the walls: this sentence was promptly executed.

This mark of fidelity might have proved fatal to Caesar: when the pope heard how his messenger had been treated, he flew into such a rage that the prisoner thought a second time that his hour was come; and in order to receive his liberty, he made the first of those new propositions to Julius II, which were drawn up in the form of a treaty and sanctioned by a bull. By these arrangements, the Duke of Valentinois was bound to hand over to His Holiness, within the space of forty days, the fortresses of Cesena and Bertinoro, and authorize the surrender of Forli. This arrangement was guaranteed by two bankers in Rome who were to be responsible for 15,000 ducats, the sum total of the expenses which the governor pretended he had incurred in the place on the duke's account. The pope on his part engaged to send Caesar to Ostia under the sole guard of the Cardinal of Santa Croce and two officers, who were to give him his full liberty on the very day when his engagements were fulfilled: should this not happen, Caesar was to be taken to Rome and imprisoned in the Castle of Sant' Angelo. In fulfillment of this treaty, Caesar went down the Tiber as far as Ostia, accompanied by the pope's treasurer and many of his servants. The Cardinal of Santa Croce followed, and the next day joined him there.

But as Caesar feared that Julius II might keep him a prisoner, in spite of his pledged word, after he had yielded up the fortresses, he asked, through the mediation of Cardinals Borgia and Remolina, who, not feeling safe at Rome, had retired to Naples, for a safe-conduct to Gonzalva of Cordova, and for two ships to take him there; with the return of the courier the safe-conduct arrived, announcing that the ships would shortly follow.

In the midst of all this, the Cardinal of Santa Croce, learning that by the duke's orders the governors of Cesena and Bertinoro had surrendered their fortresses to the captains of His Holiness, relaxed his rigor, and knowing that his prisoner would some day or other be free, began to let him go out without a guard. Then Caesar, feeling some fear lest when he started with Gonzalvo's ships the same thing might happen as on the occasion of his embarking on the pope's vessel — that is, that he might be arrested a second time — concealed himself in a house outside the town; and when night came on, mounting a wretched horse that belonged to a peasant, rode as far as Nettuno, and there hired a little boat, in which he embarked for Monte Dragone, and thence gained Naples. Gonzalvo received him with such joy that Caesar was deceived as to his intention, and this time believed that he was really saved. His confidence was redoubled when, opening his designs to Gonzalvo, and telling him that he counted upon gaining Pisa and thence going on into Romagna, Ganzalva allowed him to recruit as many soldiers at Naples as he pleased, promising him two ships to embark with. Caesar, deceived by these appearances, stopped nearly six weeks at Naples, every day seeing the Spanish governor and discussing his plans. But Gonzalvo was only waiting to gain time to tell the King of Spain that his enemy was in his hands; and Caesar actually went to the castle to bid Gonzalvo good-bye, thinking he was just about to start after he had embarked his men on the two ships. The Spanish governor received him with his accustomed courtesy, wished him every kind of prosperity, and embraced him as he left; but at the door of the castle Caesar found one of Gonzalvo's captains, Nuno Campeja by name, who arrested him as a prisoner of Ferdinand the Catholic. Caesar at these words heaved a deep sigh, cursing the ill luck that had made him trust the word of an enemy when he had so often broken his own.

He was at once taken to the castle, where the prison gate closed behind him, and he felt no hope that anyone would come to his aid; for the only being who was devoted to him in this world was Michelotto, and he had heard that Michelotto had been arrested near Pisa by order of Julius II. While Caesar was being taken to prison an officer came to him to deprive him of the safe-conduct given him by Gonzalvo.

The day after his arrest, which occurred on the 27th of May, 1504, Caesar was taken on board a ship, which at once weighed anchor and set sail for Spain: during the whole voyage he had but one page to serve him, and as soon as he disembarked he was taken to the castle of Medina del Campo.

Ten years later, Gonzalvo, who at that time was himself proscribed, owned to Loxa on his dying bed that now, when he was to appear in the presence of God, two things weighed cruelly on his conscience: one was his treason to Ferdinand, the other his breach of faith towards Caesar.

Chapter XVI

Caesar was in prison for two years, always hoping that Louis XII would reclaim him as peer of the kingdom of France; but Louis, much disturbed by the loss of the battle of Garigliano, which robbed him of the kingdom of Naples, had enough to do with his own affairs without busying himself with his cousin's. So the prisoner was beginning to despair, when one day as he broke his bread at breakfast he found a file and a little bottle containing a narcotic, with a letter from Michelotto, saying that he was out of prison and had left Italy for Spain, and now lay in hiding with the Count of Benevento in the neighboring village: he added that from the next day forward he and the count would wait every night on the road between the fortress and the village with three excellent horses; it was now Caesar's part to do the best he could with his bottle and file. When the whole world had abandoned the Duke of Romagna he had been remembered by a sbirro.

The prison where he had been shut up for two years was so hateful to Caesar that he lost not a single moment: the same day he attacked one of the bars of a window that looked out upon an inner court, and soon contrived so to manipulate it that it would need only a final push to come out. But not only was the window nearly seventy feet from the ground, but one could only get out of the court by using an exit reserved for the governor, of which he alone had the key; also this key never left him; by day it hung at his waist, by night it was under his pillow: this then was the chief difficulty.

But prisoner though he was, Caesar had always been treated

with the respect due to his name and rank: every day at the dinner-hour he was conducted from the room that served as his prison to the governor, who did the honors of the table in a grand and courteous fashion. The fact was that Dan Manuel had served with honor under King Ferdinand, and therefore, while he guarded Caesar rigorously, according to orders, he had a great respect for so brave a general, and took pleasure in listening to the accounts of his battles. So he had often insisted that Caesar should not only dine but also breakfast with him; happily the prisoner, yielding perhaps to some presentiment, had till now refused this favor. This was of great advantage to him, since, thanks to his solitude, he had been able to receive the instruments of escape sent by Michelotto. The same day he received them, Caesar, on going back to his room, made a false step and sprained his foot; at the dinner-hour he tried to go down, but he pretended to be suffering so cruelly that he gave it up. The governor came to see him in his room, and found him stretched upon the bed.

The day after, he was no better; the governor had his dinner sent in, and came to see him, as on the night before; he found his prisoner so dejected and gloomy in his solitude that he offered to come and sup with him: Caesar gratefully accepted.

This time it was the prisoner who did the honors: Caesar was charmingly courteous; the governor thought he would profit by this lack of restraint to put to him certain questions as to the manner of his arrest, and asked him as an Old Castilian, for whom honor is still of some account, what the truth really was as to Gonzalvo's and Ferdinand's breach of faith, with him. Caesar appeared extremely inclined to give him his entire confidence, but showed by a sign that the attendants were in the way. This precaution appeared quite natural, and the governor took no offense, but hastened to send them all away, so as to be sooner alone with his companion. When the door was shut, Caesar filled his glass and the governor's, proposing the king's health: the governor honored the toast: Caesar at once began his tale; but he had scarcely uttered a third part of it when, interesting as it was, the eyes of his host shut as though by magic, and he slid under the table in a profound sleep.

After half a hour had passed, the servants, hearing no noise, entered and found the two, one on the table, the other under it: this event was not so extraordinary that they paid any great attention to it: all they did was to carry Don Manuel to his room and lift Caesar on the bed; then they put away the remnant of the meal for the next day's supper, shut the door very carefully, and left their prisoner alone.

Caesar stayed for a minute motionless and apparently plunged in the deepest sleep; but when he had heard the steps retreating, he quietly raised his head, opened his eyes, slipped off the bed, walked to the door, slowly indeed, but not to all appearance feeling the accident of the night before, and applied his ear for some minutes to the keyhole; then lifting his head with an expression of indescribable pride, he wiped his brow with his hand, and for the first time since his guards went out, breathed freely with full-drawn breaths.

There was no time to lose: his first care was to shut the door as securely on the inside as it was already shut on the outside, to blow out the lamp, to open the window, and to finish sawing through the bar. When this was done, he undid the bandages on his leg, took down the window and bed curtains, tore them into strips, joined the sheets, table napkins and cloth, and with all these things tied together end to end, formed a rope fifty or sixty feet long, with knots every here and there. This rope he fixed securely to the bar next to the one he had just cut through; then he climbed up to the window and began what was really the hardest part of his perilous enterprise, clinging with hands and feet to this fragile support. Luckily he was both strong and skilful, and he went down the whole length of the rope without accident; but when he reached the end and was hanging on the last knot, he sought in vain to touch the ground with his feet; his rope was too short.

The situation was a terrible one: the darkness of the night prevented the fugitive from seeing how far off he was from the ground, and his fatigue prevented him from even attempting to climb up again. Caesar put up a brief prayer, whether to Gad or Satan he alone could say; then letting go the rope, he dropped from a height of twelve or fifteen feet.

The danger was too great for the fugitive to trouble about a few trifling contusions: he at once rose, and guiding himself by the direction of his window, he went straight to the little door of exit; he then put his hand into the pocket of his doublet, and a cold sweat damped his brow; either he had forgotten and left it in his room or had lost it in his fall; anyhow, he had not the key.

But summoning his recollections, he quite gave up the first idea for the second, which was the only likely one: again he crossed the court, looking for the place where the key might have fallen, by the aid of the wall round a tank on which he had laid his hand when he got up; but the object of search was so small and the night so dark that there was little chance of getting any result; still Caesar sought for it, for in this key was his last hope: suddenly a door was opened, and a night watch appeared, preceded by two torches. Caesar far the moment thought he was lost, but remembering the tank behind him, he dropped into it, and with nothing but his head above water anxiously watched the movements of the soldiers, as they advanced beside him, passed only a few feet away, crossed the court, and then disappeared by an opposite door. But short as their luminous apparition had been, it had lighted up the ground, and Caesar by the glare of the torches had caught the glitter of the long-sought key, and as soon as the door was shut behind the men, was again master of his liberty.

Half-way between the castle and the village two cavaliers and a led horse were waiting for him: the two men were Michelotto and the Count of Benevento. Caesar sprang upon the riderless horse, pressed with fervor the hand of the count and the sbirro; then all three galloped to the frontier of Navarre, where they arrived three days later, and were honorably received by the king, Jean d'Albret, the brother of Caesar's wife.

From Navarre he thought to pass into France, and from France to make an attempt upon Italy, with the aid of Louis XII; but during Caesar's detention in the castle of Medina del Campo, Louis had made peace with the King of Spain; and when he heard of Caesar's flight; instead of helping him, as there was some reason to expect he would, since he was a relative by marriage, he took away the duchy of Valentinois and also his pension. Still, Caesar had nearly 200,000 ducats in the charge of bankers at Genoa; he wrote asking for this sum, with which he hoped to levy troops in Spain and in Navarre, and make an attempt upon Pisa: 500 men, 200,000 ducats, his name and his word were more than enough to save him from despair.

The bankers denied the deposit.

Caesar was at the mercy of his brother-in-law.

One of the vassals of the King of Navarre, named Prince Alarino, had just then revolted: Caesar then took command of the army which Jean d'Albret was sending out against him, followed by Michelotto, who was as faithful in adversity as ever before. Thanks to Caesar's courage and skilful tactics, Prince Alarino was beaten in a first encounter; but the day after his defeat he rallied his army, and offered battle about three o'clock in the afternoon. Caesar accepted it.

For nearly four hours they fought obstinately on both sides; but at length, as the day was going down, Caesar proposed to decide the issue by making a charge himself, at the head of a hundred men-at-arms, upon a body of cavalry which made his adversary's chief force. To his great astonishment, this cavalry at the first shock gave way and took flight in the direction of a little wood, where they seemed to be seeking refuge. Caesar followed close on their heels up to the edge of the forest; then suddenly the pursued turned right about face, three or four hundred archers came out of the wood to help them, and Caesar's men, seeing that they had fallen into an ambush, took to their heels like cowards, and abandoned their leader.

Left alone, Caesar would not budge one step; possibly he had had enough of life, and his heroism was rather the result of satiety than courage: however that may be, he defended himself like a lion; but, riddled with arrows and bolts, his horse at last fell, with Caesar's leg under him. His adversaries rushed upon him, and one of them thrusting a sharp and slender iron pike through a weak place in his armor, pierced his breast; Caesar cursed God and died.

But the rest of the enemy's army was defeated, thanks to the courage of Michelotto, who fought like a valiant condottiere, but learned, on returning to the camp in the evening, from those who had fled; that they had abandoned Caesar and that he had never reappeared. Then only too certain, from his master's well-known courage, that disaster had occurred, he desired to give one last proof of his devotion by not leaving his body to the wolves and birds of prey. Torches were lighted, for it was dark, and with ten or twelve of those who had gone with Caesar as far as the little wood, he went to seek his master. On reaching the spot they pointed out, he beheld five men stretched side by side; four of them were dressed, but the fifth had been stripped of his clothing and lay completely naked. Michelotto dismounted, lifted the head upon his knees, and by the light of the torches recognized Caesar.

Thus fell, on the 10th of March, 1507, on an unknown field, near an obscure village called Viane, in a wretched skirmish with the vassal of a petty king, the man whom Macchiavelli presents to all princes as the model of ability, diplomacy, and courage.

As to Lucrezia, the fair Duchess of Ferrara, she died full of years, and honors, adored as a queen by her subjects, and sung as a goddess by Ariosto and by Bembo.

Epilogue

*T*here was once in Paris, says Boccaccio, a brave and good merchant named Jean de Civigny, who did a great trade in drapery, and was connected in business with a neighbor and fellow-merchant, a very rich man called Abraham, who, though a Jew, enjoyed a good reputation. Jean de Civigny, appreciating the qualities of the worthy Israelite; feared lest, good man as he was, his false religion would bring his soul straight to eternal perdition; so he began to urge him gently as a friend to renounce his errors and open his eyes to the Christian faith, which he could see for himself was prospering and spreading day by day, being the only true and good religion; whereas his own creed, it was very plain, was so quickly diminishing that it would soon disappear from the face of the earth. The Jew replied that except in his own religion there was no salvation, that he was born in it, proposed to live and die in it, and that he knew nothing in the world that could change his opinion. Still, in his proselytizing fervor Jean would not think himself beaten, and never a day passed but he demonstrated with those fair words the merchant uses to seduce a customer, the superiority of the Christian religion above the Jewish; and although Abraham was a great master of Mosaic law, he began to enjoy his friend's preaching, either because of the friendship he felt for him or because the Holy Ghost descended upon the tongue of the new apostle; still obstinate in his own belief, he would not change. The more he persisted in his error, the more excited was Jean about converting him, so that at last, by God's help, being somewhat shaken by his friend's urgency, Abraham one day said —

"Listen, Jean: since you have it so much at heart that I should be converted, behold me disposed to satisfy you; but before I go to Rome to see him whom you call God's vicar on earth, I must study his manner of life and his morals, as also those of his brethren the cardinals; and if, as I doubt not, they are in harmony with what you preach, I will admit that, as you have taken such pains to show me, your faith is better than mine, and I will do as you desire; but if it should prove otherwise, I shall remain a Jew, as I was before; for it is not worth while, at my age, to change my belief for a worse one."

Jean was very sad when he heard these words; and he said mournfully to himself, "Now I have lost my time and pains, which I thought I had spent so well when I was hoping to convert this unhappy Abraham; for if he unfortunately goes, as he says he will, to the court of Rome, and there sees the shameful life led by the servants of the Church, instead of becoming a Christian the Jew will be more of a Jew than ever." Then turning to Abraham, he said, "Ah, friend, why do you wish to incur such fatigue and expense by going to Rome, besides the fact that traveling by sea or by land must be very dangerous for so rich a man as you are? Do you suppose there is no one here to baptize you? If you have any doubts concerning the faith I have expounded, where better than here will you find theologians capable of contending with them and allaying them? So, you see, this voyage seems to me quite unnecessary: just imagine that the priests there are such as you see here, and all the better in that they are nearer to the supreme pastor. If you are guided by my advice, you will postpone this toil till you have committed some grave sin and need absolution; then you and I will go together."

But the Jew replied —

"I believe, dear Jean, that everything is as you tell me; but you know how obstinate I am. I will go to Rome, or I will never be a Christian."

Then Jean, seeing his great wish, resolved that it was no use trying to thwart him, and wished him good luck; but in his heart he gave up all hope; for it was certain that his friend would come back from his pilgrimage more of a Jew than ever, if the court of Rome was still as he had seen it.

But Abraham mounted his horse, and at his best speed took the road to Rome, where on his arrival he was wonderfully well received by his coreligionists; and after staying there a good long time, he began to study the behavior of the pope, the cardinals and other prelates, and of the whole court. But much to his surprise he found out, partly by what passed under his eyes and partly by what he was told, that all from the pope downward to the lowest sacristan of St. Peter's were committing the sins of luxurious living in a most disgraceful and unbridled manner, with no remorse and no shame, so that pretty women and handsome youths could obtain any favors they pleased. In addition to this sensuality which they exhibited in public, he saw that they were gluttons and drunkards, so much so that they were more the slaves of the belly than are the greediest of animals. When he looked a little further, he found them so avaricious and fond of money that they sold for hard cash both human bodies and divine offices, and with less conscience than a man in Paris would sell cloth or any other merchandise. Seeing this and much more that it would not be proper to set down here, it seemed to Abraham, himself a chaste, sober, and upright man, that he had seen enough. So he resolved to return to Paris, and carried out the resolution with his usual promptitude. Jean de Civigny held a great fete in honor of his return, although he had lost hope of his coming back converted. But he left time for him to settle down before he spoke of anything, thinking there would be plenty of time to hear the bad news he expected. But, after a few days of rest, Abraham himself came to see his friend, and Jean ventured to ask what he thought of the Holy Father, the cardinals, and the other persons at the pontifical court. At these words the Jew exclaimed, "God damn them all! I never once succeeded in finding among them any holiness, any devotion, any good works; but, on the contrary, luxurious living, avarice, greed, fraud, envy, pride, and even worse, if there is worse; all the machine seemed to be set in motion by an impulse less divine than diabolical. After what I saw, it is my firm conviction that your pope, and of course the others as well, are using all their talents, art, endeavors, to banish the Christian religion from the face of the earth, though they ought to be its foundation and support; and since, in spite of all the care and trouble they expend to arrive at this end, I see that your religion is spreading every day and becoming more brilliant and more pure, it is borne in upon me that the Holy Spirit Himself protects it as the only true and the most holy religion; this is why, deaf as you found me to your counsel and rebellious to your wish, I am now, ever since I returned from this Sodom, firmly resolved on becoming a Christian. So let us go at once to the church, for I am quite ready to be baptized."

There is no need to say if Jean de Civigny, who expected a refusal, was pleased at this consent. Without delay he went with his godson to Notre Dame de Paris, where he prayed the first priest he met to administer baptism to his friend, and this was speedily done; and the new convert changed his Jewish name of Abraham into the Christian name of Jean; and as the neophyte, thanks to his journey to Rome, had gained a profound belief, his natural good qualities increased so greatly in the practice of our holy religion, that after leading an exemplary life he died in the full odor of sanctity.

This tale of Boccaccio's gives so admirable an answer to the charge of irreligion which some might make against us if they mistook our intentions, that as we shall not offer any other reply, we have not hesitated to present it entire as it stands to the eyes of our readers.

And let us never forget that if the papacy has had an Innocent VIII and an Alexander VI who are its shame, it has also had a Pius VII and a Gregory XVI who are its honor and glory.

Printed in the United Kingdom
by Lightning Source UK Ltd.
110008UKS00001B/322